Get swept away by
Joanna Fulford's

VICTORIOUS VIKINGS

*No man could defeat them.
Two women would defy them!*

DEFIANT IN THE VIKING'S BED

Proud warrior Leif Egilsson is enslaved by his enemies and vows his revenge on the woman responsible. Lady Astrid will become *his* slave—and will pay the price in his bed!

SURRENDER TO TH~~~~

Securing ships and we~~~~ ~~~~g Finn must take a bri~~~~ ~~~~ay have to wa~~~~ ~~~~ght their unwan~~~~ ~~~~e way!

In memory of Jane Croft, writing as Joanna Fulford

DEDICATION FROM BRIAN, HER LOVING HUSBAND

To Leonie Martin, Rosie Gilligan, Sue Pacey, Carol Vardy, Ann Norman, Gaynor Roberts and Graham Godfrey, who supported Jane throughout her writing career and me since.

Joanna Fulford

—

Surrender to the Viking

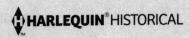
HARLEQUIN® HISTORICAL

Recycling programs for this product may not exist in your area.

ISBN-13: 978-0-373-29790-0

SURRENDER TO THE VIKING

Copyright © 2014 by Joanna Fulford

Printed in U.S.A.

Available from Harlequin® Historical and
JOANNA FULFORD

The Viking's Defiant Bride #934
The Viking's Touch #1082
Snowbound Wedding Wishes #1111
"Christmas at Oakhurst Manor"
The Wayward Governess #329
The Caged Countess #347
His Lady of Castlemora #357
*Redemption of a Fallen Woman
ΔDefiant in the Viking's Bed* #1158
Δ*Surrender to the Viking* #1190

*Part of Castonbury Park Regency miniseries
ΔVictorious Vikings

Chapter One

Rags of mist drifted across the dark waters of the fjord and hung among the trees below the promontory, and the first rays of sunlight tinted the distant mountains pink and gold. At any other time Lara might have enjoyed the scene and the peace that attended the start of the new day, but just then her thoughts were turned inwards, her body moving automatically through the drill that Alrik had taught her. Her brother was absent but she had put their former lessons to good use, rising early to practise every day until the feel of the sword in her hand was as familiar as a distaff or a drop spindle.

No one in the hall would be stirring yet, and the promontory was far enough from the buildings to make discovery unlikely. If her father learned what she had been doing these past months his displeasure would be great. Lara grimaced. The tension between them was bad enough. They had barely spoken since their last argument a week ago…

'You're eighteen years old already and like to be an old maid, yet you continue to frighten off every suitor who offers for your hand.'

'Frightened men have never held any appeal, you see.'

'Don't be flippant with me, girl,' replied Jarl Ottar. *'Indeed you would be well advised to mend your ways and cultivate some womanly charm.'*

'Am I not charming, Father?'

'I've seen she-wolves with milder temperaments than yours. No man wants a sharp-tongued harridan for a wife.'

'Then they are free to choose milksop brides if they wish.'

'It is a woman's place to be dutiful.'

Lara's eyes flashed indignation. *'Asa was dutiful, wasn't she?'*

Her father frowned. *'Your sister did what was required of her. She understood what was due to her family.'*

'Don't try to hide behind the family. Asa was forced into that marriage to satisfy your political ambition.'

'It was a necessary alliance to prevent more years of feuding.'

'You might as well have thrown her into a pit of vipers, but you will not use me as you used her.'

Lara lunged, thrusting the blade deep into the imaginary form of her erstwhile brother-in-law. It would have given her great pleasure to have disembowelled the living version but, unfortunately, he was far out of reach. She was also realistic enough to know that, were they ever to come face-to-face in combat, he would likely slay her with ease. She would never have a warrior's strength or skill with a sword, but learning the rudiments of self-defence gave her a sense of accomplishment. It was also empowering, like watching her would-be suitors fleeing.

'I will keep faith, Asa,' she murmured. 'I swear it.'

Regretfully she sheathed the blade once more and then picked up her cloak. People would be stirring now and she needed to get back. Recalcitrance didn't extend as far as ignoring the round of daily chores that fell to her lot. Those were performed diligently leaving no room for criticism. She smiled to herself. Men who were well fed and comfortable generally complained less than those who weren't. Anyway, it was good to be occupied. Idleness had never suited her.

She was just about to leave when she saw the ship rounding the promontory below her. Although it had the sleek lines and carved prow of a warship it was smaller than most of the sea dragons she had seen, with a crew of twenty or so. The lack of wind meant that the craft was under oars, the blades dipping and rising in perfect rhythm, barely ruffling the surface of the water. Lara silently acknowledged the skill of a crew working as one. Her gaze went from the rowers to the figure at the steering oar, a warrior in a mail byrnie. Her brow creased and she looked more closely. All the men on board were wearing them. Curiosity sharpened. The effort of rowing was great enough under normal circumstances; wearing mail would make it ten times harder. If they were doing so it argued that they had been under attack, that they expected to be or that they were about to launch an attack of their own.

She scanned the fjord but could see no sign of any other vessel. If they were being pursued it wasn't evident. That didn't necessarily mean that they intended to attack the steading but, all the same, it didn't pay to be complacent. Forewarned was forearmed. For that reason the landing was always guarded. Her father never took chances like that.

Seconds later she heard the sound of the watchman's horn announcing the approach of the ship. Wanting to see for herself she followed the track from the promontory but instead of turning right at the fork she bore left and headed towards the shoreline. The path led down a gentle gradient through a stand of birch before reaching the water. From the edge of the trees there was a good view of the landing and cover enough to remain unnoticed.

By the time she arrived the ship was nearing the shore. Half-a-dozen armed men watched its arrival. She heard the watchman's challenge ring out. It was answered at once. Evidently the answer must have been satisfactory because the crew were invited to tie up and come ashore.

Two men vaulted over the gunwale on to the wooden jetty and proceeded to make fast the lines while their comrades prepared to disembark. Although Lara was some fifty yards away she could see that her previous assessment had been correct: this was a warship and her crew armed to the teeth. Their leader appeared to be the individual she had seen before at the steering oar. He had his back to her at present but when he rattled off a series of instructions they were obeyed without question. Even among a group of big men he stood out. He was several inches taller than the rest and, like them, had the powerful athletic frame of the warrior. Moreover, he carried himself with the confidence of one accustomed to command and to being obeyed: a nobleman probably.

Lara was quietly amused. Most men of that class thought they had a right to instant obedience. It was ingrained in the species, like arrogance. As she surveyed the scene, the tall warrior turned around. She had an impression of a clean-shaven face with strong clean lines, framed by a mane of fair hair. He was… distinctive, she conceded. Probably he was well aware of it too.

As though sensing that he was being observed he looked up, his attention moving beyond the landing towards the trees. The questing gaze spotted her and then locked fast. Seconds later the intent expression was replaced by amusement. Lara glanced down and realised that as she was carrying her cloak the sword at her side was plainly visible against the skirt of her gown. The realisation gave her a mental jolt. It was a careless slip and she was annoyed with herself for letting it happen. Mingled with that was indignation that it should be a source of amusement to the stranger. Nevertheless, if he thought she would be disconcerted by it he was mistaken. Lifting her chin she returned his stare and held it for a moment or two. Then, unhurriedly, she turned and walked away.

Finn remained where he was, his gaze following the girl until she was lost to view among the trees. Her presence there had been both unexpected and arresting as though a curious woodland fey had suddenly appeared to investigate their arrival. The impression was enhanced by flowing brown hair and a gown of forest-green. The fey was fair to look upon but somewhat aloof in her manner. Her expression just now had been a distinct challenge, like the sword she wore at her side. He was amused and intrigued, his curiosity thoroughly roused. Had circumstances been different he'd have investigated further.

'My lord, will it please you to come with us?'

The watchman's voice brought Finn back to practicalities. 'Er, yes, of course.'

Leaving half-a-dozen men with the ship, he and the others followed their escort. It was but a short distance to Jarl Ottar's hall, an impressive timber dwelling that spoke of the status of its owner. Around it were other buildings: stables, barn, byres, pig sties, workshops and forge. Finn and his men surveyed the steading with appraising eyes.

'It's a fine place,' observed Unnr. 'Looks like Jarl Ottar's a wealthy man.'

'Let's hope he places a high value on old allegiances,' said Sturla.

'We'll soon find out, won't we?'

Any doubts they might have entertained were swiftly banished. As soon as they were announced Jarl Ottar came forward at once. He was in his forties and his red hair was faded and streaked with grey. However, his burly form suggested strength and vigour and his blue eyes were keen and shrewd. He smiled at the newcomers and then embraced their leader heartily.

'Welcome, Finn Egilsson, and welcome to your companions too.'

'I thank you, my lord.'

'Your father was a great warrior and a staunch ally. I was proud to call him friend.'

'He spoke of you too,' said Finn, 'and always with the greatest affection and respect.'

'You have the look of him.'

'My brother, Leif, also.'

'When I heard of your father's death it was with deep sorrow.' Ottar shook his head. 'There weren't many like him. Nevertheless, it's good to see one of his sons in my hall.' He shouted for the servants to fetch ale and food. 'When you have refreshed yourselves you can tell me what brings you here.'

When Lara returned the first person she saw was Alrik. He was two years her senior and he was considerably taller. Like her he had the deep red hair that was a family trait. His blue eyes held a gleam of amusement and were looking pointedly at the cloak she was holding closed over her gown.

'Been practising again, eh?' He gave her a conspiratorial wink. 'Don't worry, I won't tell.'

'I know.' She glanced round to make sure they were out of earshot. 'I need to go and put the sword away. In the meantime we have visitors.'

'I thought I heard the horn sound.'

'A vessel has just arrived at the landing.'

'A trader?'

'A warship.'

He frowned. 'How many men?'

'I counted twenty.'

'Interesting.'

'Don't you want to find out why they're here?'

He grinned. 'You mean you want to find out why they're here.'

'All right, I admit I'm curious. Are you going to pretend you aren't?'

'No, I won't pretend that.' He squeezed her arm. 'Go and hide your guilty secret. I'll go to the hall.'

With that he hurried off. Lara made her way back to
the bower. The place was empty now so she removed
her cloak and unbuckled the sword belt before laying
the weapon carefully back in the bottom of her chest
and replacing the clothing on top. No one would suspect its presence there. Having done that, she straightened her rumpled gown and brushed a few tendrils of
hair off her face. Then she went to find out what was
toward.

By the time she reached the hall the place was bus-
tling with servants carrying platters of food and jugs of
ale. Her brother and father were deep in conversation
with the guests. The servants had matters well in hand
so she was able to stay in the background and listen.

Finn and his men took the edge off their hunger with
bread and cold meat washed down by several cups of
ale. Ottar made no attempt to discuss business until
they had eaten. Then he made a gesture for the servants to replenish the cups and looked at his guests.

'Now, will you not tell me why we have the honour
of your company?'

'It is not pleasure only that brings us here,' said
Finn then, 'but rather the political turmoil in Vingulmark. The royal house did not look kindly on their
defeat at Eid.'

Ottar regarded him intently. 'You were there?'

'Leif and I fought for Halfdan Svarti. So too did our
cousin Erik and all the men you see before you. The
fighting was fierce but at the end of it King Gandalf's
army was routed. Heysing and Helsing were slain. Only
Prince Hakke survived.'

'Better if it had been the other way around,' said

Ottar. 'I always thought him the most dangerous of Gandalf's sons.'

'There's many would agree. Hakke is nothing if not vengeful. His next act was to carry off Halfdan's intended bride, Lady Ragnhild, thinking to wed her by force. Fortunately we prevented it and rescued the lady, but, in the confusion, Hakke managed to escape us.'

'That was ill luck.'

'Ill luck indeed. He bided his time until he could have his revenge. It was to take the form of a hall burning. My brother's hall to be precise.'

'That is treachery of a high order.'

'The hall was on an estate in Vingulmark, a part of the land ceded to Halfdan. It was a gift to my brother from the king—a generous gift too, but its location made it vulnerable.'

'I can see how it might.'

'Hakke intended to surround the place and trap us within before he set fire to it. But for a timely warning the plan might have succeeded,' said Finn. 'As it was we were heavily outnumbered. We decided to split up so that the enemy would have to divide his force in order to give chase.'

'Which, knowing Hakke and his adherents, they did.'

'My men and I were pursued by a big warship under the command of Steingrim. They would have overtaken us for sure but, mercifully, the fog came down and we managed to lose them.'

'As well for you that you did.'

'Steingrim won't give up easily. If we're to have any chance of defeating him we must have reinforcements.'

'Ah.'

'I was hoping you might be able to help us, my lord.'

Ottar nodded. 'Whatever can be done will be done.'

'I appreciate it.'

'You are the son of a friend and an ally. Your enemies are mine.'

'I shall not forget this,' said Finn. 'Nor do I expect such a favour for nothing. You will tell me what I may do for you in return.'

Ottar was silent for a moment, his expression thoughtful. Then his gaze met Finn's and he smiled. 'I will think on it. In the meantime I invite you and your men to remain here for a few days as my guests. Tonight you must take pot luck. On the morrow we shall feast you properly.' He looked round, his gaze scanning the room. Then it lighted on the person he sought. 'Ah, there you are. Come here, girl.'

Finn glanced round casually, assuming that his host was addressing one of the servants, but as the girl in question crossed the room towards them he stared, recognising her at once. Seen at closer quarters she reinforced his earlier impression of a fey; the face with its high cheekbones and small pointed chin was dominated by beautiful blue-green eyes. Her hair, which he'd originally believed to be brown, was actually deep red and naturally curly, spilling in a glorious mass over her shoulders and down her back to a waist he could have spanned with his hands. Despite its slenderness her figure had the alluring curves of womanhood. The green gown he had noted before was made of fine wool and belted by an embroidered girdle. The only thing missing was the sword.

'Jarl Finn and his men will be staying with us for a while,' said Ottar. 'You will make whatever arrangements are necessary.'

'Yes, Father.'

Ottar went on, 'This is my youngest daughter, Lara.'

Finn made a courteous bow. 'I am honoured, lady.'

The blue-green eyes surveyed him coolly for a moment and then she inclined her head in acknowledgement.

'The honour is mine, my lord.'

The tone was polite but also aloof. The words were not accompanied by a smile, or a blush or the lowered gaze that he might have expected. It was as though she were merely observing the outward forms of courtesy but was inwardly unconcerned about whether she pleased or not. It was far removed from his usual experience with women. Then again, the women with whom he'd associated in recent times had a vested interest in pleasing a man. This was the daughter of his host so it behoved him to make an effort.

'I did not know that Jarl Ottar had so fair a daughter.'

'Didn't you?' she replied.

Finn was momentarily taken aback, which it seemed she had intended. He recovered quickly. 'No, I regret to say I did not.'

'Why regret?'

'I could have brought a suitable gift.'

'I have no need of gifts.'

'A gift does not have to supply a need,' he replied. 'It may be given as a token of regard.'

'True, but since we have only just met the gesture would seem excessive.'

He knew he should probably drop the subject but at the same time couldn't resist pushing it a little further. 'So you would not appreciate a necklace of amber beads or a gold brooch?'

'That would depend upon the giver. If it came from my father or brother I would treasure the gift.'

'But not if it came from a visitor.'

'No, my lord, for then I should suspect an ulterior motive.'

'Oh, what motive?'

'I should have to ask myself what would be expected in return.'

It was bold and blunt and provocative. No doubt that was quite intentional too and no doubt he should let it go, but the underlying challenge was becoming irresistible. 'A gift should not come with strings attached.'

'No, but they usually do in my experience.'

'Is your experience so great, then?'

'Great enough to make me wary of gifts—and givers.'

It was politely spoken but it was a rebuff all the same. She was quite impervious to compliments of any sort and, by extension, impervious to him. Nor, he suspected, was it a ploy to increase his interest. On the contrary he was fairly sure that she didn't like him. He didn't know whether to be amused or piqued.

Before he could think of a suitable reply her father cut in. 'You must excuse my daughter, Jarl Finn. She has a sharp wit and an even sharper tongue.' He frowned at her. 'That is why she is still unmarried at eighteen and is like to remain so.'

Finn winced inwardly at that, but the girl didn't bat an eyelid. If anything he thought he saw a gleam of amusement in her eyes. However, it was so fleeting he couldn't be certain.

'Yes, do excuse me, my lord. I'll take my offending tongue elsewhere.' She inclined her head respectfully. 'Father.'

Jarl Ottar frowned. He was on the point of saying something more but evidently decided not to although his annoyance was apparent. Looking on, Finn was more intrigued than ever. Nothing here was what it seemed, he was sure of that. He was too experienced not to recognise a skilled performance when he saw one and the past ten minutes had been exactly that, but a performance to what end? His gaze followed Lara's progress across the room: it was unhurried, almost studiedly so. His lips twitched. She must have anticipated that he would be watching her. Any moment now she would look back. Women invariably looked back, which meant that they were not as aloof as they pretended.

Lara did not look back and a short time later was in conversation with two servants. When they departed to carry out whatever instructions she had given, she left the hall by the rear door. Still she did not look back. Finn sighed, feeling mildly aggrieved.

Chapter Two

When she was away from the hall Lara relaxed a little. It was hours before she'd need to face the company again and then her role would be confined to ensuring the smooth service of food and drink. She would not be required to take part in the conversation. After the past ten minutes that was a relief. Jarl Finn might have a polished manner but he also had a high opinion of himself. She conceded that he was good at holding his own in an argument. At times she had half suspected that he was enjoying himself. That probably wasn't the case; she took good care to ensure that men didn't enjoy her company so it must be that he didn't like to be bested.

As she turned the corner of the building she was rudely jolted out of thought by a small body cannoning into her legs. It bounced off and went sprawling.

'What on earth—?' She broke off, recognising the steward's son. 'Yngvi. I might have known.'

He sat up looking slightly dazed. Lara sighed and bent down to look at him.

'Are you all right?'

He nodded. 'I…I think so.' As she helped him back

on to his feet he regarded her apologetically. 'I'm sorry, my lady. Drifa and I were playing tag.'

His younger brother nodded. 'I was trying to catch him.'

'I see.'

'Did I hurt you, my lady?' asked Yngvi.

'No, you didn't. You'll be the one to get hurt if you race blindly around corners like that.'

'Yes, my lady.'

Lara smiled. 'Go on, get along with you.'

Needing no further urging they ran off. As she watched their receding figures she shook her head feeling fairly certain that her warning would go unheeded. At the age of six Yngvi was proving to be a natural risk-taker, and where he led Drifa would follow.

She reached the weaving shed without further interruption and resumed work on the length of blue cloth she had started a few days earlier. As she did so, her mind went back to the days when she and Alrik and Asa had played tag together; happy, carefree days, and all too short. Let Yngvi and Drifa play while they could; they'd grow up soon enough. When she was a child she'd longed to be grown up. Everything had seemed so straightforward then: she would marry and have children and keep her husband's house. It was what all girls did. Back then it had never occurred to her to question the matter. Now she knew better. Marriage was a trap and a handsome face was no guarantee of a good heart.

For no reason Jarl Finn drifted into her mind and lingered there. Reluctantly she was forced to admit that he was an imposing figure, no easier to banish mentally than he was to brush off physically. However, putting aside the ridiculous conversation they'd had together, she had been interested in the things he'd discussed with her father. While she knew about King Halfdan's victory at the Battle of Eid, it was the first time she'd met anyone who'd actually been present. She'd have liked to ask Finn about it. That would have been a conversation worth having. She'd have liked to ask him about the kidnapping and subsequent rescue of Lady Ragnhild too. It sounded exciting, full of action and danger. It was also the stuff of romance.

Lara caught herself there. Romance was a notion for silly young girls who didn't know any better. Nevertheless, the king must have cared very much if he was prepared to go to such lengths to get his lady back. Clearly he wasn't the kind of man who dealt in mealy-mouthed flattery and trumpery gifts. Ragnhild was fortunate. Such men were rare. Most were strutting, vainglorious fools with no thought in their head beyond the winning of fame. Some were cruel to boot. To them a woman was a chattel to be used and abused. Asa's husband had been proof of that.

Her sister had been a pawn in a deeper political game, married to seal a pact with former enemies. By the sound of it Jarl Finn had enemies, powerful ones too. Hall burning was a brutal form of revenge so it was fortunate that he and his kin had been warned in time. She couldn't wish such a fate on anyone, not even on a man as annoying as he was. Happily he wouldn't be around for much longer: once he'd got the extra swords he needed he'd be on his way.

With that happy outcome in mind Lara found it much easier to fulfil the obligations of hospitality that evening, plying the guests with mead and ale. Given the arrival of guests with no notice she'd been forced to improvise with the meal. It wasn't exactly a banquet but at least there was enough food to go around. As she had anticipated her father would feast his guests properly on the morrow as hospitality required.

'I've organised a hunt,' he said. 'Some of the men will go out first thing. A roast boar wouldn't go amiss. Maybe even some venison.'

'Either would be good,' she replied.

'You see to the rest.'

'Of course. I've already spoken to the servants about extra bread and ale.'

'I'll say one thing for you, girl, you know how to keep house and provide a good spread.'

Well, yes. It's what I've been trained to do from childhood. With an effort Lara clamped down on sarcasm and smiled instead. 'Thank you, Father.'

He regarded her suspiciously, suspecting irony, but her expression was innocent so he grunted and held out his cup. She refilled it.

'You should be putting those skills to use in your husband's hall,' he went on. 'That's the role you were intended for.'

'In the meantime I am happy to practise here,' she replied.

He snorted and turned away. Lara moved on.

'Your father is right,' said Finn as he held out his cup for a refill.

'About what?' she demanded.

'The meal was excellent.'

The jug hovered a moment and she looked up quickly, undeceived by the bland tone. It wasn't what he had meant at all but it was safer if she pretended to believe him. 'I'm glad you enjoyed it, my lord.'

'Clearly you are a good organiser.'

'Women are trained to be good organisers.'

'I suppose they are. Even so, twenty extra mouths to feed is quite a task.'

This was a first. 'Men don't usually consider such things. They seem to assume that food will magically appear at the given time. Then they eat and think no more of it until the next meal is due.'

He laughed. 'There is some justice in what you say, although, having been responsible for a ship's crew, I have learned about the importance of provisions.'

Her surprise increased. *Not a complete fool, then.* 'Yes, I imagine you have.'

'I enjoy my food as much as the next man. Besides, a well-fed crew complains less.'

'So the way to their hearts really is through their stomachs.'

'Battle loot plays its part as well.'

Lara's expression altered. *This was more like it.* Now she had the opening she'd been hoping for. 'You were at Eid, weren't you?'

'That's right. How did you know?'

'I heard you speaking to my father.'

His eyes gleamed. 'Were you eavesdropping?'

'Of course. It was an interesting conversation.'

She looked quite unabashed by the admission. Finn's lips twitched. 'Battle might be deemed an unfit topic for the ears of a woman.'

'Why should it?'

'Because it's brutal and bloody. A pretty woman should think of other things.'

She sighed. 'Like necklaces of amber beads and gold brooches perhaps? Or maybe flirtation and romance?'

'Isn't that what young women usually think about?'

Lara was silent, wrestling with irritation and disappointment. For a moment she'd really thought he might be different from the others. She looked away. 'Excuse me for asking an inappropriate question. It's just that I was hoping for an intelligent answer. I should have known better.'

As Finn watched her walk off, he uttered a soft laugh that was compounded of disbelief and annoyance, the latter directed inwards. He hadn't missed the sudden eagerness in her eyes when she asked him about Eid. If he hadn't antagonised her, she might have let down her guard and they could have had a lively and interesting discussion. Instead he'd spoken without thinking and the barriers had come up at once. He was the one who should have known better. Had experience taught him nothing?

'Pretty girl,' said Unnr.

Finn glanced up and nodded. 'As you say.'

'Difficult, though. Redheads always are.'

'So I'm told.' *Difficult* was an understatement, thought Finn. *Volatile* was closer to the truth. When that was allied to a keen intelligence and a ready wit, it made for a challenging combination. Challenging and intriguing.

'Take a bold man to tame that one,' Unnr went on. 'My oldest brother, Sveinn, married a redhead. Lovely to look at but a temper like a fiend when roused.'

Sturla frowned. 'Regretted the match, did he?'

'Certainly not. Sveinn loves a challenge—always did. A timid sort of woman would never have suited him.'

'Each to his own.'

'I'm with Sveinn,' said Vigdis, who, like several others, had been listening with close attention. 'A spirited woman has to make for a more interesting relationship.'

Murmurs of agreement greeted this.

Thus encouraged Unnr continued, 'That's right. Sveinn had fancied Halla from the start, see, because she was a real looker, but it wasn't till she went for him with an axe that he really understood the depth of his feelings.'

Vigdis nodded. 'I can see how something like that could help you make up your mind.'

'It did. He fell head over heels in love.'

'So he told her right away, then?'

'Not quite. It wasn't until he'd wrestled her to the ground and taken the axe away that he finally managed to convince her. Anyway, they made up the quarrel and married the following week. They've got five sons now.'

Ketill shook his head in admiration. 'Your brother sounds like quite a romantic.'

His companions nodded.

'I think he is,' replied Unnr, 'though of course he'd never admit it.'

'Action speaks louder than words, eh?'

'Correct. And love's a funny thing. Take my cousin Snorri for instance...'

As the others pressed closer to listen Finn detached himself from the group and moved aside. The conversation had taken an unexpected turn, evoking memories that he'd have preferred to leave alone. Unnr was right though: love was a strange thing. It entered in by the eyes and embedded itself in the heart. Its removal left a wound that never healed. Betrayal was always ugly no matter what form it took. Unnr's brother was lucky in his choice of wife: evidently deception was not part of her nature. A man knew exactly what to expect from an axe. Moreover, he could see it coming. He didn't know about betrayal until it was too late.

He should have read the signs, but he'd been so besotted with Bótey that he'd been blind. When he'd finally understood how blind, love had given way to jealousy and killing rage. She knew what his reaction would be and sought to put as much distance between them as possible. Not enough distance though, not nearly enough. He'd caught up eventually. Slaying his rival was a matter of natural justice, an act for which none would condemn him. A man must defend his rights and avenge himself on those who wronged him. That was the way of things. He had no qualms about killing his wife's lover. It was what followed that sickened him and for that, in his own mind at least, he would stand forever condemned.

He and his men slept in the hall that night, or rather his men slept and soundly too. Finn found it much harder. His mind was too busy, not least with concerns about the immediate future. If he didn't take care of Steingrim it was over. He and his men would be hunted down and slain. The mercenary force wouldn't give up until that was accomplished. However, Finn had no intention of allowing them to keep the advantage. When he had the extra swords he needed the fight would be taken to his enemies, and when they least expected it. *We'll choose our own ground.* Leif was right about that. He wondered how his brother was faring and whether he'd got his woman away safely. Presumably he had: once Leif had a goal in mind he invariably achieved it no matter who tried to stop him. Anyway, Astrid was a pretty girl.

Finn acknowledged the fact even though he felt dispassionate about it. His taste ran more towards dark hair, dark or deep red. For a moment Lara's face floated into his thoughts. It was remarkable that she was still unmarried at eighteen. She could not have lacked for suitors. Surely among their number had been those who were not deterred by the kind of challenge she represented; any red-blooded man in fact. It suggested that Lara must have rejected them. Had she used an axe? He smiled to himself. It wasn't hard to visualise such a scenario. The fey didn't seem to like men very much. She certainly didn't like him. There were admittedly some grounds for her dislike, but it didn't explain her antipathy for the male sex as a whole, and that made him curious.

When his marriage ended it had been a while before he'd embarked on any kind of sexual adventure. At first it was the sort a man paid for; uncomplicated and mutually beneficial. Later there were longer liaisons with palace courtesans; more complicated and more expensive but more enjoyable too, while they lasted. He was all in favour of the giving and taking of pleasure and was generous when it came to rewarding the objects of his attention, but he never offered more than that. His terms were made clear at the outset. That way there could be no misunderstandings and no one got hurt.

Had Lara suffered a disappointment? Was her manner a defence against being hurt again? He didn't know why his thoughts should keep coming back to her. He regretted his thoughtless words earlier: they had cost him an entertaining discussion. All conversations with her were entertaining. He had never met a woman who challenged his opinions before, or who held her own in argument with such accomplished ease, making him think on his feet. She made no attempt to flirt either and clearly resented it when he did. That too was novel. Women invariably enjoyed flirting with him. Some went out of their way to do so and the invitation they extended was blatant. Usually he was happy to oblige them with an hour of his time. He couldn't imagine Lara seeking five minutes alone with him, never mind an hour. Probably it was just as well. There was no question of any dalliance with her, even if she had been so inclined. To take advantage of his host's goodwill in that way was dishonourable. It would also jeopardise his mission here and that would be foolhardy in the extreme.

All the same Lara roused his curiosity. If he were honest she aroused rather more than that. Vigdis was right: a spirited woman was infinitely more interesting than a timid one. Finn smiled to himself. Had she been a lady of the court he'd have taken up the challenge she represented: in his experience every woman could be wooed and won; every rebel conquered—eventually.

Chapter Three

Somewhere amid these thoughts he dozed off and eventually slept until dawn. Around him his sword brothers snored on. Wanting to stretch his limbs he rose quietly, taking care not to disturb his companions, and slipped out of a side door. The morning smelled of dew and damp earth. It had rained in the night but the clouds had passed over and the new day looked promising. That was just as well when there was so much to be done. He was mentally listing it all when he glimpsed movement out of the corner of his eye.

Automatically he whipped round, his hand moving to the hilt of his sword. He wouldn't put it past Steingrim to sneak up on his foes as they slept. However, far from being the enemy's bulky form, the figure was slight and female. A proper look revealed her identity. He relaxed. She hadn't noticed him at all and was heading away from the buildings along a track that led towards the trees. For a second he hesitated, debating with himself. Then curiosity won.

Lara reached the promontory a few minutes later and, having divested herself of the cloak, drew the sword from its scabbard and began to warm up as Alrik had taught her. Then, closing her mind to everything else, she went through the drills, slowly at first, letting each movement flow into the next, then faster until the blade became almost invisible and the air hissed with its passing. Left, right, thrust, parry…left, right, block, feint, turn… Suddenly she froze, seeing the still figure just yards away at the edge of the trees. Shock was swiftly replaced by a range of uncomfortable emotions.

Jarl Finn! How in Hel's name had he found out? He must be enjoying the discovery enormously. No doubt the tale would be all over the steading by midday. She'd be a laughing stock. Her father would be furious…

Finn pushed his shoulders away from the tree he'd been leaning on, and strolled towards her. Lara lifted the sword, strongly tempted to run him through. It wouldn't be easy because he was armed, trained, battle-hardened and much bigger. All the same she'd be willing to try. He halted a few feet away. She glared at him, bracing herself for mockery.

'Not bad,' he said, 'but you need to raise your elbow a little higher when you parry.'

Lara blinked. 'My elbow?'

'Yes, like this.' He drew his sword and demonstrated. 'It prevents your enemy from delivering a downward stroke to your shoulder, you see.'

'Oh.'

He demonstrated once more. 'Now you try.'

Gathering her wits she resumed her stance and tried to copy him. It wasn't quite as easy as he made it look. He stepped behind her, placing a hand under her elbow. 'There.' The hand moved on and his fingers closed around hers, the touch warm and strong. 'Now, turn your wrist a little.' His grip tightened just a fraction. It didn't hurt in the least but her arm had no choice save to move as he dictated. Retaining his hold he took her through the manoeuvre again. Lara tried to focus on the sword, not on the man who was now standing so close to her. Gods, he was big, and disconcertingly strong with it. Had she really been mad enough to contemplate taking him on? He'd have snapped her like a twig.

'That's it.' Finn released his hold. 'Now run through that sequence again.'

He stepped away to give her space. She hesitated, torn between annoyance at the commanding tone and a wish to improve. His gaze met and held hers. One eyebrow lifted a little. The challenge was plain. Lara's chin came up at once. Assuming the correct stance, she began to repeat the moves, aware all the time of the man looking on and the cool grey eyes that missed nothing.

'Better,' he said. 'Again.'

She took a deep breath and took a firm hold of the hilt. *You can do this. You want to do this.* This time she made herself concentrate, performing the sequence once more.

'Keep your body sideways to your opponent. You haven't got a shield, remember, so you need to reduce the size of the target.'

Of course. Why didn't I think of that? Lara adjusted her position and then repeated the exercise. He watched critically, commenting on each move, instructing, encouraging and even offering an occasional word of praise. Nor could she detect anything remotely patronising in his manner. It was quiet and businesslike, requiring the like response from her. Gradually she began to relax a little and to enjoy herself. It was fun and she'd learned more in the past half an hour than in the previous three months. Knowing the basics was one thing but this had just taken the art of sword craft to a whole new level. She listened attentively now, obedient to his every command, understanding the reasons for what he was saying.

It was tempting to stay and continue for a while but the sun was above the hills now and a new day beginning. Reluctantly Lara lowered her sword.

'Is something wrong?' he asked.

'No, nothing's wrong. It's just that I have to get back. People will be stirring soon, if they aren't already.'

'You're right. I'd lost track of time.'

'I also.'

He watched her sheathe the sword. 'Who taught you to fight?'

'My brother, Alrik.'

'How long have you been practising?'

'About three months or so.'

'Not so long, then.'

'That must be obvious to you.'

'Yes, it is,' he replied, 'but Miklagard wasn't built in a day. You've made progress but you need more practice.'

She nodded, glad that he hadn't lied to flatter her and encouraged that he should think she had improved if only a little. 'I'll persevere.'

'Good.'

Lara retrieved her cloak and used it to swathe the sword before tucking it under her arm. 'I must go.'

'And I need to go to the landing and visit my ship.'

'Are you afraid something may have happened to it in the night?'

The grey gaze cooled. 'My men and I are being pursued by a large mercenary force. I take nothing for granted.'

She bit her lip. 'Forgive me. I'd forgotten about that.'

'When you're dealing with an enemy like Steingrim the day you become complacent is the day you die.'

Lara was silent, mentally berating herself. *Idiot! Now he'll think you're an empty-headed little fool.* Up until an hour ago she wouldn't have given a sheep dropping for his opinion, but now somehow it mattered.

'I beg your pardon, my lord. You speak from experience that I do not have.'

The tone was unwontedly humble and for a moment his eyes registered surprise.

'As you say.'

With that he bowed and walked away. She watched the retreating figure for a moment or two and then hurried after him.

'Jarl Finn?'

He looked round, surveying her steadily. 'Lady?'

'Thank you for your help this morning.'

The tone was sincere, unexpectedly so. He was about to make an appropriate reply but she was away, running off down the track towards the steading. He watched her go and then followed, albeit at a more relaxed pace. When she reached the fork in the path she slowed and stopped, hesitating for a moment. Finn stopped too, waiting. *Would she or wouldn't she?* Lara took another step and then another. He sighed. She checked again and then darted a glance over her shoulder. For a second or two her gaze met his then she was

off again. Moments later she was lost to view. Finn
smiled to himself and continued on his way towards
the landing.

The ship was fine and the guards on duty reported
no sighting of an enemy craft. Finn relaxed a little. For
the time being at least it looked as though they had
shaken Steingrim off their trail. Next time they met
it would be when Finn chose and he'd have the warriors to end it once and for all. Today he would settle
the details with Jarl Ottar. Tonight's feast would seal
the agreement.

As he strolled back to the steading to speak to his
host, Finn let his mind drift to his recent encounter
with Lara. When he'd decided to follow her he'd no idea
what his decision might lead to. He hadn't expected to
be so thoroughly entertained or, he admitted, so impressed. Her brother had taught her well and she'd evidently taken the lessons seriously. He hadn't lied when
he'd told her she'd made progress. However, he'd been
very careful to avoid any suggestion of flattery or flirtation, adopting the tone he might have used with his
men. It was the right strategy, although he hadn't been
entirely sure of that at first. He hadn't missed her ini-
tial hesitation but, as he'd hoped, her eagerness to learn
had overcome natural caution. She was a quick learner
too. He had but to tell her something once for her to remember it. If she'd had someone to practise with she'd
have been even further ahead by now.

He shook his head, not quite able to believe he'd
been complicit in this. Her father certainly wouldn't
approve if he knew. As far as he was concerned the
roles of the sexes were quite clear. Finn had to admit

that he found it utterly incongruous to see a pretty girl
wielding a sword. And Lara was a very pretty girl:
small, slender, fine-boned—exquisite. The very idea of
her in combat was ludicrous. It offended every mascu-
line notion of what was acceptable. However, the early
morning practices were harmless enough, providing an
outlet for a rebellious spirit. Besides, in some measure,
she had given him her trust and he would not betray it.
In any case he wasn't going to be around for very long.

As he'd anticipated Jarl Ottar was keen to speak to
him and later that morning the two men adjourned to a
quiet corner where they could speak privately. Finn sat
down and waited for his host to open the conversation.

'I have thought on the matter we discussed before,'
said Ottar. 'I will supply you with a warship and the
crew to man her. My brother, Njall, will provide another.'

Finn was momentarily incredulous. Two big warships would carry a hundred and sixty men. When
combined with his own he'd have more than enough
to defeat Steingrim.

'That is generous, my lord.'

'In addition I will ensure that each ship is well pro-
visioned and her crew armed for the task.'

'I thank you.' The cost of provisioning a warship
was considerable, never mind two. It was far more than
Finn had been expecting. He was grateful too but such
munificence came at a price. Clearly Ottar was expecting something considerable in return.

'It will take a little while to organise this, of course,'
the jarl went on, 'but not too long, I hope.'

'In the meantime I will head down the coast to my

estate at Ravndal. Our continued presence here will not
go unremarked and eventually Steingrim will learn of
it. I'll not risk subjecting this steading to an attack.'

'I appreciate your consideration. The ships will join
you at Ravndal then.'

'It is well.' Finn paused regarding his companion
shrewdly. 'And now, my lord, perhaps you will tell me
what I can do for you in return.'

Ottar's gaze met his. 'In return I want you to take
my daughter to wife.'

Finn stared at him. He'd been expecting many things
but nothing like this. Almost immediately he upbraided
himself for not having foreseen it.

'She has a fine dowry of silver and land,' his companion went on. 'I'm not going to pretend that my Lara
is a biddable young woman. We both know she isn't.
She'll need a firm hand and no mistake. The question
is, are you willing to accept the challenge?'

Finn was silent, trying to order his thoughts. At
first sight it might seem that Ottar merely wished to
be rid of a problem but the truth went deeper than that.
Marriage created enduring alliances and the jarl was
a wealthy and powerful ally. Viewed objectively, the
offer of his daughter's hand was a considerable honour. Finn had not the least doubt that her dowry was
handsome. Nor had he the least doubt that the ships
and swords he required were dependent upon his ac-
cepting this condition. Furthermore, refusal would be
regarded as a grave insult. He couldn't afford to make
an enemy when he might have a willing ally and Ottar
knew that. Finn acknowledged with grudging admiration just how cleverly he'd been manipulated. There
was only one viable response.

'Yes, my lord, I'm willing to accept.'

Ottar beamed. 'Excellent.'

'However, your daughter may be of a different mind.'

'Lara will be delighted.'

Finn had doubts about that though he didn't voice them. The matter was decided now. He had not expected to marry again or indeed felt inclined to do so, but this was not just about personal inclination. It was about survival, his and that of his family. He would do what was necessary to achieve that. The immediate future was going to be more complicated than he'd envisaged but that couldn't be helped. He turned his mind to practicalities.

'The wedding will have to take place almost at once. I sail for Ravndal two days hence.'

'The feast tonight can serve a double function,' replied Ottar, 'if you are so minded.'

Finn nodded. It made sense. 'Why not?'

'I'll go and inform Lara of the arrangement and tell her to prepare herself.'

After Ottar had gone Finn left the hall and wandered down to the promontory. As he'd anticipated it was deserted now so he found a convenient boulder and sat down, his gaze on the view. However, his thoughts were not about the scenery. By now Ottar would have informed Lara of what was toward. Her reaction was not hard to imagine. Finn smiled wryly. Part of him wished he could have been a fly on the wall for that particular interview. In spite of their temporary truce this morning he was under no illusions that Lara had any tender feelings for him. Recent developments would only have added resentment to what was already a potent mix of emotions. He wished there had been time to talk to her first and perhaps offer a few words of reassurance. He might also have said other things too, about his admiration for her beauty and intelligence and spirit, but he surmised that she would have believed none of it, dismissing it as mere flattery. It wasn't. To tell her he loved her would have been untrue. He had loved once, in another life, with a blind passion that had brought only pain and destruction. He wouldn't make that mistake again. This time his eyes were open and the forthcoming marriage grounded in practicality. However, that didn't mean affection would not grow later. It wouldn't be hard to grow fond of Lara.

For the first time he let his mind move ahead a little. He didn't deceive himself that she would be easily won, but then nothing worth the winning was ever easy to attain. Nevertheless, he did intend to win. The challenge added spice to the relationship.

Lara stared at her father in disbelief. *He can't be serious.* 'I'm to marry Jarl Finn? Today?'

'That's right.'

'That's absurd.'

'Not in the least. I offered him your hand and he has accepted.'

For a moment she was silent, trying to take it in. *He has to be joking.* But as she looked into his eyes she knew he wasn't. Her stomach lurched.

'You…he…' She strove to find the words to express a raft of emotions and failed. Only one word came immediately to mind. 'No.'

'It's an excellent match, Lara.'

'For the two of you I have no doubt.'

'And for you. Thor's teeth! You're eighteen years old. You should have been wed long since.'

'I will not wed at your behest.'

'You damned well will. I've put up with your games for long enough.'

'A game? Is that what you think it is?'

He glared at her. 'Isn't it? Are you trying to tell me you haven't enjoyed sending your erstwhile suitors packing?'

Lara's chin tilted at a militant angle. 'No, I won't tell you that. I did enjoy it and good riddance to the lot of them. I'll enjoy it even more when I send Jarl Finn packing.'

'Are you really so simple as to imagine you could?'

She closed her eyes for a moment, trying to gather her scattered wits. It wasn't easy while she was trying to fight a sensation of rising panic as well. Deep down a part of her suspected that what her father had said was true. Finn Egilsson wasn't the kind of man who could be sent anywhere if he didn't wish to go.

'This man isn't like the others, Lara. If I'd thought so I wouldn't have offered him your hand.'

No, he isn't like the others. He isn't like any man you've ever met and that is the problem.

'I can't marry him. I barely know him.'

'Don't you?'

'How could I? We only met yesterday for goodness' sake.'

He surveyed her with a level gaze. 'And do you find him lacking in wit or intelligence?'

Gods, hardly. The man is sharp enough to cut himself. 'No, of course not.'

'Well, then, is his manner uncouth?'

'His manner is highly polished, as well you know.' *It's practically got a gloss on it.*

'Do you fear mistreatment at his hands?'

She shook her head. In spite of their short acquaintance she knew he would never be violent to a woman. Just how she knew was hard to say but the knowledge came from somewhere deep inside her. 'No, I don't fear that.'

'Do you find him displeasing to look upon?'

Just for a moment his face appeared in her mind's eye; a face composed of strong lines and planes, a blade of a nose, a firm mouth, square jaw and piercing grey eyes. The kind of face you couldn't forget: arresting, disturbing. 'He is not ill-looking.'

'Perhaps it is something about his birth or rank that you find lacking.'

'He is of good birth. I know that.'

'What is it that you so dislike, then?'

Lara was silent for a moment. Then she met her father's gaze. 'What I dislike is being treated like a chattel. I am not some possession to be disposed of at your whim, Father.'

'I never make a binding agreement on a whim and I have never considered you as a chattel, or your sister, hard as that may be for you to believe. That alliance was made because it had to be, but it was made in good faith.'

'Good faith?' She uttered a shaky laugh. 'Is that what you call it?'

'I regret the outcome as much as you do. That's why your future husband is a different kind of man.'

'He is not my future husband. I will not marry him.'

She steeled herself for the explosion of rage that must surely follow, but it didn't happen. Her father continued to regard her calmly. It was more disconcerting than any outburst of anger would have been.

'You'll marry him,' he replied. 'You can either do it with a semblance of grace or you can be dragged into the hall by main force. It's up to you.'

Her hands clenched at her sides as she conquered the urge to scream, rage, shout defiance. It wouldn't do any good. His word was given and he would not be forsworn. If she tried to disobey him he would have her forcibly brought to her wedding all right, and under the gaze of the assembled company and, worse, Jarl Finn's mocking grey eyes. The humiliation would be unspeakable.

She swallowed hard. 'The use of force will not be necessary.'

'I'm glad to hear it. Incidentally, I shall expect you to wear your finest gown this evening and do honour to your husband. Is that clear?'

'Very clear, Father.'

'Good. I'll leave you to it, then.' He moved towards the door but as he reached the threshold she stayed him.

'Does he even like me?'

'He has not confided the matter.' He paused. 'However, you have looks and wit enough to win a man's affections if you choose. Use them.'

'Perhaps I do not choose to.'

'Then you're a fool.'

She looked away blinking back tears. Her father's gaze never wavered.

'Marriage is not easy even when both parties are making an effort. You cannot afford to be at odds.'

'The situation is not of my making.'

'True, but half of what happens hereafter will be of your making. Remember that.'

After he had gone Lara seized the nearest object and hurled it at the wall. The horn cup shattered into a dozen pieces. As though at a signal, the water in her eyes spilled over and for a while she paced the floor, uttering a protracted growl of fury and frustration. It was all happening again! In spite of her best efforts it was happening again. She'd been so determined that it wouldn't. She'd promised Asa but in the end it was an empty promise. The matter had been decided without any reference to her or any consideration for personal inclination. She was powerless.

At length she sank down on the edge of the bed and shakily dashed away the tears with her sleeve. Tears were weakness and, anyway, they wouldn't help her. She had to think. The trouble was that rational thought had never seemed so far away. The only thing that was clear was just how naive she had been to imagine her father would allow her to remain unmarried. When she'd refused to make a choice he'd done it for her. *This man isn't like the others.* And, gods, wasn't that the truth?

Lara drew in a ragged breath as Jarl Finn's face impinged on her thoughts. He was all the things she had admitted before and yet she felt no closer to knowing who he really was. Her mind returned to the scene on the promontory. That man had been very different from the one she'd spoken to the day before but which was real, the smooth-tongued admirer or the warlord? Or were they just different facets of the same character?

She'd known how to deal with the first but the second was another matter entirely. The warlord was charismatic but he was also dangerous. Some of that was about his sheer physical presence, but it went deeper. It was concerned with the aura of power he wore as effortlessly as the sword at his side. Everything about the warlord spoke of a natural leader, of a man familiar with command and to being obeyed. She'd already glimpsed his strength; he'd controlled her without even trying. In a few hours from now he would be her husband and his power over her would be total. As the realities of what that meant began to sink in the knot of apprehension tightened in her stomach.

Chapter Four

Finn half expected that his intended bride would refuse to appear that evening. As her father had said, Lara was not a biddable young woman and only a fool would imagine that she viewed this marriage with favour. She was more than capable of creating a spectacular scene. The possibility created a knot of tension in his gut. He had no idea how he would handle such a scenario never mind trying to visualise how her father would react if she exposed him to ridicule. The situation had all the potential for disaster. The only thing he could do now was to play his part and see this through.

His men had greeted the news of his impending marriage with amused interest but also with absolute understanding of the reasons for it.

'With all those extra swords we'll crush Steingrim like a louse,' said Unnr. 'Jarl Ottar is proving to be an invaluable ally.'

'Quite so,' replied Finn.

'He does you much honour in wishing for a closer alliance. In fact, it does all of us honour.'

The others voiced their agreement. It pleased them

greatly that their lord should be offered a noble bride with a fine dowry. Quite apart from the fitness of such a match it was indisputable evidence of their host's good faith.

'The gods must be smiling on us,' said Sturla, 'and especially on you, my lord, since your bride is fair into the bargain.'

Finn nodded. *Lara is fair all right, and difficult and unpredictable.* 'That she is.'

'And a redhead.'

Vigdis grinned. 'No man can foretell the future but I'd be willing to wager that yours will not be dull, my lord.'

Dull was the very last word that Finn would have used to describe it. The coming years would take care of themselves; it was the next few hours that weighed on his mind. Needing occupation he bathed his hands and face and combed his hair. Having done that he changed his clothes, swapping his worn hose and old brown tunic for the best blue and replacing the current leather belt for the one made of interlinking silver discs. Then he buckled on his sword and slid the seax into his belt. A red cloak completed the costume, fastened with a gold brooch wrought in the likeness of a dragon. Whatever happened this evening it would be evident that he meant to honour his bride.

His men likewise prepared themselves and dressed in their best. They were in high good humour now, exchanging jests and banter. Ordinarily Finn would have joined in but as the hour drew nearer his nervous tension increased. It also occurred to him that he had not thought about a morning gift for the bride. Silver and land were the most usual offerings. He realised it would have to be the former since that was what he had to hand. He'd have liked to offer her a more personal gift as well but there hadn't been time to arrange it. He'd have to address that later. Right now he had more pressing concerns.

Would Lara be compliant or would she publicly reject him? Would she even turn up for her wedding or was he going to have to fetch her? Uncertainty created a sense of anticipation. He realised then that he would fetch her if he had to. He hoped it wouldn't come to that but one way or another she was going to be his wife.

Considering the limited time available the servants had done well: they had contrived to clean and sweep the hall and the delicious smells of cooking testified to the coming feast. When Finn and his men arrived they were greeted by their host. He too had changed his clothes and donned his best in honour of the forthcoming nuptials. Under his smile however, Finn detected tension. He thought he could guess the reason for it. A swift glance around revealed no sign of Lara.

'The bride will be here shortly, my lord,' said Ottar.

Five more minutes passed and still she did not appear. The men laughed and talked among themselves, apparently quite at ease. No one seemed to find anything amiss. Finn took a deep breath, trying to ignore the knot in his gut. *She isn't coming.* It seemed he wasn't alone in that suspicion because Ottar's unease became increasingly apparent.

'What in the name of the All-Father is keeping the girl?' he demanded.

Finn summoned what he hoped was a soothing

smile. 'It's a lady's privilege to keep the groom waiting, my lord.'

Ottar grunted but looked unconvinced. When another five minutes passed his expression grew more annoyed. Some of those standing nearest began to notice and to exchange glances. Finn maintained an outward show of ease. Inwardly his thoughts were quite different. *She definitely isn't coming and this is getting more awkward by the second.*

Ottar's frown deepened but he kept his voice low. 'If this is one of her Loki tricks I'll thrash her before the entire company.'

Finn smiled as though at some pleasantry. 'Let us be patient a little longer, my lord.'

'You are gracious, Jarl Finn.'

'It is but a slight delay. I'm sure there's a good reason for it.' *The reason being that she has no intention of being married.*

'Two minutes more,' growled Ottar. 'Then I'll go and find her and drag her here by the hair if I have to.'

Finn closed his eyes. This was about to become unpleasant. The question was how to prevent it. Somehow he was going to have to forestall his companion before matters spiralled out of control.

The two minutes passed. Ottar's face was thunderous. 'Right! She's asked for it…'

He began to head for the bower but after two paces he stopped in his tracks, staring at the doorway opposite. Finn followed his gaze and then he too stared.

Lara! His heart gave a peculiar lurch as he watched her cross the room towards him. The green gown was gone now and in its place a fine dress of deep blue edged with red and gold at the neck and sleeves. A matching girdle rode her waist. Her beautiful hair was worn loose. A slim gold torc adorned her neck and there was a matching bracelet on her wrist. She looked a little pale but otherwise composed. It didn't detract from the fact that she was stunning.

She eventually reached them and dropped a polite curtsy.

'What in Thor's name took you so long?' growled Ottar.

She regarded him steadily. 'A torn hem, Father. It took a little while to mend.'

Finn recovered his wits and smiled. 'It was worth the wait.'

Her gaze flicked to his face. 'You are all kindness, my lord.'

Realising that the groom was not offended, Ottar relaxed, apparently mollified. 'Well, let's get on with it.'

Lara shivered inwardly. It had been in her mind to defy her father earlier and not turn up at all. The torn hem had been a lie, an excuse to cover delay caused by mounting dread. Minutes in which her imagination had suggested various means of escape, each wilder than the last. In the end common sense reasserted itself. If she tried to run she would be followed and eventually she would be caught. At the very least she could expect a thrashing. If that had been the end of it she might have taken that option, but it wouldn't be the end of it. She would still be forced to obey her father's will. *You can either do it with a semblance of grace or you can be dragged into the hall by main force.* She'd opted for a semblance of grace but it was a thin disguise.

The sight of her future husband set her heart pounding like a fuller's hammer. He had never seemed more imposing a presence than he did just then. The blue tunic was ideally suited to his colouring and by some fluke it almost exactly matched her gown. The costume also showed off his broad shoulders and athletic frame to considerable advantage, enhancing the suggestion of leashed strength. It was impossible not to feel intimidated. The other feelings he inspired were more complex and much harder to define. Nor was she inclined to explore them.

Ottar took her hand and placed it in Finn's much larger one. Her hand was cool and it trembled a little. He glanced down at her but she wasn't looking at him now and her expression revealed nothing. *Is she afraid? Fear* wasn't a word he'd have associated with Lara. A little nervous possibly, and that was understandable. He squeezed her fingers gently. She did look up then, the blue-green eyes meeting his for a moment. Then she lowered her gaze again but not in time to conceal the strong emotions there.

It took only a short time to exchange the vows that would bind them henceforth. Ottar supplied the ring, knowing that the groom wouldn't have had time to get one made. It was made of gold filigree, the workmanship delicate and beautiful. It was also tiny. Finn knew it would barely fit his little finger. However, it slid on to Lara's hand with ease. Then Ottar declared them man and wife and called upon those present to attest the fact. It was done. Expectant silence descended.

Ottar looked at Finn. 'Aren't you going to kiss your new wife?'

Finn sensed rather than saw Lara stiffen but when he took her in his arms he was in no doubt. However, there was nothing for it now but to carry this to the expected conclusion.

Lara knew this had to come and steeled herself. She had thought herself prepared; prepared for that inevitable proximity; prepared for the strong warm hands on her waist; prepared for the symbolic seal of possession. However, as his lips brushed hers she was definitely not prepared for the resulting shiver along her spine, a shiver that had nothing whatsoever to do with nerves. His lips continued to flirt with hers, light, almost teasing. Her pulse quickened. The pressure on her mouth increased a little. She lifted her hands to his breast to push him away but his arm slid around her waist and tightened, pulling her hard against him, trapping her hands. The other arm closed round her shoulders. She gasped as her body was pressed against the lean hard length of his. Before she had a chance to protest his mouth closed on hers in a passionate kiss that ignored resistance until she abandoned the attempt and her mouth opened to his. His tongue tilted with hers, intimate and shocking like the sudden rising tide of warmth inside her. It rippled through her body to the core.

He took the kiss at leisure. As it went on a roar of approval erupted around them. When eventually he drew back she was breathless, the pallor in her face replaced by a rosy flush. Grey eyes looked down into hers and she saw him smile, almost as if he knew about that sudden flood of heat in her blood. *He couldn't know. She was imagining it.* What she wasn't imagining was his evident enjoyment of the situation. Nor was he alone. All around was a sea of grinning faces. Even her father was smiling. Embarrassment mingled with confusion.

Ottar raised his arms. 'Let's drink to health for the bride and groom.'

He gestured to the waiting servant who brought the ceremonial silver mead cup. Lara took it and then offered it to Finn. He drank and passed it back. She took a mouthful of liquor and swallowed it. It was cheering but it was also strong, particularly when taken on an empty stomach. She handed the cup back to her father. To get drunk was not part of her plan at all; she needed to keep all her wits about her.

'Now we shall feast,' said Ottar.

Finn held out his hand to Lara and obediently she placed her fingers in his, allowing herself to be led to the high table. When she had taken her seat Finn sat down beside her with Ottar on his left. The rest of the company took their places and the servants filed in with platters of food. Although she hadn't eaten since morning Lara had little appetite. However, the meal gave her a reason to avoid looking at the man beside her, so she took refuge in the pretence of eating, forcing each morsel down and taking her time over it.

In contrast, Finn ate heartily, evidently quite untroubled by the anxiety she felt. However, he was attentive too, offering various dishes to her or enquiring whether she would like more meat or bread. Unwilling to let him see her unease she accepted another slice of the roast boar. Usually she would have enjoyed it but this evening it tasted of ashes.

The last time she had attended a wedding it was to see Asa married, an occasion that had given rise to similar feelings of impotent anger and bitter resentment. At the time she had felt them on her sister's behalf. Tears and pleading had accomplished nothing: Asa was bound to a man she detested and who cared nothing for her. She was a means to a political end and no more. Lara's fingers tightened on her cup.

'Will you have something more to eat?'

Finn's voice jerked her out of thought. 'No, I thank you.'

'You haven't eaten much thus far. I'd hate to have you waste away.'

'I'm not very hungry.'

He leaned back in his chair surveying her steadily, an unnerving scrutiny that brought creeping warmth to her neck and cheeks.

'This has been a difficult day for you, hasn't it?'

Difficult doesn't begin to describe it. 'That's one way of putting it.'

'I regret the suddenness of this arrangement but circumstances dictated it.'

'Why should you regret it? You have the ships and swords that you came for.'

'So I have, but I've achieved far more than that,' he replied.

'Ah, yes, a bride with a rich dowry.'

'A *fair* bride with a rich dowry.'

Lara looked away and took another sip of mead to try to quell the surge of resentment that his words had revived.

'That wasn't flattery by the way,' he went on. 'It was a statement of fact.' He continued his scrutiny. 'That gown becomes you very well incidentally.'

When she made no reply he smiled faintly. 'That was your cue to say, *Yes, I know.*'

She did look at him then, her gaze smouldering. 'Must I speak on cue now for your entertainment?'

'There is no *must*, Lara, although you are invariably entertaining.'

'I'm glad I amuse you.'

'How could you not when your company is so enlivening?' His eyes gleamed. 'Company that I greatly look forward to sharing.'

'I wish I could say the same.'

He laughed softly. 'That's better. For a while there I was afraid you had laid down your sword.'

The warmth in her cheeks intensified. 'If you thought that, then you were gravely mistaken, my lord.'

'I'm delighted to hear it.'

'You are pleased to mock.'

'Not at all. I really am delighted. The greatest enemy to a relationship is boredom but I feel quite sure ours will never suffer in that way.'

'Possibly not. Steingrim may slay you long before boredom sets in.'

Finn laughed out loud. 'I'm sorry to disappoint you there. Steingrim will not slay me.'

'If he doesn't perhaps I will.'

'You have already slain me with your incomparable beauty and sharp wit.'

'Would it were so easy.'

'I am not an easy man to kill, sweet Lara. You are destined to remain at my side.'

'What a rousing prospect.'

'Indeed I do hope to arouse you—very soon now.'

The implications of that produced a tide of heat that

rose from her feet to her face. *The man is outrageous. Utterly without shame.* He was also very big and very strong and he was her husband. In reality he could do whatever he chose now. However, that didn't mean craven surrender on her part.

'You will never arouse me, my lord.'

'Another challenge, Lara? I accept it, gladly.'

He is truly impossible. She sought for a witty and crushing retort but wit had temporarily fled and she had to make do with the latter. 'You are loathsome.'

'I'm sorry you should think so. I'll do my best to change your mind.'

'I will never change my mind.'

'Shall we have a wager on that?'

'There's no point. You have already lost.'

'Have I?' He surveyed her speculatively. 'I wonder.'

'No need to tax your brain so, my lord. You may take my word for it.'

The grey eyes glinted. With quiet deliberation Finn set down his cup and got to his feet. Lara blinked, staring up at him in surprise. Had she routed him at last? A glimmer of hope kindled in her breast. It was shortlived. Without warning he bent and lifted her bodily off the chair. Ignoring the laughter and amused glances all around them he turned to Ottar.

'I find myself impatient to be alone with my bride. Perhaps a private place has been prepared for us?'

The hall erupted with cheers and raucous laughter. Lara went hot and cold by turns, struggling furiously.

'Put me down, you brute!'

Finn grinned, adjusting his hold a little so that he had a surer grip. 'I shall, sweet Lara, as soon as we reach our bedchamber.'

The words elicited renewed efforts to escape. He held her with insulting ease and, surrounded by a laughing crowd, carried her from the hall.

Chapter Five

A small hov had been made ready for the bridal couple so that this night at least they might have privacy. Lara fought her captor every step of the way but to no avail: she was borne inexorably on until they reached their destination. Before anyone had a chance to intervene Finn carried her inside and heeled the door shut behind him. Then he set her down and barred it securely. At once a chorus of indignant voices rose from outside and heavy fists pounded on the wood. He ignored them, and turned towards his bride.

For several heart-thumping seconds they surveyed each other in silence. Lara darted a look around: lamplight revealed that the hov was sparsely furnished, the single room dominated by a large bed covered with furs. The window was shuttered fast. The only door was the one by which they had entered and Finn was between it and her. She moistened her lips. In the confined space he seemed much larger than before, a dominating and virile presence whose attention was now entirely on her.

'Alone at last.' He smiled and removed his cloak,

tossing it over a chair. Then he looked at Lara and threw his arms wide. 'Come here, sweet wife.'

She made no move to obey. 'I will not. I agreed to wed you, nothing else.'

He evinced complete surprise. 'Are you saying you will not share my bed?'

'Yes, I am saying that.'

'It's a serious matter to deny a man his marital rights.'

The teasing tone was much more disconcerting than an outright display of anger, and much harder to deal with.

'You've got what you wanted. This was about ships and swords and nothing else.'

'Didn't anyone mention that it's actually about more than that? Would it surprise you to know that you must run my hall and perform all duties connected with that?'

Her eyes sparkled with indignation. 'Of course it wouldn't.'

'Oh, good. That'll save confusion.' He paused in apparent contemplation of some mental list. 'In addition I must mention, in case anyone else didn't, that I shall want half-a-dozen fine sons to continue my line and that you must produce them. Not all at once of course,' he amended. 'I don't wish to be unreasonable.'

Lara experienced a fresh surge of indignation. Along with that were other more elusive emotions that she didn't want to explore. 'I am not a brood mare to be used at your pleasure.'

'You know, it would be very much my pleasure,' he replied. 'In spite of your vile temper you're a comely wench. Bedding you will not be an unwelcome obligation.'

Lara backed a pace. 'Stay away from me!'

'You don't mean that.'

'I said stay away.'

'What are you afraid of, Lara?'

'I'm not afraid of you.'

He advanced unhurriedly. 'No?'

'No.'

It was a downright lie. Just then she'd never felt so scared in her life. All the same she'd rather have died than admit it. She would also have given anything to have had a sword in her hand.

'Then come and kiss me, sweet wife.'

'I will *not* kiss you.'

'I really would like it if you did.'

Her stomach wallowed. Then her back met the wall. Desperately she edged along it, her eyes seeking some weapon, anything that might be used to hold him off. Her leg brushed a stool. She bent and grabbed it, hurling it at his head. Finn ducked and the missile flew past, crashing against the door. She heard him chuckle. Anger temporarily replaced fear and the stool was followed by a jug and a wooden bowl. He avoided them easily and came on. Heart pounding, she retreated step by step until she reached the corner. Seeing the danger she tried to dodge away but Finn was faster, dodging in front of her, forcing her back again, forbidding escape.

'I really would like that kiss, Lara.'

'Never.'

'Never is a long time.' He moved closer, trapping her there with an arm on either side of her shoulders. 'Too long.'

'Don't you dare to touch me!'

'Do I dare?' He contemplated it briefly. 'Yes, I believe I do. Otherwise what a world of pleasure would be lost.'

She had no idea what he meant and didn't care. All she could see was the face looming above hers, a handsome arresting face wearing an infuriating smile.

'I'm warning you. Get away from me.'

'No, for if I do that I cannot pleasure you, and I do wish to pleasure you, very thoroughly.'

The words were beyond outrage and she struck him hard. His eyes glinted. Her attempt to launch a second blow ended in a gasp as her wrist was caught in an iron grip.

'It's no good, Lara. You won't drive me off as you did all the others.'

'Let *go* of me.'

'No.'

He evaded a kick. Lara struggled, writhing in his hold, every particle of her being in revolt. He held her without any undue effort. His evident enjoyment of her predicament did nothing to calm her rage.

'How dare you treat me like this?'

'You have chosen the method.'

'I?' She kicked out again and missed. 'Don't try to blame me for your shortcomings, you devious rogue.'

'Harsh words, ill suited to a bride.'

'Well-deserved words! You *are* a rogue—an opportunist, a pirate, a low, cunning, smooth-tongued, scheming underhanded villain.'

'Sweet Lara, did no one tell you that you must show respect when you speak to your husband, and that you must be obedient to his wishes?'

'You'd like that, wouldn't you?'

'It would have a certain novelty value, I'll admit.' He strode across the room propelling her towards the bed. 'Since you will not kiss me we shall have to omit that and just retire instead.'

Her heart leaped towards her throat. 'I will not.'

He sighed. 'Either you can remove your clothes or I will.'

She glared at him. 'How I hate you!'

He ignored the words as if she hadn't spoken. 'If I do it you will likely never be able to wear that gown again, which would be a pity. The colour suits you.'

Her chin lifted. She wanted to defy him but knew that, if she did, it would end in humiliating defeat and a ruined dress. Throwing him a look of detestation she got to her feet and with fumbling fingers began to unfasten her girdle. As it came loose she let it fall to the floor. Then she drew off the shorter overdress. She paused, her eyes meeting his.

He raised an eyebrow. 'Keep going.'

The under-gown followed. Clad only in her shift now she waited, dread vying with fury. Was he going to demand that she strip? Was that to be her punishment for defiance? It occurred to her then that making her strip was likely to be the least of it. She was completely in his power and that wasn't a comfortable thought. Was he going to hit her? Did he intend to hurt her? Once she had thought he wouldn't offer violence to a woman, but now certainty was tainted by creeping doubt. She had never felt more vulnerable or more afraid in her life but she wouldn't have let him know it for a shipload of silver. Her chin lifted.

The grey gaze never left her. 'The bed awaits.'

Reluctantly she obeyed him, perching gingerly between the cool linen sheets, hugging her knees protectively. For a moment or two he remained quite still. Then he bent and retrieved his cloak, throwing it over his arm. Lara followed the movement in silent bemusement, confusion evident in her face.

He smiled mockingly. 'Don't worry. I shan't rape you, Lara, easy as that would be. I prefer my women to be willing participants. When you tire of your cold, virginal bed and decide to become a real woman let me know. In the meantime sleep alone if you will.'

Speechless, she watched him cross to the door and unbar it. He paused on the threshold.

'You had best secure this after me. I cannot vouch for what drunken pranksters may attempt later.'

With an effort she found her voice. 'Then you're not… You don't mean to return?'

'No, I don't mean to return.' His smile lost some of its mockery and was replaced by something much like regret. 'Goodnight, Lara. Sleep well.'

With that he was gone, pulling the door to close behind him.

Chapter Six

For a few moments Lara was too stunned to move. Then she crept to the door and listened, half expecting a trick. The sound of retreating footsteps assured her otherwise. With shaking hands she barred the door and then leaned against it, trying to assimilate what had just happened. Never in a thousand years would she have expected the evening to end like this. Her imagination had supplied a more graphic image in which she was pinned to the bed while he did his will. She swallowed hard. He could have raped her; he was frighteningly strong. Her wrist still bore the imprint of his fingers. All her efforts to resist had done no more than afford him some light amusement. His taunts were still ringing in her ears. Even his avowed wish to have sons had been nothing more than provocation. He wasn't concerned with getting sons at all: what mattered to him were ships and swords. That was why he had agreed to this marriage. He had no interest in her; he didn't even like her. Quite possibly, when he had resolved his immediate problem with his enemies he would put her aside citing her refusal to consummate the marriage.

No one would blame him or question his right to do it either. If he put her aside she would be returned to her father. The consequences of that would be dire. Alternatively she could crawl back to Finn and beg him to take her. Her jaw tightened. *I'd rather be in a midnight fire at sea.* She would never submit to him or go willingly to his bed.

Finn sat down on a rock at the end of the promontory and watched the rising moon silver the dark water of the fjord. The night was still. Even the sound of revelry from the hall didn't carry this far. The participants were no doubt imagining him locked in a passionate embrace with his bride. He grimaced. The only way that could have happened would have been to give way to baser urges. Thor's teeth but he'd been tempted; tempted to give the little spitfire something to think about. The possibilities afforded him fierce momentary satisfaction. Had he given in to temptation it would have been no more than she deserved. If ever a woman needed to be taught who was master it was she. In the whole history of the world there had never been such a proud, contrary, wilful, infuriating little hussy.

He let out a long ragged breath. As he'd been expecting her to reject his advances tonight he ought not to have felt disappointment. It was utterly illogical and it was the fault of that earlier kiss. While he'd thought to enjoy it he could never have anticipated that he would find it so deeply arousing.

That wasn't all he found arousing either. A man would have to be dead not to be aware of her fiery beauty. Most of all it was the challenge she represented, a challenge he'd been unable to ignore from the outset. However, physical mastery wasn't enough. When he took Lara—and he would take her—it was going to be with her willing consent. She would submit; would yield all of herself to him. It was a heady prospect and, he admitted, a distant one. In the meantime he had more pressing concerns. When he had defeated Steingrim there would be time enough to vanquish Lara.

Having clarified his thoughts he eventually left the promontory and, since a return to the hall was out of the question, he went to the barn and found a convenient pile of hay. It was dry and comfortable at least, even if it wasn't where he'd envisaged spending his wedding night.

Lara had fallen into an uneasy sleep and woke at dawn. For a few seconds she was disorientated, trying to think where she was. Then, slowly, memory flowed back. Along with it came resentment. She was married now and to a man who cared nothing for her save as a means to an end.

When she opened the window shutter it was to admit grey light. The only sound was birdsong. It was hardly surprising. The revelry had gone on late and no doubt the company would be sleeping off the effects. It occurred to her to wonder where Finn had slept last night. Had he returned to the hall to continue drinking? It seemed likely. Quite probably he was lying across the table in a stupor along with his companions. She shrugged it off. His whereabouts were of no interest.

Collecting up her discarded clothing she dressed once more and, when she was decent again, unbarred the door. She had no wish to remain. The hov held too many disturbing associations and the sooner she was out of the place the better. Instead she returned to the women's bower. As she'd hoped, the occupants were still asleep enabling her to avoid their curious looks and knowing smiles. Quickly and quietly she changed back into the green gown, returning the blue one to the chest. As she did so her gaze went to the sword at the bottom, but this morning she had no desire to practise. Nor had she any desire to remain in the steading. She didn't want to speak to anyone nor was she of a mind to be the butt of other people's humour. The marriage had happened but she wasn't going to pretend to like it. Until she had firm control over her anger she was better out of the way.

Taking the path through the lower meadows she headed for the hill above the farm. She would find fresh air and solitude up there and if there was any company it would only be a few sheep. That was fine by her. The less she had to see of humankind the better.

On leaving the barn at dawn Finn took a detour to the promontory but the place was deserted. Either Lara was in no mood to practise sword craft or else she had no wish to be found there. He had a pretty shrewd idea which of those suppositions was correct and was sorry for it. Their previous training session had been fun. Unfortunately, recent events were not calculated to win her confidence or soften her mood. Just then he had no idea how that was to be achieved. Lara was unlike any woman he'd ever met. It was a pity she hadn't come to the promontory this morning because there were things he needed to impart, not least about their forthcoming departure. Since she evidently had no intention of seeking him out he'd have to go to her.

* * *

When he reached the hov he found it empty. That left the bower as the most likely line of retreat. From his point of view, she couldn't have made a more awkward choice because he couldn't impose his presence there without creating uproar. He'd have to send a female servant to fetch her and that in turn would arouse all manner of speculation that he could well have done without. No doubt Lara was fully aware of that and probably enjoying the thought of his chagrin. He gritted his teeth. How was it that she always managed to make his life more difficult at every turn?

He was rounding the end of the hov when he saw her, but, far from hiding in the bower, she was heading away from the steading along a track that led towards the hill behind. For a second, it occurred to him to wonder if she was running away, but she wasn't moving like one in furtive haste; nor was she dressed for travel or carrying anything with her. Whatever her intention it wasn't flight. The little witch was good at keeping him guessing. But this way at least they could have a private conversation.

He set off after her, his longer strides closing the distance between them. For a while she didn't notice that she was being followed but as he gained on her some sixth sense must have given warning of his presence and she glanced over her shoulder. He saw a flicker of surprise and then annoyance in her face. Somewhat to his surprise she stopped and waited for him to catch up. They surveyed each other in silence. He saw that she had changed back into the green gown and that the jewellery was missing too. In fact all trace of bridal finery was gone. She looked pale but otherwise composed, her expression impassive now.

'Where are you off to, Lara?'

'For a walk.'

'Alone?'

'As you see.'

'I looked for you on the promontory earlier.'

'Did you?'

'There are things we need to discuss.'

'Such as?'

He sighed. Clearly she had no wish to talk to him at all although in the light of recent events he couldn't entirely blame her. All the same this could not be avoided. She had just become part of the arrangements.

'Tomorrow I leave for Ravndal.'

He had her attention now. 'But that is several days' sailing from here.'

'That's right.'

He didn't miss the glimmer of hope that flickered into her face. The thought of his departure was pleasing to her. If she was anticipating his protracted absence she was doomed to disappointment.

'My continued presence here is unwise,' he went on. 'Steingrim won't be far behind and when I meet him it will be on ground of my choosing.'

She could see the point. 'What about the other ships, though?'

'Alrik's will accompany us. The second will meet us a little later.'

'I see.'

'We'll be leaving early.'

She nodded, controlling a sudden surge of jubilation. He was leaving tomorrow. He would be gone for days; weeks with any luck. Perhaps the gods were redressing the balance a little.

'Was there anything else, my lord?'

'No, nothing else—for the moment.'

'Then I beg you will excuse me.' She would have continued on up the path but his voice stayed her.

'Lara.'

She paused, surveying him quizzically. 'My lord?'

'My name is Finn. It would please me if you were to use it.'

'As you wish.'

'You know, it seems to me that life would be easier if we were not at odds.'

'Ah, yes. I'm quite sure you would prefer a meek and obedient little wife who would never open her mouth and who would perform your every command with alacrity.'

He smiled faintly. 'That would indeed be a novelty though I fear it would quickly wear off.'

'What do you want, then? It cannot be a wife such as me for you have already declared me to be lacking in obedience, respect and temper.'

'So you are. Perhaps I should prefer a woman whose character is somewhere in between?'

'You should have sought her earlier. It is too late now. You are stuck with me.'

'I can conceive of worse things that might befall a man.'

'Well you do have the compensation of ships and swords.'

'There is that of course.' He reached out and lifted a fiery lock of her hair, testing its softness between his fingers. 'Though I think there are potential rewards far greater than those.'

His hand brushed across her gown, an apparently accidental touch but no less disturbing for that. As disturbing as his proximity now. Not that she intended to let him see it. 'You think that if it pleases you.'

'It does please me, Lara.'

'Well, then, at least one of us is happy.'

He raised an eyebrow. 'Does it not occur to you we might both achieve that state?'

'How should it? In my experience marriage is not conducive to happiness.'

It struck a chord but he had no wish to rake over his past. However, he was curious about hers. 'In your experience?'

'My sister was given in marriage as a peace woman in order to end a long-running feud. The match was much against her will. Her husband was a cold, hard, unfeeling brute and our father knew it. Nevertheless, he gave Asa to this man anyway.'

He could not miss the bitterness and anger in her tone and understood it. The lot of a peace woman was neither easy nor enviable. However, he resisted the temptation to comment on that since anything he said would sound like a platitude. In any case there was a more fundamental point here that needed to be addressed.

'And do you think me a cold, hard, unfeeling brute?'

For a moment she was silent, evidently wrestling with strong emotion. Then her gaze locked with his. 'What do you care? You have already stated that my opinion is of no importance.'

Finn grimaced and his hand fell to his side. *She*

*knows how to turn the tables on me. She's damnably
good at it. All the same she isn't going to slide out of
this.* 'Answer the question, Lara.'

'When it comes to achieving your ends I think you
are as cold and hard as any other man. Feeling doesn't
come into it.' She paused. 'However, I…I do not think
you a brute.'

'I'm overwhelmed.'

'You did ask.'

'So I did.'

'Would you rather I had lied to flatter you?'

'No, I would never wish you to lie to me.' He paused.
'Nor would I wish to lie to you.'

'Indeed I hope you will not. In that way we will both
know exactly where we stand.'

Finn had a fairly good idea of where he stood with
her just then but decided not to voice his thought. If
he did she would be quick to confirm it and there was
only so much truth a man could take in one day.

'I give you my word that I will always try to be honest with you,' he replied.

She inclined her head in acquiescence. 'Good.'

'Now if you will excuse me there are things I need
to arrange.'

For a moment or two Lara watched his retreating
back, then turned and resumed her walk. The news of
his approaching departure was more than pleasing. She
had no doubt that he would defeat his enemies eventually but that wouldn't be accomplished overnight. In
the meantime she would be relieved of his constraining
presence. She smiled, her spirits lighter than they had
been since the whole sorry business began.

On reaching the top of the hill she found a convenient rock to sit on. From here the view was impressive but her mind was more agreeably engaged. Eventually she would have to accompany Finn to his hall but, given the nature of this marriage, it seemed entirely possible that he might often be away from home. Since she had no intention of sharing his bed she had no doubt that he would take his pleasures elsewhere too. That was fine by her. Indeed it was the best that might be hoped for.

Finn spoke to his men and made the necessary arrangements for the morrow. It was good to have something to do and for a while it took his mind off Lara. However, she was proving to be an invasive presence. Their conversation had been disturbing and in spite of his best efforts it kept coming back. The reason for her antipathy towards marriage was now much clearer and he could well understand how her sister's fate had affected her thinking on the subject. To see someone you loved made desperately unhappy was intolerable. Being married off to a total stranger in her turn had only further fuelled her resentment. A stranger whom she regarded as being cold, hard and unfeeling. Just short of being a brute in fact. He drew little consolation from that. It wasn't the first time a woman had thought the worst of him.

Bótey had been in no doubt. Of course he was younger then and so arrogantly self-assured, concerned only with following his own wishes regardless of how his actions might affect others. For him the lengthy absences from home were something he took in his stride, relishing the adventure and the change of scene and the companionship of his sword brothers. For Bótey those times meant loneliness and boredom. She'd lacked the inner resources to be content with her own company. If he hadn't been so self-absorbed he might have foreseen what that would lead to. Finn's jaw tightened. He couldn't right the past but if he'd learned anything from that time it was about the folly of taking someone for granted. He wouldn't make that mistake again.

The company was in lively good humour that evening, the hall filled with conversation and laughter. Lara could feel the buzz of anticipation in the air around her as she moved from group to group filling the mead cups. These men were looking forward to the coming adventure and the prospect of a fight. The possibility of death had no power to deter them; what mattered was the winning of battle fame. Then a man's name would live after him on earth while he entered Valhalla and feasted with the heroes in Odin's hall. As she looked around at the eager faces she wondered how many of these men would be slain in the coming enterprise. Steingrim was a dangerous and determined foe. What if he were to win? What if it were Finn who was slain?

By rights the notion ought to have been mighty pleasing but oddly it wasn't. In spite of all that had happened she could not wish that. He was so much larger than life that it was hard to imagine a world without him in it. Somehow he had made an impression at an altogether deeper level than she'd realised. She could barely recall the faces of the other men who had sought her hand, but, if Finn walked out of her life tomorrow, she knew she'd never forget his.

'You seem thoughtful this evening,' said Alrik as

she paused to refill his cup. 'Are you anxious that your handsome husband is soon to go into battle?'

'No, of course not. Why should I be?'

'You are but recently married after all.'

'Finn looks like the kind of man who can take care of himself.'

'That he is. His reputation is considerable.' Alrik glanced across the room towards the subject of their talk. 'He is a man whom others will follow.'

Lara's gaze followed his and came to rest on the tall figure across the room. In any company Finn would stand out, she thought, and he would always be at the centre of things, as now.

She smiled faintly. 'Including you?'

'Aye, including me. It will be an honour to fight at his side.'

Lara regarded him curiously. At twenty Alrik was an able commander in his own right. He and his crew would accompany Finn, a prospect he evidently relished since there was no mistaking the sincerity in his tone and looks.

'What makes you so eager to join his cause?' she asked.

'We are kin now so his cause is mine, but it's more than that. I respect him and so does every other man here.'

'But you barely know him.'

'I know that I could not have a better man at my back in a fight.'

'You trust him, then?'

'Aye, I do.'

'How has he managed to inspire such loyalty in so short a time?'

'It's obvious, isn't it? The man has presence, intelligence and courage.'

'Perhaps.'

'There's no perhaps about it,' he replied. 'He does.'

'Very well, but the possession of those qualities doesn't necessarily mean you can trust him.'

'Look at his crew, Lara. Don't be deceived by the jovial smiles and friendly banter. They're as tough as boiled leather, and every man among them has made a name for himself in battle. Would such men follow one whom they believed to be untrustworthy?'

'I suppose not.'

Alrik snorted. 'You suppose right. If they'd had any doubts on that score they'd have cut his throat and left his body for the crows.'

'I will admit he is a natural leader.'

'He's also a likeable one. It's a rare combination.'

Lara made no reply but her brother's words had left her with plenty to think about. The present situation had caused her to see Finn in an unflattering light but it was evident that others didn't share those views. Respect was not given on demand. Reluctantly she was forced to concede that their high opinion of him had been earned. Of course, he would appear different to men because they inhabited a different world in many respects; a world in which trust and mutual reliance were all-important. Battle forged a bond like no other. They didn't think about women in the same way. When they thought about them at all it was to satisfy a physical need, to get sons or to attain a political ambition; perhaps all three. Such terms as trust and liking didn't feature.

She left Alrik and continued filling cups. Out of the

corner of her eye she could see Finn talking to his companions. As always he looked completely at his ease, radiating quiet confidence. He must have said something amusing because his words were followed by a burst of laughter. It elicited several quips in return and she heard him laugh. It was infectious and she found herself smiling too. Finn looked up and for a moment his gaze met hers. She saw amusement there and then it faded to be replaced with something that caused her pulse to quicken. A flush of warmth crept from her neck to her cheeks. Disconcerted now, she looked away.

Finn called across the room, 'Is there any more mead in that jug, woman?'

The tone was unmistakeably provocative and it stopped Lara in her tracks. Several grinning faces turned her way, their owners waiting for the coming explosion. She ignored them. Glancing down into the jug she favoured Finn with a smile.

'Yes, there is.'

Having answered the question she turned away, feigning to look for empty cups elsewhere. Finn's eyes glinted.

'Then bring it here and be quick about it.'

The words drew several indrawn breaths. Lara surveyed him coolly.

'Right away, my lord.' Without the least semblance of haste she made her way to his side. 'Here it is.' She held up the jug. 'Would you like me to refill your cup perhaps?'

His lips twitched and he looked around at his companions. 'What it is to have a wife with sharp wits.'

Several chuckles greeted this. Lara smiled sweetly. 'It's good to be appreciated, my lord.'

He held out his cup. 'Oh, I could scarcely fail to appreciate you.'

'The sentiment is mutual, believe me.'

'I'd be tempted to take that for flattery if I didn't know better.'

'Keen perception is one of your strengths.'

He laughed softly which, in its way, was far more disturbing than annoyance would have been. She poured the mead, concentrating on keeping her hand steady, supremely conscious of the man and of having his undivided attention.

'You imply that I have more,' he said.

'Well, let me see.' She pretended to consider. 'Although our acquaintance has been short I could not fail to note that you are single-minded in pursuit of a goal—that you possess a cunning brain and that you have considerable skill at barter.'

He nodded. 'I also enjoy a challenge.'

'How very fortunate.'

'And I like to win.'

'Dear me! You must have known your share of disappointment.'

'I am rarely disappointed.'

'That must be why humility doesn't feature among your personal qualities.'

His grin widened. 'I do confess it.'

'Never mind, it is amply compensated by arrogance.'

'A crushing blow to my self-esteem.'

'Nothing could crush that, my lord.'

Finn laughed out loud. 'I'm sure you will persevere anyway.'

Lara stared at him. The man was impossible. Noth-

ing deflated him. Nothing daunted him. It was definitely time to beat a dignified retreat.

'If you will excuse me I must go and fetch some
more mead.'

'What a pity.'

'Yes, but I'm sure you'll get over it.'

Finn watched her departure with mixed feelings. Although her assessment of his character was decidedly
unflattering he had enjoyed the repartee that went with
it. In spite of his best efforts that day he hadn't been
able to dismiss her from his mind altogether. Once or
twice he'd even found himself looking around in the
hope of seeing her. Annoyed with himself he'd made
a more determined attempt to focus on the business in
hand. He had a battle to fight. Now was not the time
for distraction of any sort, least of all for a troublesome
little vixen like Lara.

Even in the hall tonight she had done her best to
avoid him, leaving others to fill his cup. It should have
been a matter of complete indifference to him, but it
wasn't. Even while he tried to focus on the conversation his gaze obliquely followed her progress around
the room. Knowing that she would not come to him
he'd had to resort to outright provocation just to be sure
of getting her attention. It had worked, although he
didn't get the response he'd been expecting. He never
knew which way she would jump. With her he had to
be continually on his toes, ready for anything, but it
was the element of unpredictability that he found so
stimulating. In the short time he'd known her he'd experienced a wide range of emotions but boredom wasn't

one of them. She represented an entirely different kind of challenge and one that would be met. Just let him deal with Steingrim and then they would see.

Chapter Seven

Next day, just after dawn, the men began loading provisions and war gear on to the waiting ships. Although Lara watched the preparations from a distance, she felt the familiar thrill of excitement that the sea dragons always inspired. They were beautiful and deadly, their long clean lines built for speed enabling them to bear down on their prey with the ruthless power of swooping hawks. Their shallow draughts made them ideal for exploring inland waterways as well, something her brother had taken advantage of many times.

'I'll bid you farewell, Daughter.' Her father's voice jerked her out of her reverie. She'd been so engrossed in the ships that she hadn't even noticed his approach.

'My lord?'

He clasped her shoulders and bestowed a kiss on her cheek. 'I wish you a safe journey and contentment in your new life.'

'Thank you but—'

'Be a good wife and obey your husband in all things.' He squeezed her shoulders and then stepped back. 'I expect your brother will bring me word in due course.'

He glanced around and spied Alrik on the jetty. 'That reminds me, I need a word with him before he leaves.'

She looked after him in bemusement. Before she had time to ponder too deeply Finn appeared at her shoulder.

'Are your things aboard yet?'

'No, why?'

'The ship will be leaving very soon. I'll have someone fetch your box.'

'To what end?'

'I should have thought that was obvious.'

'Not to me.'

He surveyed her steadily. 'Surely you didn't think I would leave you behind?'

Lara blinked. It was exactly what she had thought. It had never occurred to her that he might have other plans.

'But you're going to meet Steingrim.'

'Don't worry. I'll keep you safe.'

Something in his smile caused her breathing to quicken. 'I'll be safer here and indeed I am content to remain.'

'But I am not. Indeed, the idea displeases me greatly.'

'I am flattered that you should so desire my company but in truth I have no wish to impede your plans, my lord.'

'You won't impede my plans. You're very much a part of them.'

'I should prefer to stay here.'

'And I should prefer you to go.'

This was getting trickier by the minute. He seemed impervious to even the strongest of hints. She was going to have to be blunt. 'I don't wish to go.'

'That is unfortunate.'

'What would I do on such an expedition?'

'Whatever I command of you.'

It was blatant provocation again but knowing that didn't diminish her annoyance. Her gaze smouldered.

'Not likely.'

'I think you'll find it otherwise. Incidentally, the penalties for disobedience are harsh on board a ship.'

'I'm not going on board your ship.'

'A wife's place is at her husband's side. Where is your box?'

'It's in the bower where it's staying.'

Finn called to one of the passing crewmen. 'Sturla, go to the bower and fetch the lady's things. One of the women will show you.'

'Right away, my lord.'

Lara glared at Sturla. 'Don't you dare touch my things, you oaf.'

The man ignored her as though she hadn't spoken and strode off for the steading. Furious, she rounded on Finn.

'You can't do this.'

'I just did.'

'And I just told you I wasn't going.'

He raised an eyebrow and then slowly advanced. Reading his intention, Lara turned to run but he caught her in two strides. There followed a few heated seconds of loud protest and futile struggle and then she was tossed over his shoulder and carried bodily to the waiting ship. As they reached the jetty they passed her father. Having observed the spectacle for a moment he nodded to Finn.

'Good man. Start as you mean to go on.'

Lara heard the words with impotent and speechless wrath. Moments later she was aboard the ship. Once there she was deposited in the stern and, despite a furious resistance, was pinned to the deck with a knee in her back and then bound hand and foot. Finn surveyed her steadily.

'I'll untie you again when we're underway.'

'Then I'll swim back, you bastard.'

'Try it and you'll be tied up for the rest of the journey. That's after I've tanned your backside, of course.'

She glared at him. 'Only you would be low enough to think of such a thing.'

'Low enough to do it and enjoy it as well.'

Just then she had no doubts about his sincerity on either count. The ramifications sent a flush of heat the length of her body. As a result she bit back the insults she wanted to hurl at his head and remained silent.

Finn had no trouble reading her expression. 'I think we understand one another.' He straightened, looking down at her. 'Now, if you'll excuse me, I'll get this ship underway.'

With that he left her. A short time later the man Sturla returned carrying her chest. As soon as he came aboard she heard the shouted commands and saw the lines cast off. Slowly the ship began to move away from shore. As it did she was aware of covert glances coming her way from the crew. Fuming, Lara fought the rope but it had been most expertly tied. Her bonds yielded not a whit. In the end she gave it up, realising that she was going to have to stay there until it pleased Finn to release her. It was but a small demonstration of his power but it gave rise to more sombre reflections. Soon now they would be in his territory, a wild and potentially dangerous place cut off from everything that was familiar. In that place his authority was absolute.

It was another hour before Finn came near her again. By then the ship was under sail in open water, the coast a dark smudge on the horizon. Even had she felt so inclined, Lara knew it would be impossible to swim back to shore. In fact she wasn't so inclined. The fury that had consumed her earlier had died down to a resentful glow and then gradually burned itself out. Resentment was futile. Besides, Finn would most likely enjoy it. She sighed and shifted a little as the edge of a strake dug into her shoulder. All she wanted now was to be able to stretch her cramped limbs. Involuntarily her gaze returned to the tall figure in the bow, taking in every lean hard line of him. Imagination suggested a physical manifestation of the fearsome creature depicted in the carved prow, fierce, predatory and dangerous. He looked completely at home in this environment, master of the world he inhabited. Technically he was her master too.

Her breath caught in her throat as he turned and made his way unhurriedly along the deck, pausing to exchange a word or two with his men on the way. None of them paid her the slightest heed. It wasn't unusual for a woman to travel on a ship and, though they might not have expected it to be a sea dragon, it was the only choice available. As to the method of her arrival on board... Not only would they not question his orders they clearly didn't question his actions either. In their view a disobedient wife could take what came to her. They probably thought he'd been lenient. When she thought of what he might have done she realised that,

in many ways, he had been. In all their dealings so far
he had never physically hurt her. Would that change
now? Once away from her father's jurisdiction Finn
would have no need to practise restraint. He could do
what he liked. It wasn't a comforting thought.

As he drew closer she tried to read his expression
but it gave nothing away. Had he come to free her or to
gloat? Whatever happened she wasn't going to beg. He
stopped a few feet away, surveying her keenly.

'If I untie you are you going to do anything stupid?'

She shook her head.

'Do I have your word on that?'

'Yes.'

He bent down and began to loosen the rope round
her ankles. His fingers were strong and sure, making
short work of the knots. When her legs were free she
altered her position and he turned his attention to the
rest. He was very close now, near enough for her to
feel his body heat and to catch the smell of wool and
smoke from his tunic. Beneath it was the subtle and
disturbing scent of the man.

As the bonds came free she breathed a sigh of relief
and flexed her cramped wrists. He hadn't bound them
tightly enough to cut off the circulation but it was good
to have freedom of movement again. More than anything she wanted to stretch her legs. However, when
she tried to stand the combination of rolling deck and
stiffened limbs caused her to stagger. A firm hand
caught her arm and steadied her.

'You'll get your sea legs in a little while.'

She nodded, every particle of her being aware of
the man beside her. In self-defence she looked away
towards the distant coast.

'Will we put in to shore tonight or stay on the ship?'

'We'll go ashore. It gets cold on the water at night.'

'You must be used to that.'

'We are but we still prefer to sit around a fire when we can.'

She shot him a sideways glance. 'Is this a suggestion of softness? I don't believe it.'

'Even the hardest of men like their creature comforts from time to time.'

'Even the likes of Steingrim?'

'Of course.'

'Popular report says he's made of stone.'

'He'd like people to think so, but he's still a man for all that and therefore no more immune to the attractions of comfort than anyone else.'

'A fire, hot food and a cup of mead would suffice to soften him?'

'They would help,' he replied, 'but you'd need to add a soft dry bed to the list—and a woman to warm it.'

The conversation was heading into deep water. It was time to steer it back again. 'Have you met the man before?'

'Our paths have crossed once or twice.'

'But you did not fight him.'

'I had no reason to then.'

Now he did have a reason and one that could not be disputed. The coming conflict had to happen but the thought filled her with foreboding. Finn must have read it in her face because he drew her gently round to face him.

'Are you afraid, Lara?'

She would have liked to deny it but she had promised to be honest with him. 'A little.'

'Do you doubt my ability to protect you?'

'No.' Her gaze met his. 'My doubt is not about your courage or prowess in battle but rather the evil nature of the man you must meet. I think him capable of the foulest trickery.'

'So do I and I will be ready for it.' He smiled faintly. 'All the same I appreciate your concern, and your good opinion of my skills.'

'Don't mock, Finn. I was being serious.'

'So was I,' he replied.

They put into a small cove that evening. Nevertheless, Finn organised a small contingent of four to remain on board. Lara eyed him quizzically.

'You fear an attack?'

'No, though I won't rule it out entirely,' he replied. 'Even so, there's always a guard on the ship. Then if she slips her mooring and drifts, or if any other problem arises, there's someone at hand to deal with it.'

'I see.'

They stood by the side watching as the rest of the crew vaulted over the side into the surf and waded ashore. Lara eyed the water dubiously. It was thigh deep on the men which meant it would likely reach her waist. While she would have no hesitation about getting wet feet the thought of a soaking had less appeal. It would ruin her gown and she'd have to sit around in wet things all evening. On the other hand she wasn't about to complain to Finn. After her earlier experience she wouldn't put it past him to throw her in if she annoyed him again.

'Are you ready?' he asked.

She took a deep breath and nodded, hoping that she looked more enthusiastic than she felt. 'Yes, of course.'

'I'll go first. It's quite a long way down.'

He lowered himself over the side and then looked up at her. 'All right.'

Gingerly she sat down and swung her legs over the side. Finn reached up and caught her by the waist. Resting her hands on his shoulders she took a deep breath, bracing herself for the cold water. He lifted her clear of the side and for a moment she had a sensation of gossamer lightness; the next she was settled in his arms.

'Put your arms around my neck and hold on.'

Meekly she obeyed him. His lips quirked slightly, then he headed towards the shore. All thought of cold water was forgotten now; everything vanished except the hard-muscled body holding her close. The nape of his neck was warm beneath his hair, the curve a natural resting place for her hands. Now that she was so close she realised that his hair wasn't just a dark shade of blonde: it was gold and bronze shot through with sun. It brushed her skin, the touch light and sensual inviting other, more dangerous, thoughts like how it would feel to run her fingers through it. The possibility sent a curl of heat into her belly.

Happily for her peace of mind they reached the strand a few moments later and he set her down above the waterline. For the space of a few heartbeats they surveyed each other in silence. Then she recovered the use of her voice.

'Thank you.'

'You're welcome.'

His arm was still resting lightly on her waist. It should have felt intrusive but somehow it didn't, any more than his nearness now. The feeling it engendered was quite different; different and disquieting. Every instinct advised retreat. She moistened her lips.

'I…I'll go and help collect some wood for a fire.'

'Good idea.'

He released his hold then and she walked away letting out the breath she had been holding and trying to ignore the fluttering sensation in the pit of her stomach. It was a ridiculous overreaction to a simple act of kindness. And it had been kind, she reflected, quite unexpectedly so. The man was nothing if not unpredictable. It was impossible to guess what he might do next. For a moment she'd suspected that he might demand recompense for carrying her ashore but once again she was wide of the mark. That should have come as a relief but for some reason relief wasn't her dominant emotion just then. Rather than explore that any further she turned her attention to finding some wood.

A short time later the other ship arrived in the cove and they were joined by Alrik and his men. When the fires had been lit and provisions broken out the company settled down for the evening, the men talking quietly among themselves. Gradually the light faded and the first stars pricked out. Lara finished her portion of bread and meat and then sat awhile looking out to sea, her eyes following the silvery trail of light across the water beneath the waxing moon. The air smelled of salt and wood smoke and pine from the trees that fringed the bay, reassuring and familiar scents that enhanced the present sense of well-being.

Presently Alrik strolled over and settled himself beside her. For a moment or two he surveyed her in silence then he too turned his gaze seawards.

'Are you all right?'

Lara nodded. 'Yes, I thank you.'

'That's good. After what happened earlier I feared you might not be.'

'There is no reason to be concerned.'

'He did not hurt you, Lara?'

'No, he did not.'

'I'm glad to hear it. The thought has been much on my mind.'

The words produced a twinge of guilt. 'I'm sorry if you were worried. I did not intend it so.' She sighed. 'What happened was my own fault. I should not have lost my temper. It was foolish.'

'Well, on that we are agreed.'

'Don't worry. I've learned my lesson.'

'Indeed I hope so. Jarl Finn is your husband now and your place is at his side. There is no point in stubborn rebellion. If you try to fight him you'll lose.'

She made no reply but kept her gaze on the moon-tracked sea. However unpalatable they might be she knew the words for truth.

'Is he really such bad choice of husband, Lara?'

She turned her head to look at him. 'You forget. I did not have a choice.'

'Is there another man you'd rather have? One of your erstwhile suitors perhaps?'

'Don't be ridiculous.'

'Well, then, do you equate Jarl Finn with them?'

'Of course not. He's nothing like them.' She reddened a little. 'He's…he's…well, I don't yet know what he is.'

'Not yet perhaps.'

'You evidently like him well.'

'Yes, I do,' he replied. 'In fact after today I like him even better.' He gave her shoulder a gentle squeeze and then went to rejoin his men.

When he had gone she was left to ponder on what he had said. Alrik had a strong streak of common sense and the habit of quiet plain speaking that she respected. She could not reflect on her earlier behaviour with any satisfaction. It was not only foolish: with hindsight it seemed petulant as well. She had only herself to blame for the consequences. Finn had made it clear that he would not be crossed but at the same time he had tempered the punishment. It seemed he didn't bear a grudge either or she'd be shivering in wet clothing now. Perhaps it was merely that he rated her defiance as nothing more than a minor inconvenience. Certainly the signs pointed that way. It was frightening to recall how easily he'd dealt with her.

She glanced furtively across the campsite towards the other fire and the group of men gathered around it, locating Finn at once. He was speaking with his companions but she didn't catch the words and didn't try. Her attention was on the man. The light of the flames fell across him casting part of his face into shadow and accentuating the rest with fire. The result was dramatic and arresting. He was more than distinctive, she realised. *He's not like the others.* That had never been more apparent. He was as unlike them as mead was from swamp water. At the same time she knew so little about him. Suddenly she would have liked to know more, to know what made him who he was. She sensed that there was so much more beneath the surface; far more than he ever revealed. She had never met a man who was so self-contained and yet who conducted himself with such ease in company. Conversations with him were stimulating. Even when they argued, she enjoyed pitting her wit against his.

When she thought about it more carefully it was apparent that every challenge she threw out had been met and overcome. He'd accomplished it without seeming to try too hard either. Nor had his relationship with her deflected him one inch from his purpose. While he had made a major impact on her life she suspected that the reverse wasn't true at all. He'd married her because it advanced his plans and he'd taken the whole business in his stride; it had made no personal impact on him.

For the first time, it occurred to her to wonder what kind of woman would have that effect on him. Such a man must have known many women in his time. It could not be otherwise. Had he cared for any of them? Loved any of them? What was his ideal of womanhood? Tall, buxom and blonde most like, and with a placid nature. At all events not a slight, hot-tempered little redhead. Some considered her fair but beauty was in the eye of the beholder. *You have wit and looks enough to win a man.* She sighed. Even if she'd wanted to she had no idea how to win this man.

Chapter Eight

Finn glanced across the camp towards Lara and Alrik, wondering what the conversation was about. Not that it was any of his business. Had it been anyone else he might well have made it his business. His men wouldn't attempt to engage his wife in private conversation, but the others were an unknown quantity. However, it seemed unlikely that they would behave with undue familiarity to Ottar's daughter even if they had known her for years. Alrik had a privileged position. He could speak to her whenever he liked without it being taken amiss. Nor was he likely to be rebuffed. The closeness between brother and sister was evident. None of which improved Finn's present humour.

Although she'd since bowed to the inevitable it was clear that Lara didn't want to be with him and that she would cheerfully have watched him sail away. Perhaps she had even been secretly hoping that when confrontation came Steingrim would be the victor. He sighed, mentally upbraiding himself for that. It was unfair and it contradicted what she'd said earlier about the evil nature of the foe. He ought to be glad that she had acknowledged his prowess as a fighter. It wasn't much but at least it suggested that he wasn't completely sunk in her estimation.

When he'd determined to bring Lara with him he hadn't anticipated having to bind her hand and foot to do it. She'd left him no choice in the end. He wouldn't have put it past her to make good the threat to jump overboard. Even so, he didn't want a relationship with her that was based on coercion. She would learn to respect him as a wife should respect a husband, but he didn't want her to fear him. He wanted her willing cooperation. He wanted her to be relaxed in his company, to enjoy his company, to desire his company. Finn grimaced. He knew how far he was from that particular goal. Yet it had been on his mind since he'd carried her ashore that afternoon. By rights he should have let the little witch get wet but if he had he would have missed an opportunity. For a few short minutes he'd got Lara exactly where he wanted her and without a fight. He hadn't been too sure he'd succeed in getting her to put her arms around his neck but the ruse had worked. It had also rebounded on him spectacularly. He hadn't anticipated his response to her nearness, to the touch and the scent of her. He hadn't anticipated the urge to kiss her again, this time until she begged for mercy.

Fortunately, he hadn't yielded to temptation. Things between them were difficult already without his making them worse. He would honour his promise not to force himself on her. What he wanted could not be compelled. They needed time to grow accustomed to each other. Besides, there was still the matter of Steingrim...

His train of thought was broken when he saw Alrik

move away. Lara remained where she was, apparently contemplating the view. It was a fine night; he might almost have said a night made for romance. With any other woman he'd have taken full advantage of that but Lara wasn't any woman. She was his wife and just then she looked small and forlorn and strangely vulnerable. The sight awoke his protective instincts. It shouldn't have: it was weakness and he knew it. That apparent fragility contained a core of steel. By rights he should keep his distance, keep her guessing.

He turned back to his companions and tried to concentrate on the conversation but his attention kept wandering back to the lonely figure on the strand. The air was cooler now and she was some distance from the fire. He hesitated, torn…

The scrunch of stones underfoot alerted her to his presence. At first she thought it was Alrik returning but when she looked up it was a very different figure standing there. The sight of him set her heart beating a little faster.

'Finn.'

'You'll get cold sitting there. Come closer to the fire.'

The invitation carried a faint hint of command. However, he was right. The air was chilly now and beginning to make itself felt. The thought of some warmth was not unwelcome.

'All right.'

He held out a hand to help her up, a casual gesture of courtesy that she had not expected. After a brief hesitation she placed her fingers in his and was drawn effortlessly to her feet. Retaining his hold he led her up the strand. His hand was strong and warm, the touch both possessive and reassuring. Part of her wanted to disengage from that disconcerting contact but, deep down, something else countermanded the urge and she allowed herself to be led to the fire.

As they arrived, the men sitting there glanced up. Some of them smiled but they made no comment and continued their conversation.

Finn gestured to the makeshift seat afforded by his sea chest. 'Please....'

Somewhat self-consciously she sat down and then Finn took his place beside her. It was far more comfortable than cold stone but in the limited space bodily contact was inescapable. Lara stretched her hands to the blaze and tried not to think about the strong thigh pressed against hers or the arm brushing her shoulder. Her flesh tingled where they touched and the sudden heat in her face had nothing to do with the fire.

'Better?' he asked.

'Oh...er, yes. Thank you.'

'It would be most inconvenient if you were to catch a chill.'

The quietly acerbic tone both rallied and reassured. Her lips twitched and she shot him a sideways look. 'I should have known this was not an altruistic gesture.'

'Yes, you should. I am not given to altruism. I prefer to look to my own interests.'

'Most of the time I have no doubt, but not always.'

'What makes you say that?'

'If you were truly as self-interested as you claim you would not be championing your family's cause. You'd have set sail for the safety of foreign parts and let them take their chances.'

'The thought did occur to me.'

She uttered a soft laugh. 'No, my lord, it did not.'

It elicited a reluctant smile. 'In truth you are right.' He paused. 'How did you know?'

'Such a course of action would be cowardly and dishonourable.'

For a moment he was silent, his gaze returning to the fire. 'Am I to infer then that you think me above such deeds?'

'Yes, I do think that.'

'I am honoured, my lady.'

He sounded sincere. At least on this occasion the words carried no discernible edge. Lara too had been sincere: she could not imagine this man leaving his kin or his friends in the lurch to save his own skin. He was many things but dishonourable wasn't one of them. Why he should have suggested otherwise was a mystery, unless of course it had been intended to provoke. That was entirely possible.

'I was under the impression that your opinion of me was much lower,' he went on.

'Not that low, my lord.'

The smile returned. 'I am relieved.'

'I didn't know that my opinion mattered.' When he did not immediately reply she went on, 'That was your cue to say that it doesn't.'

'To say that would be false and I have given my word to be honest with you.'

'And yet you compelled me to come with you today.'

'So I did.'

'Don't worry, I'm not about to contest the point any further. I have learned the folly of disobedience.'

'I wonder.'

'Well, I'm sure I can rely on you to remind me if I forget.'

His eyes gleamed. 'Certainly. However, that wasn't the reason for insisting on your company.'

'A wife's place is with her husband?'

'Yes, it is. It's a lesson I learned the hard way. Only a fool makes the same mistakes twice.'

She blinked. 'Twice? Then…you were married once before?'

'Yes, I was married before, but I was too often away from home and for long periods of time. In consequence my wife found consolation elsewhere.'

'Oh.'

It was as though the ground had suddenly disappeared from under her feet. Yet why should it be so hard to believe? He was older than her by seven or eight years, certainly old enough to have been married before. He was handsome, noble and moderately wealthy. It was naive to imagine that such a man would not have a past. With an effort she gathered her wits.

'I see.'

'Do you?'

'It's obvious, isn't it? You think that if you had left me behind I would have amused myself behind your back.' She paused, regarding him coolly. 'Hardly a flattering assessment of my character but at least it's honest.'

'You leap too swiftly to conclusions.'

'Do I?' Suddenly the proximity was too much, the heat from the fire too great. She got to her feet. 'You will excuse me.'

She left the circle of firelight and hurried away, grateful for the cool air on her face. However, before she had gone a dozen paces a large hand closed on her arm, arresting her progress. Lara's gaze smouldered.

'Let go of me, Finn.'

His grip didn't alter. 'The conversation isn't finished yet.'

'It is as far as I'm concerned.'

He drew her round to face him. 'Will you calm down and listen, you crazy little hothead, instead of storming off like that?'

She glared at him. 'So I'm a hothead now as well as a slut.'

'I did not call you a slut.'

'You implied it.'

'That was not my intention and I'm sorry if you thought so.'

'Then say what you want to say and have done.'

'Neither of us sought this marriage but it happened. Nor were the circumstances ideal. In addition there is a ruthless enemy to confront and overcome. Nevertheless, it seems to me that these are not insurmountable obstacles—that, ultimately, we can determine how this works out.'

'We?'

He took a deep breath. 'I don't want to fail a second time, Lara, but I'm only half of this relationship.'

It chimed uncannily with what her father had said before and it gave her pause. However, there were inconsistencies. 'Your words imply that our roles are equal but your actions imply the opposite.'

'My actions today were a last resort. I prefer reason to the use of force, but when reason fails I'll do what I must. I wanted you with me and so I chose the most direct method of achieving that end.'

'It is unlikely to take very long to settle accounts with Steingrim. You could have returned for me afterwards.'

'A few weeks? A few months? Who knows? By then we would have become well and truly estranged,' he replied. 'I wasn't prepared to let that happen. The only way we're going to get to know each other better is by spending time together.'

'Such things cannot be forced.'

'No, they can't, but at this stage of the proceedings time together offers more hope than time apart. In my experience absence doesn't make the heart grow fonder.'

'Might not familiarity breed contempt?'

'Only if there is something inherently contemptible in the character to begin with. Time shows us the man.'

'Are you not afraid of what you may learn?'

'No. I prefer to keep an open mind.' He surveyed her steadily. 'Are you prepared to do the same?'

She nodded. 'Very well.'

Finn released his hold on her arm. 'Good. Then we are agreed.'

By tacit consent they returned to the fireside for a while but, as the hour grew late, the men left off their conversation and began to prepare for sleep. While some made use of cloaks and blankets, most had sealskin sleeping bags which were both snug and waterproof. Finn lifted his from the wooden sea chest and shook it open, laying it out on the strand. A rolled cloak served as a pillow. Lara watched these preparations with quiet dismay. Her mind hadn't moved as far ahead as sleeping arrangements, an oversight which hit her forcefully now.

Her companion straightened and smiled. 'My sleeping bag is large enough for two if you feel inclined to share it. Alternatively there's a spare blanket.'

She swallowed hard. 'I'll take the blanket.'

'How did I know you were going to say that?' He retrieved the item from the chest and tossed it over.

She caught it awkwardly. Finn turned away and unbuckled his sword belt, laying the weapon within easy reach. Then he climbed into the sleeping bag. Recollecting herself she hurriedly prepared her own bed and lay down.

Finn laced his hands behind his head, looking on with interest. 'You know, you'd be a lot warmer in here.'

She had not the slightest doubt about that. Just thinking about it sent a wave of heat the length of her body and she was glad of the darkness that hid the telltale blush in her cheeks.

'I'm quite content I assure you.'

'It can get very chilly in the early hours.'

'I'll be fine.'

'Well, if you change your mind…'

'I won't.' She turned on her side and pulled the blanket higher around her shoulders. 'Goodnight, my lord.'

As he bade her goodnight in return she could have sworn his voice trembled on the edge of laughter.

Chapter Nine

Lara woke from an uneasy doze in the first grey light of dawn. Not even a bird call broke the heavy stillness. She sat up slowly and looked around, her gaze sweeping the quiet camp, moving down the strand to the water. Through the early mist the prows of the sea dragons loomed like mythical beasts arisen from the deep. A night on the hard ground had left every part of her stiff and aching and she felt chilled to the bone. The fire had burned down to embers now and the comforting warmth was gone. She glanced resentfully at the sleeping figure nearby. The handsome face was as striking in repose as it was in wakefulness. He looked peaceful lying there, entirely untroubled by cold or discomfort. Briefly her imagination took flight and she wondered how it might have been to share his sleeping bag last night. The result of that was a physical tremor quite unrelated to the morning chill.

Wrapping the blanket around her shoulders she banished the thought and moved quietly away. The need to answer the call of nature was pressing now so she headed for a clump of bushes on the edge of the cove.

After that she hesitated, unwilling to return and sit around in the cold until the men awoke. A little exercise would be welcome and might help her warm up. She wouldn't go far, just to the top of the rise and back.

The hill wasn't particularly steep but the uneven and rocky slope required concentration. Her stiff legs stumbled once or twice and she winced as the ground jarred her feet, but she persevered. A short time later she reached the top and looked around to get her bearings. The low hill on which she was standing formed a peninsula between the cove and the open sea. Off to her right wooded slopes ended abruptly in grey rock. The fog was low and patchy, rolling slowly across the surface of the still water. The stillness was all-enveloping. Just then she might have been the only person on the face of the earth.

She was about to turn away and return to the camp when her ears caught a sound. Listening intently, she identified the soft, rhythmic rise and dip of oars. She tried to pinpoint the direction, her gaze scanning the fog. And then her heart missed a beat as she saw the carved prow of a sea dragon glide out of the mist. Her immediate thought was that the third ship had arrived to join Finn and Alrik but a closer inspection revealed a vessel she had never seen before. Nevertheless, the carved figurehead and long sleek hull identified a warship, like the rows of shields along her sides. She carried a large crew. Lara estimated fifty men at least. Her attention moved on from the rowers and the steersman to the figure in the bow, motionless, intent. Was he watching out for rocks and hazards or looking for something else entirely?

As she studied him he turned his head as though

scanning the shore. Instinctively, Lara ducked out of sight behind a boulder. Had he seen her? Still no sound broke the silence, no call or alarm that would suggest her presence had been detected. Heart pounding she risked a glance round the edge of the rock. Her eyes widened as a second warship glided out of the mist. She was as big as the first and equally quiet. Lara felt gooseflesh prickle along her arms. Suddenly everything about their silence seemed predatory. The ships reminded her of nothing so much as hunting raptors. She also had a shrewd idea of their intended prey. Casting a final glance in their direction she retraced her steps and hurried back down the slope.

Finn woke at dawn. A glance towards Lara's sleeping place revealed only empty space. In moments he was on his feet, looking around. Although one or two others were stirring now the camp was still quiet and he could see no sign of her. Common sense suggested that she couldn't be far but alongside that lurked the memory of her unwillingness to be here at all. He frowned. Surely she wouldn't have done anything foolish? There was nowhere to run to. Besides, there were bears and wolves in the woods to say nothing of human predators.

His gaze swept the cove again. As it did so he glimpsed a figure on the slope opposite. She was almost running, slithering and sliding down without any regard for safety. Not that such a consideration as safety would weigh with her. He watched anxiously, breathing a sigh of relief when she reached the bottom in one piece. Then she was racing across the strand towards him with what looked like a large cloak billowing behind her. Several amused glances followed her progress. As she drew near he realised that what he'd taken to be a cloak was the blanket he'd lent her, still clutched in one hand. The other seized his arm.

'My lord, you must rouse your men.'

'Lara, what is it?'

'Two warships,' she gasped. 'I saw them from the hill.'

His smile faded. 'Two? Are you certain?'

Had it been only one he'd have felt a lot better. One would likely have meant the arrival of his reinforcements. Two had very different ramifications.

'Quite certain.' She hesitated. 'They're not our allies, are they?'

'I seriously doubt it.'

Without further ado he roused the men nearest and told them to wake the rest. Within a minute the quiet cove was astir. Like all fighting men they were alert at once, hurriedly gathering round to find out what was toward. As Finn summarised they exchanged glances.

'Which way were the ships headed, Lara?' asked Alrik.

'This way,' she replied, 'but moving slowly and keeping good watch, as though they were looking for something.'

Her brother frowned. 'Steingrim?'

'It has to be,' replied Finn. He looked at Lara. 'How many men?'

'I estimated about a hundred in all, my lord.'

The intelligence was greeted with grim silence. Finn's jaw tightened. Without the reinforcements on the third ship they were going to be outnumbered. The only hope now was to be proactive and take the fight to the enemy. Steingrim expected him to run. The element of surprise might help improve the odds a little. Only a little, but it was better than nothing. He glanced round the assembled group.

'Arm and make ready. Alrik, I need a couple of men to take care of Lara. The rest of you get to the ships.'

They didn't need to be told twice. Finn too threw on his war gear, shrugging into the mail byrnie and then buckling on his sword. He glanced up at Lara.

'You'll remain here in the cove.'

Disappointment welled. 'Let me come. I can fight.'

'You'll do no such thing.'

'But…'

'No buts, Lara. Conceal yourself and stay hidden. Do you understand?'

Recognising the finality in his tone she swallowed her disappointment. 'Yes, my lord.'

'I'll leave a small guard here as well.'

'I'll be all right. You need those men.' Without the third ship he and his crew were going to be badly outnumbered.

'We'll manage.'

Suddenly everything she'd ever heard about Steingrim returned with horrible clarity. 'Be careful, Finn.'

'Always.' He squeezed her shoulder gently. 'I'll be back as soon as I can.'

With that he donned his helmet, slung his shield over his shoulder and grabbed the rest of his gear. Then he was gone, running down the strand to the waiting ship. She saw him climb aboard. The decks were anthills of ordered activity and within two minutes the crews were bent to their oars and the vessesl were moving away from the shore. With thumping heart Lara watched them go. Never in her life had she felt as helpless as she did now. She had never felt this afraid either although the fear was not for herself. What if the fight went badly for the allies? What if Finn and Alrik were slain and their men with them? The possibility chilled her to the marrow. She had to think positively. They weren't going to lose. They were going to come back.

'Best find a place to hide, my lady.'

She glanced round, recognising the speaker and his companion. Geirr and Eystein were kin by marriage. She had known them almost all her life. They had grown up in Ottar's hall and, being of an age with her brother, had formed a close bond there, eventually becoming Alrik's shield brothers when the three of them reached manhood. She knew that close affinity was the reason he had chosen them for this duty.

'I thank you both for staying behind,' she said. 'I know you'd rather have gone with the ships.'

'It is an honour to be chosen to protect you, my lady,' said Geirr.

'I doubt that but I appreciate it all the same.' She looked around, mentally assessing the possibilities of the terrain.

Geirr followed her gaze. 'The rocks over yonder would afford good cover.'

'They would,' she agreed, 'but if we climbed the hill we might be able to see the battle.'

'My lord's instructions were clear.'

'And we shall obey them. There's cover up there. I found it earlier.'

They hesitated and exchanged glances. Lara pressed home the advantage.

'It will be quite safe but we'll also be able to see

what's happening. If we remain down here we can only guess.'

Eystein grinned. 'What are we waiting for?'

They reached the top of the hill a short time later. As they gained the summit all three checked in dismay, staring at the drifting bank of fog beyond the point. Already visibility was reduced to a few hundred yards.

'Damn it,' muttered Geirr. 'It'll catch them out for sure.'

Lara frowned, her gaze following the progress of the two ships. All sailors feared fog and with good reason. It concealed hazards of all kinds. Just then it wasn't the underwater variety that worried her.

'Can you see Steingrim's ships?'

Eystein shook his head. 'No, my lady, and in a little while we won't see anything.'

Lara knew he was right. Their vantage point was about to become an island of rock in the encroaching mist.

'Now what?' she asked.

'They'll head out into deeper water,' he replied. 'They daren't do anything else.'

Sure enough a few moments later the ships changed course, away from the coast. Then, slowly, the fog closed around them and they were gone.

The ship had cleared the cove and was rounding the point when, without warning, visibility diminished to a stretch of grey water and a rolling bank of fog. Finn frowned, his gaze automatically moving ahead to Alrik's vessel some fifty yards in front. Within moments its outlines grew indistinct and then faded completely as the mist swallowed it. Of the enemy there was no sign at all.

'Thor's thundering war hammer this is all we need,' muttered Unnr.

'Head us out into deeper water,' said Finn. 'The shoals along this stretch of coast are treacherous.'

Unnr nodded and moved the steering oar over. The ship began to change course. They had travelled about a hundred yards before the mist rolled over them. Finn controlled an urge to swear. Instead he gave the command to stop rowing. The men leaned on their oars, listening intently. Barely a ripple disturbed the surface of the water and the stillness was all-enveloping.

Finn guessed that Alrik would have headed his ship away from shore in similar fashion. He knew this coastline and knew of the deadly rocks lying just beneath the surface waiting to rip a hole in the side of an unwary vessel. He wouldn't risk staying in too close when he couldn't see the hazards. And rocks weren't the only peril. It was small comfort to know that their enemies were blind too. At present they could literally run into each other before either group was aware.

'Keep your eyes peeled,' he said quietly.

A collision was to be avoided at all costs. Apart from the inevitable damage to the ship such an encounter would mean hand-to-hand fighting. Without the support of their allies Finn's crew would be dangerously outnumbered. With the best will in the world Alrik would be hard put to help. The one consolation was that Lara was safe. Steingrim didn't know of her presence on this trip and Finn was determined it should stay that way. If the worst happened her two guardians would get her home. In that case the marriage would likely rank

as one of the shortest in history. He couldn't imagine
that she would feel much regret about that. Then he
reflected that she had volunteered to fight alongside
him, a ridiculous offer, albeit a brave one.

'Fog seems to be thinning, my lord,' said Unnr.

In a little while it became evident he was right.
Gradually it dissipated around them leaving the ship
in an area of open water. A few moments later their
companions reappeared to starboard. Then, slowly,
part of the coast came into view again. The enemy was
nowhere in sight.

'Let's find out what Alrik knows,' said Finn.

As they drew level with the other ship his brother-
in-law appeared at the side. 'We heard their oars. They
must have come close but we didn't get a sighting.
You?'

'Nothing,' replied Finn. 'They must have gone right
past without realising we were here.'

'My thought exactly.' Alrik grinned. 'Now we're
after them.'

'I can live with that.'

'What do you want to do now?'

'We'll let them get clear and then follow,' replied
Finn. 'Wait here while I go back for my wife.'

'By all means.'

Lara and her companions were waiting at the water's
edge when the ship returned. As it drew near Eystein
called out, 'What happened?'

'Nothing,' replied Sturla. 'Bastards rowed right past
us.'

Lara's companions shook their heads in disbelief.

She took a deep breath, conscious only of flooding relief.

'We saw the fog roll in,' said Geirr, 'but after that not a ruddy thing. We couldn't hear anything either.'

Sturla shook his head. 'There was nothing to hear save for the sweet sound of their oars as they rowed away.'

'Are you two going to stand there chatting all day or are you coming aboard?' demanded Unnr.

Eystein grinned. 'We're coming. We're coming.'

'Good,' said Finn. 'Quite apart from the pleasure of your company I'd like to have my wife back. Perhaps one of you would like to assist.'

'Gladly, my lord,' said Eystein. He turned to Lara. 'With your permission, lady.'

Clearly he took it as given because before she had time to say a word she was lifted off her feet and borne to the side of the ship. Finn reached down to relieve Eystein of his burden and lifted her aboard.

He smiled. 'Welcome back, my lady.'

The grey eyes met hers and warmed. For no good reason her pulse quickened. It didn't help that he seemed in no hurry to put her down either. She could feel the links of his mail through her gown, the metal hard and unyielding, like the powerful muscles beneath. He smelled of steel and leather and musk, a combination that was suddenly both dangerous and exciting.

With an effort she found her voice. 'I'm glad to be back, my lord. I think the gods must be on your side.'

He grinned. 'I think they were today.'

'They're valuable allies.'

'Indeed they are. I'll do my best to keep their regard.'

As Geirr and Eystein clambered aboard, the ship moved slowly away from the cove. Finn set Lara on her feet and placing a hand under her elbow, led her astern. Now that the immediate danger was over reaction began to set in and she shuddered.

He glanced down at her. 'Are you all right?'

She nodded. 'It's just the release of tension, that's all.'

'I knew better than to suggest you were afraid.'

'I was afraid, Finn. I don't mean to cast doubt on you or your men or on my brother either, but the numbers were so unevenly balanced that I dreaded what might happen.'

'And yet had I been slain you would be free.'

'Free to do what?' she replied. 'My father would find me another husband soon enough. Besides, I would not purchase such a temporary freedom with men's lives.'

'Not even with mine?'

'Of course not.'

He regarded her steadily, his expression unreadable. 'Incidentally, I thank you for your offer to fight today.'

'I meant it.'

'I know you did.'

The quiet tone was entirely free from mockery like the eyes studying her now. Taken aback she lowered her gaze, aware of him to her fingertips.

'With hindsight I suppose it must have seemed foolish.'

'It was many things but not foolish.'

'And yet you would never allow it, would you?'

'It's my responsibility to keep you from harm. Steingrim doesn't know you're here and I'm not about to enlighten him. You'd make too tempting a target.'

'Oh.' That aspect of the matter hadn't occurred to her but now that he'd said it she conceded he did have a point.

'Your courage was never in doubt.'

Uncertain how to respond she remained silent. Did he mean it or was he just letting her down gently? Probably the latter, she decided. All the same, he could have been scathing. She'd met plenty of men who would have been; most of her former suitors for a start. *He's not like the others.* Suddenly those words had never seemed truer.

Chapter Ten

For the next three days they made steady progress down the coast keeping close watch for Steingrim's ships. Once when they put in to shore for the night they found evidence of the enemy's former campsite in heaps of grey ash from their fires. Finn was content to let the mercenaries stay well ahead until the remainder of his reinforcements arrived. It was a growing concern that they hadn't.

'Where in Frigg's name are they?' demanded Unnr. 'Surely they should be here by now.'

'Perhaps they aren't coming,' said Sturla.

'They'll be here,' replied Ketill. 'Ottar gave his word, didn't he?'

'Well, I wish they'd get a move on. This isn't a ruddy trading expedition.'

Murmured agreement greeted this from those nearby.

Finn interjected. 'Ketill's right. They'll be here.'

The words sounded more assured than he felt. He didn't think Ottar would let them down; something unforeseen must have happened to delay the other ship.

Now he just had to hope it wasn't a serious problem. They needed those extra swords.

The men lapsed into silence but he knew the doubt was taking root in their minds. It was one thing to face an enemy when there was a good chance of winning, and quite another to face a battle when there was every chance of annihilation. It was not unknown for crews to mutiny over such things. Finn had a strong bond with his men but he was reluctant to test it so far. Like all Viking warriors his companions were brave but they weren't stupid. And like all Viking warriors they were essentially opportunists who seized the advantage when they saw it and walked away when they didn't. Had he dwelt on that long enough it might well have brought him out in a cold sweat.

Presently the conversation turned to different things but he knew it wouldn't be forgotten. He glanced at the open water beyond, letting his gaze return the way they had come but there was no sign of a ship. He sighed. If the worst happened he was going to need an alternative plan, a very good plan if he hoped to sell it to his men.

'I'm sure it will be all right.'

He turned swiftly to see Lara at his shoulder. 'You heard the conversation I take it.'

'Yes, I heard. The uncertainty is understandable but I'm sure it's unfounded.'

'You say that very confidently.'

'The bond between my father and his brother is strong. My uncle won't let the side down. There's nothing he likes more than a battle, which means there must be a good reason for his absence.'

In spite of himself Finn smiled. 'He sounds like a real character.'

'He is.'

'Does he resemble your father?'

'Not really, apart from the red hair of course. I should explain that Uncle Njall is roughly the size of a barn door and strong enough to tear the head off an aurochs.'

'Well, let's hope he gets here soon. He sounds like the sort of man I need. Dare I hope that his crew takes after him?'

She laughed. 'He's one of a kind but he leads some tough men.'

'That's encouraging.' It really was, although that wasn't the reason why his breath suddenly caught in his throat. Laughter suited her, he decided. It suited her very much.

'My uncle fought a bear once. He'd gone out hunting and it attacked him. He still has the scars to prove it.'

'I'll wager he has. Did he kill the beast in the end?'

'Yes, but it nearly killed him as well. It chewed his ear off and its claws tore his arm and ripped his shoulder to the bone. Fortunately his men had the sense to wash out the wounds with mead before they sewed him up. Apparently it took six of them to hold him down.'

'I can well imagine.'

'My father says he's never heard swearing like it. Even their berserker friends were impressed.'

Finn chuckled. 'I don't suppose your father repeated that part of the story.'

'Unfortunately not, although we importuned him most strongly.'

'We?'

'Asa and Alrik and I.'

'Ah.'

'Anyway, Uncle Njall survived. He kept the bear's skin too, as a bed cover.'

'Practical as well as brave, then?'

'He earned his trophy.'

'Yes, he did.'

She sighed. 'I wish I'd been there to see it but it happened many years before I was born.'

'Has anyone ever told you that you have a blood-thirsty turn of mind?'

She threw him a sideways glance. 'It may have been mentioned once or twice.'

Finn laughed, enjoying her. The look in her eye was beguiling as well as mischievous and it seemed to him that her lips had never looked as kissable as they did just then. He resisted the temptation, unwilling to destroy the present mood.

'Was it your uncle who inspired you to learn sword craft?' he asked.

Her expression grew sober again. 'No, that was after Asa left.'

Finn hesitated. This was uncertain territory and he didn't want to alienate her, especially when she had been so communicative before.

'Forgive me, I didn't mean to pry but I should like to understand.'

To his relief Lara seemed more surprised than offended. For a second or two she was silent but he made no attempt to fill the gap. He would not force her confidence.

'It was a symbolic gesture for the most part,' she replied, 'because it didn't do anything for Asa—she died anyway. All the same it made me feel less helpless.'

'How did she die?'

'In childbed. Her husband got a child on her soon after the marriage but it was a difficult birth. She died in fear and pain among strangers.'

'You loved her very much, didn't you?'

'Yes, I loved her.' The blue-green eyes burned. 'And if I could I would take a sword and slay the man responsible for killing her.'

'By that you mean her husband?'

'He.'

'Unfortunately it is not uncommon for women to die in childbed. Her husband could not have prevented it.'

'Childbed was the last element of the tragedy. She died a little every day she was with him.'

They lapsed into silence. He could feel the anger flowing out of her. Not just anger either but also sorrow and loss. He understood it. Had he too not felt all of those things? Only the circumstances were different. He wondered then if Bótey had died a little with each day of his absence. If he'd been there, if he'd been the kind of husband she'd needed the whole sorry mess could have been avoided. Whatever happened he didn't want to repeat the mistake.

'It doesn't have to be like that,' he said.

'True. I know of people who are happily married.'

The next question formed in his mind but he knew better than to ask it. To do so would put Lara between the cliff and the maelstrom. Besides, he already knew the answer. All he could hope for was that time might change it.

'I should like—

He broke off as the look-out hailed the camp. 'Ship approaching!'

Immediately the men leaped to their feet and ran to the water's edge. Finn's heartbeat quickened. The vessel was some distance away so it was impossible to make out the details but there was a better than even chance it was the one they were waiting for.

As the distance shortened they could make out the clean lines and dragon prow of a warship, her oars dipping and rising in unison. She was travelling fast. Lara looked at Alrik who had appeared beside them.

'Is it our uncle?'

'I damned well hope so,' he replied.

Finn silently echoed the sentiment. Once he had the reinforcements he could implement the next part of the plan. Without them…

An expectant hush descended, every man there straining to identify the rapidly approaching vessel. As her crew had sighted the two moored ships she altered course slightly, making straight for them. As they came closer Alrik beamed.

'It's the *Sea Snake*!'

A cheer greeted the words. Finn let out a long breath, mentally thanking the gods. It really did look as though they might be on his side after all. The *Sea Snake*'s crew stopped rowing and the big ship glided in and slowed.

'Can you see Uncle Njall?' asked Lara.

Alrik shook his head. 'That's Guthrum in the prow.'

'Guthrum?' asked Finn.

'A cousin,' replied Lara. 'My uncle's third son and the one most like him in looks.'

Finn didn't care about her cousin's numerical ranking or his physical appearance; all that mattered was his arrival. Guthrum cupped his hands and called across to them.

'Hail the camp!'

'Hail yourself!' replied Alrik. 'What the blazes kept you?'

'Long story.'

Guthrum swung himself over the side and, flanked by a dozen of his crewmen, waded ashore. He engulfed Alrik in a hearty hug and then seized Lara by the waist, lifting her up to bestow a resounding kiss.

'It's good to see you both! Lara, you're even prettier than I remembered.' He returned her to earth and looked around, his gaze meeting Finn's. Lara hurriedly introduced them.

Finn smiled. 'I'm glad to see you, Guthrum. You and your men are most welcome.' He thought he'd never said truer words in his life.

Guthrum smiled in return. 'Good to be here, my lord.'

'We'd almost given you up for lost,' said Alrik.

'We only got Uncle Ottar's message three days ago when we got back from Sogn,' replied Guthrum.

'What were you doing there?'

'Business trip.'

Alrik eyed him speculatively. 'Lucrative?'

His cousin grinned. 'Not bad. Anyway, when we returned we found out what was toward. Then it was a case of loading up with fresh provisions and turning the ship around and heading straight out again.'

'Well, better late than never. Where's Uncle Njall?'

'Fell off a ladder and broke his leg while he was mending a roof last month. You should have heard him swear.'

'I can imagine,' said Alrik.

'As it is, he won't be going anywhere for a while.'

'Pity. Still it's good to see you, Cousin.'

'That it is,' said Finn. 'Will you and your men join us in a cup of ale?'

Guthrum nodded. 'Gladly. Then you can tell us all the details about this venture.'

When the ale was poured and the men had sat down around the fire, Finn obliged. They listened intently, grim-faced.

'Steingrim's reputation for treachery is well known,' said Guthrum when at length the tale was told. 'It'll be a pleasure to settle accounts with the swine.'

Growls of approval greeted this from the listening men.

'We shall,' said Finn.

'Do we know where he is?'

'About half a day in front of us, or a little more. He sailed right past us in the fog.'

Guthrum grinned. 'Excellent. Now we have the element of surprise.'

'Quite so.'

'What's the plan then, my lord?'

Lara sat a little apart, listening quietly while the men talked. She could not but feel relief at her cousin's arrival and guessed that Finn and Alrik must be feeling the same. They had not spoken of their concern but she had seen it in their faces. She had also sensed the un-

derlying tension in Finn. This wasn't just some petty
raid he was planning; it was a matter of life and death.
Steingrim wouldn't give up. He had to be confronted
and killed or they would spend the rest their lives looking over their shoulders. That wasn't the kind of future she wanted. Thus far she hadn't considered the
future in any detail; the advent of marriage had been
so traumatic that she had been lost in a black fog of
anger and resentment, existing only from day to day.
Now she found herself thinking ahead to a time beyond Steingrim when she and Finn would settle properly into married life. Although she couldn't view it
with unbounded joy, the idea wasn't as unwelcome as
it had once been. Without her even being aware of it
the dark gloom had lifted and she no longer felt its suf-
focating, oppressive weight. Nor was she inclined to
rail any more against what could not be altered. Finn
was not as Asa's husband had been. That much was apparent. *It doesn't have to be like that. I should like...*
What? A well-run hall, perhaps? Domestic harmony?
She sighed. It didn't seem such a bad idea. They didn't
love each other but they might learn to rub along together. It had to be better than continual strife.

She wondered what his first wife had been like,
apart from unfaithful. Had she been very beautiful?
Had he loved her or was theirs another marriage of con-
venience? The latter seemed most likely. If she'd loved
him she couldn't have been unfaithful. He wasn't brutal
or coarse so was it rather that she'd found him lacking
as a lover? Lara didn't have to ponder that very long:
the recollection of his kiss created doubt enough. Her
experience was limited but if the mere idea of shar-

ing his bed had caused a hot flush what would the reality be like?

The question caused a whole raft of disturbing thoughts. For the first time she admitted the inevitability of physical union with Finn. They were husband and wife. Eventually he would want sons to continue his line. That he had not already enforced his marital rights was astounding even if he did have other things on his mind. *When you decide you want to become a real woman let me know.* Lara bit her lip. Not only did he not think of her as a real woman he didn't even find her desirable. Now that resentment had cooled she was forced to admit that Finn would have had his pick of women in the past. He hadn't picked her, though. It didn't even bother him when their marriage wasn't consummated. A couple of days ago that situation had seemed quite satisfactory; now what she felt was more like mortification.

Her private musing was interrupted by Guthrum's arrival. 'Well, my little cousin, you are a married woman now I hear.'

'Oh, yes. That's right.'

'You finally took the plunge, eh? Word is you were mighty hard to please.'

'Is that right?'

'I know some of your rejected suitors, remember.'

'Ah.'

'Well, why should you not take your time? It's a pretty woman's prerogative after all.' He lowered his large frame on to a rock beside her. 'And you've made a fine choice.'

Although choice had never entered into the arrangement it seemed politic not to mention it. Nor did she wish to go into the details. Guthrum could keep his illusions. 'I'm glad you think so.'

'Jarl Finn's reputation is well known and, unlike Steingrim's, for all the right reasons. You're a lucky girl.'

'As you say, Cousin.'

'I'll wager there are plenty who would like to be in your shoes.'

'It's a wager I'm sure you'd win.'

'What woman could object to sharing her bed with such a man?'

Lara gave him an ambiguous smile. Trust him to leap to that conclusion. It was time to shift the focus of the conversation. 'I hope that Greta is well.'

He nodded. 'Well enough, I thank you. She's carrying our third child now.'

'Goodness, is she?'

'The baby's due in another month, more or less.'

'Well, congratulations.'

'Thank you.'

'How long have you two been married now?'

'Five years.' He grinned. 'At this rate I'd say we're going to have a large family. I don't suppose it'll be very long before you've a few children of your own.'

Her cheeks grew warmer. 'Guthrum, I've only been married a few days.'

He chuckled. 'It takes less time than that to conceive a child.'

Her blush deepened. The man was incorrigible. 'I bow to your superior knowledge.'

'As well you should.'

'Get your mind out of the midden, Cousin, and tell me the rest of the family news,' she replied.

He laughed but, to her relief, complied and the conversation moved into less hazardous waters.

Finn kept up his part in the conversation with his present companions but he couldn't stop his gaze from wandering across the intervening space to where Lara was sitting. She looked pensive, completely lost in her own world. He'd have given a good deal to know her thoughts. Did he feature there at all? Her manner seemed less distant than it had erewhile; once or twice even friendly, but he didn't want to read too much into that. He saw Guthrum get up and go to sit with her. They were speaking quietly so he couldn't hear the conversation but they seemed to be very relaxed in each other's company. Their shared laughter was a pointed reminder of the gulf that lay between himself and his wife. It also created a twinge of something suspiciously like jealousy. He fought it. Why on earth he should feel jealous over something so trivial was beyond him. They were cousins for goodness' sake.

However, his self-control was tested further when half-a-dozen others came over to sit with Lara and Guthrum. Clearly all of them were known to her because she greeted them with a smile and fell readily into conversation. Members of her uncle's household no doubt. Some were older men but by no means all, and while their manner was unmistakably respectful he didn't fail to see the admiring looks directed her way. It pleased him that other men should find his wife attractive but he'd have preferred their admiration to be at a greater distance. He sighed. That kind of thinking had been entirely absent in his recent dealings with women;

he wooed them, bedded them and moved on. Not since Bótey had he experienced such raw possessiveness.

The discovery of her perfidy had been a knife in the guts. He hadn't suspected a thing until he found her gone. The swift interrogation of a frightened servant established the facts. The affair must have been going on for months until in the end she'd decided that a future with her lover looked better than the one she might have had with her husband. He'd been jealous then all right, and made furious with the pain of betrayal. But no matter how great his rage he'd never have harmed Bótey. His purpose in pursuing her had been to get her back. He'd been prepared to kill the man who stood in his way but never to do her physical harm. He'd thought she would have known that but it seemed she hadn't known him at all. He should have sheathed the sword before he tried to approach her but it hadn't occurred to him that she might think he intended to use it on her.

'Your lovely wife is a real asset,' said Unnr.

Finn snapped back to awareness. 'What was that about my wife?'

'I said she's an asset.'

'Oh. Oh, yes, she is.'

'It was a cunning move to bring her along, my lord.'

'You think so?'

'Of course. Men will fight better with a woman looking on.'

'She won't be looking on,' replied Finn. 'She'll be in a much safer place.'

'I didn't mean literally,' said Unnr. 'Stands to reason you wouldn't put her at risk. All the same, every man here will want to give a good account of himself in the fight because she'll be the first to hear the story afterwards.'

'You mean they'll want to boast of their battle fame.'

'What man doesn't want to impress a lovely woman, especially when she's the wife of his jarl? Her approval adds to the prestige.'

'Does it really?'

'Yes, my lord, especially when that approval is not easily won.'

'It sounds to me as if you inherited your brother's romantic streak. Either that or the ale's stronger than it seems.'

Unnr sniffed. 'You may mock, my lord, but you'll see if I'm not right.'

Chapter Eleven

The men rose early the next morning in preparation for a reconnaissance mission. Lara watched Finn arm.

'Let me come with you.'

'No. You'll stay here with a small guard.'

Recognising the tone she didn't try to argue. However, he heard the stifled sigh. Taking her shoulders in a firm clasp he met her gaze.

'I don't know how this will end, Lara. I'm intending to reconnoitre and lay my plans when I know where Steingrim is, but if we were to happen upon him suddenly anything could happen.'

'I understand.'

'It is well.' He dropped a kiss on her forehead. 'I'll return as soon as I can.'

She nodded. The prospect of a long day spent in uncertainty without occupation or news filled her with dismay but whining about it would serve no purpose, except to annoy him, and she didn't wish to do that. It sat ill that he might think her spoilt and petulant. This undertaking was important to him and if her part was to remain behind then she would do it without complaint. So she looked on in silence as he completed his preparations, her gaze missing no detail. Gods, but he was imposing, in fact downright intimidating. The chainmail byrnie enhanced every line of that virile form, accentuating the impression of lithe strength. Sword and seax did nothing to detract from that. His face, so arresting before, was now partly concealed by the guards of the helmet and had acquired a dangerous distinction that made her catch her breath. Privately she thought he looked magnificent and, somewhere deep inside her, a flicker of pride kindled into life.

Becoming aware of her scrutiny he eyed her askance. 'Have I forgotten something?'

Lara cleared her throat. 'No, my lord. I am sure you have not. Your war gear is a second skin to you.'

'That's well put.'

He smiled and her heart gave a dangerous lurch. She had never been so aware of a man in her entire life, had never met one who aroused such sensations in her. His company both excited and perturbed. How amused he would be if he knew that. Get a grip, Lara. You've seen men in war gear before for goodness' sake. Seeking another outlet for her attention she focused instead on the sword at his side.

'That looks like a beautiful weapon. May I see it?'

'If you wish.' He drew the blade and then, altering his hold, offered it to her. 'Here.'

Carefully she closed her hand around the grip and lifted the sword. At once she was aware of its weight, heavier by far than her own. The crescent-shaped pommel was silver, beautifully wrought and inlaid with niello. The guards were silver too and similarly decorated. However, it was the blade that took her breath away. Its forging had created wondrous rippling patterns that flowed down the surface of the steel like water, shining grey-blue in the light. It was magical, like a sword out of a saga. Odin might have had a weapon like this. She didn't need to be told that its edge was sharp enough to split a hair.

'It's magnificent—truly a warrior's weapon. Does it have a name?'

'Foe Slayer.'

She smiled. 'Very apt.'

'I thought so.'

'Was the blade made for you?'

'It's one of a pair specially commissioned for me and my brother, Leif. We named the swords accordingly. His is Foe Bane.'

'A most appropriate choice.' She traced a finger lightly along the central fuller. 'The smith was a cunning workman.'

'One of the best.'

'Evidently.' She handed the weapon back. 'I can see why you chose him to make this.'

Finn returned the blade to its scabbard. 'It has served me well and no doubt will do so again.'

'No matter how fine the sword it's only as good as the man who wields it.'

'Should I take that as a compliment?'

'Very much so.'

The words came so naturally that they were out almost before she was aware. It was only then that their implications occurred to her. Somehow another shift had taken place in her thinking about him. His momentary silence suggested that the significance hadn't escaped him either. Under the weight of that penetrating gaze she felt her colour mount.

'I'll strive to deserve your praise,' he replied. Then seeing the men beginning to embark the ships he smiled ruefully. 'I must go but, with any luck, not for long. I anticipate finding Steingrim very soon. When a hundred and eighty men are hunting each other they're likely to be successful rather than not.'

She tried to look pleased for him; tried to ignore the knot of anxiety in her stomach. 'Go well, my lord.'

His hand brushed her cheek. 'Go well, Lara.'

Watching the ships pull away from the shore she felt strangely bereft. Not so long ago it would have pleased her to see them leave.

'Never fret, my lady, they'll be back.'

She glanced round to see Torstein. He was one of half-a-dozen guards who had remained behind. They were older men from among the contingent who had arrived the previous day with Guthrum, hearth companions who had been entrusted with her safety.

She summoned a smile. 'Of course they will.' *Gods, that had better be true.*

Time hung heavily that morning. The guards paid her no further heed and sat talking quietly together. Lara took the opportunity to bathe her hands and face and then comb her hair. It took a while but she was disinclined to hurry knowing that lack of occupation would afford too much opportunity to think. As it was the campsite seemed forlorn. She missed the company of the men and their cheerful banter and laughter. She missed her brother and cousin and, she was forced to admit, she missed Finn's dynamic and enlivening presence. When he was nearby the very air seemed charged with invisible energy. Now he was gone it was as though light and colour had somehow leached away with him. The result was an unwonted lowering of the spirits.

Eventually she could stand the inaction no longer. If she didn't find something to do, she would go crazy. Making up her mind she went to speak to Torstein.

'If you don't mind I'll go and collect some wood for the fire this evening.'

He nodded. 'Aye, why not?'

'I won't go too far.'

'All the same I reckon Gorm and I'll come along and lend a hand.'

Gorm got to his feet and the three of them headed off together. Pleased as she was to be doing something it didn't stop Lara from thinking. How far had the ship travelled? What was Finn doing now? In her imagination he was walking the deck or taking a turn at the oars or perhaps standing in the prow, scanning the horizon for a sighting of Steingrim. Given the number of islands along the coast that might not be so easy. There were plenty of hiding places where a vessel might lie in wait. Finn had the advantage now but the situation might change at any time. The consequences of that didn't bear thinking about. She sighed and bent to pick up another log.

Somewhere among the trees ahead a twig snapped underfoot—the sound like a cracking whip in the quiet air. Lara turned quickly, her gaze moving to the thicket. Her two companions did likewise.

'What was that?' she asked. 'A bear perhaps?'

'I don't know, my lady.'

Torstein remained quite still, listening intently. Nothing moved. Lara darted swift looks around. The thought of a bear so close to the camp was not reassuring.

'I don't hear anything,' she murmured.

Even the birds were quiet now but it was not a peaceful silence. As it drew out she felt the skin prickle on the back of her neck. Nor was she alone in feeling uneasy. Torstein slowly laid down his bundle of firewood and drew his sword.

'Best you go back, lady,' he said, 'while we—'

He broke off as half-a-dozen men stepped out of the thicket, all of them clad in war gear and all of them fully armed. One look was enough to ascertain that they weren't friends. Gorm drew his sword. Then Torstein spoke again, this time his tone low and urgent.

'Go, lady. Now.'

Dropping the firewood she turned and ran. Behind her she could hear the clash of steel. Her mouth dried. Torstein and Gorm would have no chance against such odds. She had to alert the others. However, she had barely gone fifty yards when more armed men stepped out of the thicket in front of her. She checked abruptly, looking desperately around for an escape route. There was none. She was surrounded. Her mouth dried as they closed in, a pack of grinning wolves with steel teeth.

As the sun rose above the hills, Finn's frustration mounted too. They'd made good speed but still an intensive search had revealed no trace of Steingrim. He wasn't that far ahead of them so they ought at least to have sighted his ships by now. The fact that they hadn't so much as glimpsed a sail made Finn increasingly suspicious. It didn't pay to underestimate an enemy like Steingrim and especially not when he was out of plain view.

Finn glared at an empty horizon. 'Where in Frigg's name is he?'

'Hiding out among the islands maybe,' said Unnr.

'The hunter hiding?' replied Vigdis. 'It doesn't make sense. What he wants is battle and slaughter.'

'Unless he's lying in wait somewhere.'

'If he'd been waiting we'd have come near him by now and he'd have launched an attack,' replied Finn. 'It doesn't stack up. We ought to have found him.'

'Maybe he was thinking the same thing, my lord,' said Vigdis. 'It must have occurred to him by now that he could have passed us. If so he might have doubled back.'

That uncomfortable thought had been in the back of Finn's mind too. Hearing it spoken aloud only lent it greater weight.

'If he'd doubled back then surely we'd have seen him,' said Unnr.

'Not necessarily,' replied Finn. 'Steingrim is cunning. He wouldn't risk sailing right into us without knowing our strength first. He'd be stealthy about it.'

Vigdis nodded. 'Under cover of darkness maybe? Remaining unseen and safely out in open water while he looked for the light from our campfire? Having located it, all he'd have to do would be to wait just out of sight and plan his next move.'

An uneasy silence descended. Finn's frown deepened. He knew that it was entirely possible and he didn't like the implications one bit.

'Turn around. We're going back.'

* * *

It was over very quickly in spite of furious resistance. In less than a minute Lara was overpowered and slung over a mailed shoulder like a sack of meal. Ignoring struggles and curses her captor took her back to camp. He set her down then, albeit retaining a vice-like grip on her arm. Breathless and dishevelled she looked around. With a sinking heart she saw the two sea dragons lying just offshore and realised that the invaders must have doubled back and then overrun the place. The four remaining guards were dead, their bodies lying where they had fallen. Of Torstein and Gorm there was no sign.

Her captor hauled her in front of a mail-clad warrior seated on a rock nearby. He was an older man, in his early forties perhaps, his lined face as hard and angular as a hatchet. Strands of grey mingled with black in his hair and beard. The latter was plaited, the braid interwoven with a strip of red cloth. A helmet, crested with the likeness of a charging boar, reposed beside him. A naked sword rested lightly across his knees.

Conversation faded and the place grew quiet, the air laden with expectation as the weight of attention turned their way. Lara tensed, her heart thumping unpleasantly fast as she realised who was sitting in front of her. He surveyed her in silence. Under the scrutiny of those dark and feral eyes her skin crawled. Then he inclined his head in acknowledgement.

'Well met, Lara Ottarsdotter.'

She forced herself to meet his eye. Whatever happened she had to hide her fear. 'You are well informed, Jarl Steingrim.'

'One hears things,' he replied. 'Intriguing things sometimes.'

She evinced polite interest. 'Indeed?'

'Ordinarily a marriage alliance wouldn't be of much interest to me but when it concerns an old acquaintance I find myself curious.'

She remained silent hoping her face wouldn't reveal the dismay she felt inside. Her first thought was to wonder how he'd found out. Just as quickly she dismissed it. *Never mind how he found out. He knows and that's it.*

'Curious to see Finn Egilsson's bride,' Steingrim went on. His gaze stripped her and then he shrugged. 'Well, each man to his own.'

Soft laughter issued from the crowd. Still she remained silent, refusing to rise to the bait. Let Steingrim insult her. It didn't matter what he thought. It didn't matter what any of them thought.

'Of course, it may be that his first concern wasn't your looks. Most likely it was fighting men.' He paused. 'How many men, I wonder?'

Her heart sank as she saw which way this tended. Whatever happened she wasn't about to give him the information he sought. She knew she was going to have to tell him something and make it plausible, just not the truth.

'Enough,' she replied.

Steingrim rose from his seat and casually lifted the sword. The point hovered an inch from the base of her throat.

'How many?'

She knew better than to think he was bluffing. If she defied him openly he'd cut her all right—into slivers if need be. 'Twenty of his own men and...' she hesitated, hoping it sounded reluctant and therefore more convincing. If she misjudged it…

'And?'

She swallowed hard. 'My brother's crew as well. He…he has fifty men.'

'Who else?'

'No one else.'

The point of the sword came to rest against her skin. 'I'll ask you just once more. Who else?'

Does he know of Guthrum's involvement or does he just suspect? Gods, let it be the latter. Her gaze met his and held it. 'I told you, no one else.'

'I don't believe you.'

The point pressed closer and a bead of blood welled on her skin. Her stomach wallowed but she forced herself to keep looking at Steingrim.

'Suit yourself. Killing me won't change the facts. Anyway, fifty men will be more than enough to slay the lot of you.'

His eyes glinted and for a moment she thought she was dead. Then anger was replaced by grudging admiration and he laughed and the blade was withdrawn a little way.

'Fifty will not defeat eighty, Lara Ottarsdotter.'

She heard the note of self-satisfaction in that and played up to it. 'Yes, they will, and then my husband will kill you, Jarl Steingrim.'

'Your faith in him is touching. Unfortunately, the reality will be rather different. I shall kill him and then sell his wife into slavery.'

The thought was chilling but she wasn't about to let him know that. 'You must catch the bear before you skin it.'

'Oh, I won't need to catch the bear.' He lowered the sword. 'He will come to me now, especially when he finds out that his honour has been trampled into the dirt.'

'His honour is more than proof against you.'

'We'll see, won't we? However, I have a feeling he's not going to be best pleased when he finds out that all my men have taken turns with his wife.'

Lara's cheeks went deathly pale. He was quite right. It was a deadly insult and no man would rest until he had avenged himself on the perpetrators. First though the outrage had to be committed. Likely she wouldn't survive the ordeal, but she'd survive long enough to afford Steingrim considerable satisfaction; long enough for him to be able to taunt his enemy with the details afterwards. Details whose vileness brought her out in a cold sweat.

Steingrim's gaze never wavered. If anything he looked speculative now, as though waiting for her reaction. Waiting for her to scream perhaps? Anticipating the outward manifestation of the fear he knew full well she was feeling. Instinct brought her chin up. If the brute thought she was going to fall weeping at his feet and plead for mercy he could take a running jump into the Skagerrak. Besides, no amount of pleading would help her now. She could feel the increasing tension in the air; could sense the slavering eagerness of the pack around them. One scream, one sign of terror and they'd attack. If she had to die she would choose the method and it would be a lot quicker than theirs.

'How very unoriginal,' she replied. 'Worse, it's not even sporting.'

'I think it'll provide sport enough,' he replied.

Murmurs of agreement greeted this.

'Give me a sword and I'll make it much more interesting, I promise you.'

Amusement rippled through the crowd of onlookers. Even Steingrim smiled. 'Perhaps we have a Valkyrie in our midst. A very small one.'

Amusement turned to sycophantic laughter but Lara stood her ground. 'Does the thought frighten you?' She regarded them coolly then turned back to Steingrim. 'Surely there must be one among this crowd of nithings who has the guts to face a woman in combat?'

On hearing this insult their laughter faded. Steingrim pursed his lips.

'Nithings, eh? What say you to that, lads?'

A voice spoke out. 'I say it's time to teach the bitch a lesson.'

'If you think you're man enough,' she replied.

Steingrim raised an eyebrow. '*Are* you man enough to fight the Valkyrie, Kal?'

'Aye, and to defeat her in short order,' said Kal.

'Very well,' replied Steingrim. 'Give her a sword.'

Lara experienced a brief fierce exultation. Her ploy had worked. Moments later the weapon arrived point first, quivering in the earth at her feet. She took it without hesitation, closing her hand firmly round the grip.

Steingrim glanced at his men. 'Back off. Give them some room.'

They obeyed forming a large circle around the two combatants.

Kal glanced at his companions and grinned. 'This won't take long.'

The mocking jests and ribald laughter that ensued indicated their total belief in the prediction. Lara let it wash over her, quietly enjoying their misplaced confidence as much as the reassuring weight of the weapon in her hand. What she felt now was not fear: it was empowerment. By agreeing to this combat Steingrim had just foiled his own plan and given her back control of her destiny. Kal was right; this wouldn't take long but it didn't need to.

Lifting the sword she adopted the fighting stance that Finn had shown her. The memory brought with it a strong twinge of regret that she would never see him again. She set it aside. It was too late for that. The best she could hope for now was to die with honour. Then, in time to come, he might at least remember her with pride.

Kal lifted his sword. 'Ready, Valkyrie?'

She inclined her head. 'Ready, nithing.'

His smile faded and was replaced by a much uglier expression. Lara took a deep breath as her opponent began to advance.

Chapter Twelve

Finn and his men moved silently among the trees, circling round towards the campsite. They were within two hundred yards when they found the bodies of Torstein and Gorm. Both had received half-a-dozen wounds, any one of which would have been fatal on its own. It was a clear and chilling message and did nothing to dispel the sense of foreboding that hung in the air like an invisible pall. The men exchanged troubled glances. No one mentioned the other four companions who had been left behind and they didn't mention Lara either, but their silence was eloquent.

Finn's jaw tightened. 'Move in slowly and stay sharp. They'll likely have guards posted.'

However, as they advanced no voice rang out to challenge them or to sound the alarm. Suspecting a trap they looked warily around but the only sound seemed to be coming from the camp itself. It sounded like laughter interspersed with cheering. As they neared the place they stopped at the edge of the thicket, staring in slack-jawed astonishment at the circle of men in front of them.

'What in the name of the All-Father is going on?' muttered Vigdis.

Unnr shook his head. 'Dunno. Looks like some kind of contest to me.'

No one ventured a comment about what the nature of the contest might be. The sound of mocking laughter and jeering voices told its own tale and Finn's gut knotted.

'We'll move in closer. Archers to the fore. Wait on my signal to shoot.'

As another burst of laughter erupted from the crowd up ahead his misgivings grew. Several thoughts flashed through his mind, each seeming more implausible than the last. He was pretty sure that none of the usual reasons applied. Whatever form of amusement was taking place it boded ill. Steingrim had a reputation among the darker elements of the warrior caste; those renowned for ruthless cruelty and brutality. The thought that Lara might have fallen into their clutches filled him with cold dread. Was he too late? Had he lost her?

In the event not even his wildest imaginings prepared him for the reality when they got near enough to see what the crowd was watching. His men stopped in their tracks.

Unnr stared. 'Thor's stones.'

'They would stoop to fight a woman? Those cowardly scumbag nithings!' said Vigdis.

As his horrified gaze took in the spectacle of the unequal combat, Finn's heart leaped towards his throat and for the second time in his life he felt truly afraid. Then cold rage replaced fear and the warrior's instinct superseded both.

Raising his sword aloft, he signalled to the archers.

In response a dozen arrows flew from the thicket and whicked into the wall of exposed backs. In that densely packed throng it was impossible to miss. As the victims fell, those nearest to them looked round. Before they even had time to yell a dozen more arrows found their targets. Then the alarm went up and Steingrim's men fumbled for their swords. The blades had barely cleared leather before the air was rent by a mighty battle roar torn from a hundred throats. Finn and his companions hurtled down on the foe.

Hearing the sudden commotion Lara glanced up. That moment's inattention gave Kal the opening he sought and his blade landed with vicious force under the guard plate of her sword. With a yelp of pain she let the weapon fall, cradling her numb hand. He smiled, menacing her with the point of his blade.

'You just lost, bitch. Now it's time to pay up.'

Lara backed away looking frantically around, but all she could see was a swaying chaos of fighting men. With sick horror she realised that she was trapped between the main line of battle and the water. She backed another pace and then another, her gaze on the sword hovering above her breast, until her heel caught on a rock and she stumbled. Kal grabbed her arm and twisted hard, throwing her to the ground. Then he followed her down. Pinned underneath him Lara fought with desperate fury, writhing and kicking. He smiled but the expression stopped well short of his eyes.

'Fight all you like. It won't change the outcome, bitch.'

She spat at him. 'You'll have to kill me first, you nithing.'

'I'm not going to kill you—at least not yet.'

* * *

Finn slew his first three opponents without conscious effort, fuelled by emotions he hadn't realised he possessed. Then he paused briefly, his gaze moving past the fighting throng, desperately seeking Lara. When he couldn't find her he was filled with dread. Then, over the din, he heard a woman scream. He carved a path towards the sound, dispatching two more enemies on the way. Then he saw her. As he took in the scene before him dread turned to molten rage.

Lara struggled harder and got a hand free. Her nails raked down her assailant's cheek raising red welts. He swore and slapped her hard. The iron taste of blood filled her mouth. Two seconds later her wrists were above her head, clamped in a large fist. The other hauled her skirt up around her thighs. She shrieked, writhing helplessly beneath him, every part of her in revolt. *This couldn't be happening. It couldn't.*

Suddenly a dark shape loomed over them blotting out the sun. Lara gasped. Her assailant cried out and she felt his body jerk violently. A strange choking sound issued from his mouth and the hold slackened on her wrists. Seconds later his weight lifted altogether as a large fist hauled him away and flung him aside. Then she was staring at a bloodstained sword. Her wide-eyed gaze travelled to the warrior who held it, a huge and terrifying figure silhouetted against the sky. She stifled a sob and tried to scramble away but he reached down and seized her arm. Panic-stricken, she kicked out at him.

'Get away from me! Don't touch me!'

'Lara! Lara, it's all right. Don't be afraid.'

For a few seconds she stared at him in heart-pounding disbelief before the familiar tones began to sink in. 'Finn?'

He pulled her upright. Almost faint with relief she flung herself against him, clinging close despite the hard chainmail shirt pressing into her flesh. And then his arm was around her, a solid reassuring bulwark between her and harm. For a little while they remained thus. Then he glanced down. 'Are you all right?'

She nodded, unable to speak and still scarcely able to credit the narrowness of her escape. Finn had come back. Somehow he had come back and he had saved her. As it began to sink in she became aware of clashing steel and shouting and running men.

Outnumbered and trapped between the enemy and the water Steingrim's warriors had realised that their best hope was to reach the boats. Those nearest were making good their escape while their companions fought a rearguard action against Finn's men. The mercenaries were hard pressed every step of the way and as soon as they reached the water they turned and fled, splashing through the shallows to the waiting ships. Many of the fugitives were cut down. The remainder were hauled aboard by their companions. With that the ships put off from the shore and pulled away rapidly.

'To the ship!' bellowed Guthrum. 'We follow!' His men pulled back and raced off through the trees towards the mooring.

Alrik shouted across to Finn, 'We need to finish this, my lord.'

Finn nodded. 'Go! I'm with you.'

Alrik raced off, summoning his men. Finn looked at Lara. 'He's right. I have to finish this now, while my enemy is weakened.'

Tears pricked behind her eyelids but she blinked them away. Tears were weak. Finn didn't need a clinging vine. She was safe. Kal was dead. Nothing happened.

'I know.' She dredged up a wan smile. 'Do what you must, my lord.'

The grey eyes registered surprise and admiration. He squeezed her arm gently. 'I'll be back very soon.'

Then he too was summoning his men and the whole force was racing away through the trees.

Five minutes later their ships were in hot pursuit of Steingrim. Lara shivered as she watched them go, her body trembling. The strand around her was littered with bodies. More floated in the shallows, their blood staining the water red. The stench of death hung on the air. *This is the reality of battle. This is what you envied men for.* She let out a ragged breath. Imagination had never come close to the truth. Worse, it wasn't over yet. All the same she knew Finn was right: he did have to end it, now, today. And while he did his part she must do hers. Self-pity had no place here. There were wounded men to tend to.

Fortunately the casualties among the allies were few. Only eight men had been injured and although the wounds were temporarily incapacitating they were not life-threatening. Lara set about helping as best she could, using strips of torn shirt to bind wounds. The men submitted to her ministrations without complaint and smiled their thanks. One small bright spot in the proceedings was the discovery that Folkvar was still alive. He'd been one of the six men who had comprised the original guard detail and, like them, had come under attack when Steingrim arrived. Although he was luckier than his companions, he had still lost a lot of blood from the deep slashes to his shoulder and ribs and lower leg. The wounds needed to be sewn but Lara had no equipment to hand and wouldn't until the ships returned so she improvised in the meantime.

'When the others get back I'll tend these cuts properly,' she said. 'In the meantime just lie still and rest.'

He smiled faintly. 'I'll do that, my lady.' His gaze held hers. 'I heard you stand up to Steingrim and his men. Bravest thing I ever saw. I wanted to help but…'

'It's all right. Don't try to talk now, Folkvar. Save your energy to help you recover.'

He closed his eyes. Lara regarded him anxiously, thinking she'd give a great deal for a needle and thread and a pot of honey salve.

'Don't worry, my lady. He'll survive.'

She looked round to see Ketill standing nearby. A bloody bandage stanched the cut on his thigh. He limped the last few feet to join them.

'Folkvar is my cousin,' he went on. 'They breed 'em tough on that side of the family.'

'I think that toughness isn't just limited to one side of your family, Ketill.'

He reddened and smiled sheepishly. 'I'll sit with him awhile, my lady, until the others get back.'

Lara nodded hoping that her face wouldn't betray the trepidation she felt inside. *Gods, please let them all come back. Let Finn come back.* Suddenly nothing in the world seemed as important as that.

It was mid-afternoon when the three ships returned. As they came into view Lara leaped to her feet, her gaze following them every inch of the way. Ketill and the other walking wounded came to join her as the

ships glided in towards the shore. Lara breathed a sigh
of relief when she saw Alrik and Guthrum. Then her
gaze moved on, scanning the remaining vessel for a
glimpse of Finn and failing to find him. Perhaps he was
taking a turn at the oars and she'd somehow missed him
among the other crewmen. Craning her neck to try to
get a better view she looked again. *He has to be there.
He has to be.* When she still didn't find him her heart
sank and dread began to replace anticipation. *Please,
gods, don't let him be dead.*

Then Ketill's voice rang out, asking the question she
feared to pose. 'Where's Jarl Finn?'

Unnr called back, 'He's here, with the other wounded.'

Lara paled and her stomach seemed to tie itself in
knots. 'How badly is he hurt?'

'He took a sword cut to the leg,' replied Unnr. 'We
bound it as best we could but he's lost a lot of blood.'

'I want to see him. Help me aboard, somebody.'

Two minutes later she was standing on the deck.
She found him then, propped against the strakes in
the stern. He was conscious but his face was deathly
pale. A blood-soaked bandage was bound about his left
thigh. She swallowed hard. *He's alive.* Relief mingled
with anxiety to produce a tremulous smile.

'Finn?'

As she knelt beside him he became aware of her
presence and the grey eyes brightened a little. For a moment they faced each other in silence. Her smile faded a
little when she saw the blackening gore splashed across
his arms and breast. Interpreting her expression cor-
rectly he smiled faintly.

'It's all right. It's not mine.'

'I'm glad to hear it. It seems to me that you can ill

afford to lose any more.' She looked at the injured leg. 'That will need to be cleaned and sewn up.'

'By and by. First we'll bury our dead and collect our wounded. Then we'll find another place to make camp. This place has too many unpleasant associations.'

It was a fair point and she didn't want to start an argument, but at the same time she was reluctant to delay treating the wound. He saw the inner struggle in her face.

'I'll survive a little longer.'

'Please don't tease, Finn. Not now. The past few hours have been among the longest of my life.'

He took her hand. 'Are you telling me that you were worried?'

'Of course I was worried. I...I didn't know if I'd ever see you again.'

His gaze warmed. 'If you thought that you were well wide of the mark, my sweet.' He raised her hand to his lips. 'I apologise for such a tame offering but it's the best I can do at present. Besides, that cut lip looks painful.'

'It's nothing.'

'Not to me it isn't.'

He retained his hold on her hand and she made no attempt to withdraw it, needing the solid reassurance of physical contact.

'Tell me what happened?'

'We caught up with Steingrim and slew a goodly number of his men, although they delivered their share of blows.' He glanced at his leg. 'This was a parting gift from one of them, delivered from behind while I was otherwise engaged. Steingrim was wounded in the fighting but in the confusion he and some of his followers escaped.'

'Oh.' It wasn't what she'd hoped to hear but it pleased her to think that the enemy hadn't escaped unscathed. 'But surely he can't be much of a threat now.'

'His force is smashed, that's for sure.'

'Did you lose many men?'

'Fifteen in all. A small fraction of Steingrim's losses.'

'I'm sorry you lost any.'

'So am I, but it could have been much worse.'

It was bad enough. In truth she didn't want to think about how much worse it could have been or what she might have been feeling now if it had.

The sun was sinking before the new camp was established and Lara could set to work on the wound. It was deep but clean. Finn made no sound while she sewed the cut though his pallor worried her. His skin felt cold to the touch. If only she'd had access to the herbs and salves from home she could have offered him some relief from the pain. When they reached Ravndal she would find out what might be done in that respect. In the interim a few mouthfuls of mead had to suffice. When the wound was bound again she unbuckled his sword belt and co-opted a couple of men to remove the chainmail shirt and help him into the sealskin sleeping bag, which she had laid out ready near to the fire.

When she had made him as comfortable as possible she went to attend to Folkvar's injuries. He made light of them but his ashen face spoke louder. Nevertheless, he dredged up a wan smile of thanks as she finished tying off the bandage. Once again she found herself wishing she had some medicines to hand.

Having finished the task she asked if anyone else needed help, but it seemed that the majority of their wounds were slight. She had half expected the enquiry to be met with mocking smiles and perhaps some teasing comments: it was a point of pride with fighting men to make light of all but the most serious injuries. Somewhat to her surprise their mockery was conspicuous by its absence and, although they declined her assistance, it was declined courteously. She supposed that they must be feeling too tired to engage in the usual banter. Gathering her things she prepared to return to Finn. Weariness was setting in now, a reaction to the rigours of the day, and she guessed it wouldn't be long before the men turned in too.

She was on her way back when she met Alrik. Like the rest he was dirty and dishevelled but, happily, unhurt.

'Shall we reach Ravndal soon?' she asked. 'We need some medicines and clean linen for bandages. I would not have any of these men succumb to fever or wound rot.'

He nodded. 'We should be there tomorrow in the afternoon.'

'I'm glad to hear it.'

He looked around at the men now talking quietly among themselves. 'The enemy came off far worse today I'm pleased to say.'

'But Steingrim escaped.'

'Aye, he did, unfortunately. The man's as slippery as an oiled viper. Still, his fangs are drawn so he won't be giving us any more trouble for a while.'

'I hope you're right.'

'I'm sure of it.' Alrik paused. 'How does Jarl Finn?'

'Poorly at present. I need to get him back to civilisation where I can look after him properly.'

The words elicited an expression of keen interest. 'Spoken with wifely concern. Can it be that you're warming to him, Lara?'

Her reply was short and pithy.

His grin widened. 'Well, well. Who'd have thought it?'

Lara's cheeks reddened. 'If all you can do is make sarcastic remarks I shall leave you alone.'

Alrik laughed softly. With as much dignity as she could muster she suited action to words and began to make her way back across the camp. Really her brother could be tiresome on occasion. He always knew how to annoy her. She ought to know better by now than to rise to the bait.

On her return Lara liberated the blanket from Finn's sea chest and wrapped it around her shoulders against the evening chill. Then she settled down nearby. Finn was still very pale but he was sleeping now. For a little while she watched him, her heart full of conflicting emotions. He had fought for her today; he had saved her from Kal and from intended violation. It was a husband's role to protect a wife and no man worthy of the name would suffer another to trespass in that way, but had that rescue been only about possessive instinct? Suddenly she wanted to think that it had not.

Finn might not love her but his behaviour today, his whole manner, suggested something other than indifference. The fear she'd felt when she'd thought that she

might have lost him also compelled her to acknowl-
edge what she had so steadfastly tried to ignore, what
she had been trying to ignore from the first. *You're not
indifferent to him. You never were.* Alrik was right.

The admission was profoundly troubling on many
levels and she had absolutely no idea what she was
going to do about it. She had no experience to call on,
nothing that might help her in the present predicament.
If only she could have talked to Asa. Even if her sister didn't have a solution it would have been wonderful to be able to confide the matter and to know that
the confidence would be respected. There was no one
now. Much as she loved Alrik she couldn't speak to
him about this. *You're on your own.* She glanced again
at Finn. *All right not on your own exactly, but it's not
the same thing.* If he guessed he would be amused or
else he would pity her. The idea was unbearable. He
was the last person she could tell. Anyway, at present
there were more important considerations.

Finn fell into an uneasy slumber from which he
awakened intermittently because the least movement
was agony. He felt cold too despite the sealskin bag and
his proximity to the fire. Once or twice he glanced in
Lara's direction. She looked calm and untroubled in
rest. The cut lip was all that remained to testify to the
events of the previous day. The sight of it filled him
with anger. Only twice in his life had he enjoyed killing a man but yesterday had been one of those times.
The brute had been well served and lucky too. Finn's
imagination supplied a dozen slow and painful deaths
that would have been fitting punishment for such a
crime. Fitting, and far more satisfying too. As long as

he lived he wouldn't forget the sight of Lara in those predatory clutches. Nor would the image lose its power to chill. Her vulnerability had brought all his protective instincts to the fore. Along with that was admiration for her courage. He had no idea what madness had possessed her to take on one of Steingrim's thugs but there was no denying the bravery of the deed. Until that moment he hadn't realised it was possible to feel pride and terror simultaneously. From now on he was going to do a better job of taking care of her.

He grimaced. At the moment he was incapable of taking care of anyone. In fact the boot was on the other foot. He had a sense of things sliding out of control but he lacked the ability or even the will to do anything about it.

Chapter Thirteen

In spite of her concern for Finn and her eagerness to arrive at their destination Lara found herself enjoying the voyage the next day. The morning was fair and the breeze keen so that white caps chased each other across the wide expanse of grey-green water. The air was sharp and smelled pleasantly of brine and rope and wood. It was good to be away from danger and the stench of death. The thought of Ravndal no longer daunted her. On the contrary she found herself looking forward to some peace and quiet and a more settled way of life.

She looked at Finn and pulled the sealskin closer around him. He was sleeping again and he was still very pale but his flesh had lost some of its alarming chill. Moreover when she'd checked his wound earlier there was no sign of fresh bleeding. With care and rest he would recover. In the meantime a settled life would mean a chance to get to know him better. Suddenly she wanted that very much. Familiarity hadn't bred contempt; far from it. All her former hopes that he might often be absent had entirely disappeared. But what if

he didn't want a settled life? What if he wished to follow the whale road as he had before? Why should he
not revert to his old life? He'd married her because it
was expedient and, although he'd treated her well, that
didn't necessarily mean he'd be staying around. He'd
never pretended love and she had no power to hold him.
Even the wife he had loved hadn't been able to do that.

There were so many questions she wanted to ask
him about the past and the future but they were going
to have to wait. What mattered now was to restore him
to full health.

As Alrik had predicted they reached Ravndal the
following afternoon. The arrival of three ships could
not fail to cause a stir but when the watchers on the
jetty identified who the visitors were their arrival was
greeted with words of welcome. Willing hands helped
to carry the injured ashore and then the whole company
trooped up to the hall. The majority of the men would
sleep there later; the rest would make shift in the barn.

Finn was carried to a separate building that was
clearly intended for family sleeping accommodation.
One end had been curtained off to provide the jarl
with a measure of privacy. It contained a large bed, a
stand holding a wooden basin and a jug, a stool and
a wooden storage chest. The servants set Lara's box
down next to it and stowed Finn's sea chest and his war
gear in one corner.

When she had seen Finn laid carefully in the bed
Lara had lost no time in bespeaking clean water and
bandages and in finding out exactly what medicinal
plants were available for use. One of the women ser-

vants showed her the store which, mercifully, was well stocked. Lara's gaze scanned the small room.

'Do you have some willow bark?' she asked.

'Yes, my lady.'

'Do you know how to prepare an infusion?'

On receiving an answer in the affirmative Lara instructed the woman to do so. After that she arranged for a pallet to be brought to Finn's sleeping quarters so that she could be on hand if he needed her. If anyone had told her a fortnight ago that she would volunteer to sleep close to this man she'd have laughed. Now it seemed the natural thing to do. Natural and right. The thought of Finn in pain was something she couldn't countenance, particularly when she had the means to alleviate his suffering. It was the least she could do when she owed him so much.

He hovered between sleep and waking in a restless doze. Mercifully she had seen no sign of fever in him but it didn't pay to be complacent. When he did open his eyes he seemed disorientated but she put that down to loss of blood and to pain. She used the opportunity to give him a drink of willow-bark tea. After that he slept better.

He slept for the better part of three days during which time she left him only when she had to. He was still pale and the lines of his cheek and jaw were more pronounced, the latter stubbled with a new growth of beard, but the frightening waxen hue had gone. So too had the chill in his flesh. Only the small furrow in his brow remained to tell of pain. She reached out a hand and stroked his face. He would get well again. He must get well.

* * *

When Finn awoke it took him a second or two to work out where he was. Gradually the familiar details of the room reasserted themselves and memory returned. All the same he had little recollection of the voyage, or of being carried ashore, or of how he came to be lying in bed under a pile of furs. He felt warm now and, although his leg still throbbed, as long as he was still the savage pain could be held at bay. He looked around and became aware that he wasn't alone.

'Lara?'

'How are you feeling?'

'I've known worse.'

'Drink this. It'll help with the pain.'

'What is it?'

'Willow-bark tea.'

She held the cup to his lips and, little by little, he drank the liquid within. It tasted of honey underlain with bitterness.

'Are you hungry?' she asked. 'There's a pot of soup on the fire.'

'Maybe later.'

'All right.'

He sighed. 'This wasn't exactly how I'd anticipated our arrival at Ravndal.'

'If it's any consolation it wasn't how I'd anticipated it either.'

'I'll wager it wasn't.'

'Never mind. We're here now.'

'Yes.'

They lapsed into silence both aware of unspoken questions hanging in the air but neither wishing to utter them. There would be a time for that, he decided, but it wasn't now. In spite of having slept so much he still felt deathly tired. Maybe blood loss had something to do with it. He hadn't even seen the attack coming. The perpetrator was already wounded, lying among his slain companions, but he'd summoned enough strength to get to his knees and deliver one last malicious thrust. Being engaged in a separate combat Finn's attention was to the front. He'd had no suspicion of the danger behind him until he felt cold metal bite deep into his flesh. With a yell of fury he sped the present opponent and then turned to deliver a death blow to the snake behind. Only then had he noticed the pain and the hot blood pouring from the wound. Even so he knew he'd been lucky: with the full weight of the enemy behind it the blow would have severed the limb completely.

'Try to sleep some more,' said Lara. 'It's rest that will help the leg to mend now.'

'I haven't even thanked you for sewing the wound.'

'No thanks are necessary. Think of it as returning a favour.'

He smiled faintly and nodded. 'Will you come back later?'

'Of course.'

His gaze followed her to the curtained doorway. When she had gone he shut his eyes again but for a while sleep eluded him. He had understated the case when he said this wasn't how he'd planned things. In his imagination he had welcomed her properly and shown her around and made sure she was accorded the status she deserved. When she'd had a chance to adjust to her new home he'd have set about wooing her as she ought to have been wooed in the first place. He could not reflect on his behaviour with any satisfaction at all. He should have been protecting her from danger not dragging her into it.

Incredibly, she hadn't uttered a word of criticism, even though she'd had good cause. She hadn't railed or wept or treated him to female hysterics. Bótey had done all of those things. No doubt he had deserved it too, but Lara's self-possession moved him much more. He was proud of her, but his admiration went a lot further than her beauty. She touched something deep inside him that he hadn't known he possessed. For that reason he couldn't define the sensation or pin it down. It remained elusive, a lingering resonance like a chord that hung in the air after the harper's hand had left the strings, and it engendered a spark of recognition as though spirit had somehow spoken to spirit.

As soon as occasion permitted they were going to talk. Quite apart from anything else he owed her an apology.

Lara sank into the tub with a sigh of relief. The bathhouse had been a welcome discovery and one she'd been longing to take advantage of. So much so that she'd hauled the water and heated it herself. Days of rough living and nursing duty had left her feeling grubby and dishevelled—something she fully intended to remedy. However, her urge to bathe wasn't merely about wanting to restore a sense of well-being. It was about wanting to look attractive too. She sighed. *Who are you trying to fool? You want to look attractive for him.* Not so long ago, she wouldn't have cared two straws for Finn's opinion one way or the other, but now it mattered a great deal. She wanted him to look at her not as part of a bargain struck but as a man looks at a woman, the way he had looked at her in those first seconds when she appeared before him on their wedding day. Seconds before he had time to conceal his thoughts behind an urbane manner and mocking humour. He wore that manner like a mask. Just occasionally it slipped to reveal a different person, someone who intrigued and attracted her, someone she wanted to know better.

She could hardly fail to note his dismay over the present state of affairs. For the first time since she had known him he appeared vulnerable, even a little uncertain. He wasn't used to being dependent. In many ways it was touching to see the man beneath the persona of the warrior and commander. He need not have been concerned about the manner of her reception here. It hadn't taken long to establish her identity or to assert her authority with the servants. There at least she did have plenty of experience to call on. In any case Finn's needs had made it essential to step into her new role immediately: the jarl's new wife. Lara grimaced. Not truly a wife, not yet.

That thought gave rise to sensations that she no longer wanted to deny. She had never expected to enjoy a man's touch or to like his kiss or to want more of both. *When you decide that you want to become a real woman let me know.* She knew she did want that. Even if Finn didn't love her, even if he wasn't going to be around all the time, she still wanted that. Of course, knowing it was one thing, letting him know was quite another. Facing Steingrim and his thugs was nothing in comparison.

Hearing footsteps in the passageway beyond the curtain Finn looked up eagerly. Instead of Lara though, it was Unnr who appeared on the threshold. For a moment or two he surveyed Finn in silence then he grinned.

'You're looking better than you did. How's the leg?'

'Better than it was before. The willow-bark tea helps.'

'That's what Folkvar said.'

'Folkvar? I feared he had died with the others we left behind.'

'By rights he should have but he was lucky. All the same he's got a wicked slash to the shoulder. Right down to the bone. Got another nasty cut across the ribs too.'

'I feel for him. Did any of the other five survive Steingrim's attack?'

'No, he was the only one. Your little wife sewed him up a treat.'

'She has a talent with a needle.'

'That's not all she's got a talent for.'

'I beg your pardon?'

Unnr looked sheepish. 'Sorry, poor choice of words. What I meant was courage. Folkvar told us all about it and I don't mind admitting we were impressed. It's the bravest thing I ever heard.'

'What is?'

'Why, Lady Lara standing up to Steingrim like that.'

'Like what?'

Unnr blinked. 'She must have told you about it.' Then, seeing Finn's expression he looked a little embarrassed. 'Or maybe not.'

'Does this have something to do with that crazy sword fight we interrupted?'

'Well, yes.'

Finn's eyes glinted. 'I think you'd better tell me what you know.'

'If she hasn't said anything I'm not sure I should…'

'All of it, Unnr. Now.'

As he listened, Finn felt himself turning cold again. He'd been so preoccupied with slaying the would-be rapist that he hadn't thought to enquire why Lara had been in combat in the first place. Had it not been for her wits and her courage she might have been raped before he and his men arrived on the scene. It also occurred to him that she couldn't have known he would be back in time to save her. Had she been planning to use the sword for another purpose entirely? The more he thought about it the likelier it seemed. She wouldn't let herself be used by Steingrim's crew if there was a way out. Finn was appalled. Not only did it highlight his failure to protect her properly, it also revealed how close he'd come to losing her. He'd once thought it wouldn't be hard to grow fond of Lara. He realised now how far he'd understated the case.

'I'm glad you told me, Unnr.'

'You won't say it was me, will you? Otherwise she might decide to try to run me through as well.'

'Don't worry. Your secret is safe.'

When Lara had bathed and changed her gown and combed her hair she returned to check on her patient. He was awake and though he smiled when she entered the atmosphere seemed subtly different. If he noticed her altered appearance he didn't comment on it. However, when she suggested he might like to have some soup he accepted.

'I'd offer to feed you as well,' she said, 'but I feel sure you'd dislike it.'

His expression was eloquent. 'Don't even think about it.'

She concealed a smile. 'Let me rearrange the pillows then so that you can sit up.'

When it had been accomplished she handed him the bowl and the spoon and then perched on the stool while he ate.

'It's good,' he observed.

'It will help you make new blood and get your strength back.'

'A truly marvellous soup, then.'

'Let's hope so.' She paused. 'Has the willow-bark tea helped the pain?'

He nodded. 'I thank you, yes.'

'I'll bring you some more later on. That bandage will need changing too.'

'You're a competent nurse.'

'I've had the practice. At home there were always injuries of some sort to attend to, everything from broken limbs to a gash from a boar's tusk. Men are imaginative when it comes to hurting themselves.'

'I hadn't thought of it that way but I suppose we are.'

Lara smiled but made no reply so he finished the majority of the soup and handed the bowl back. As she rose from the stool he stopped her.

'Don't go. Not yet.' He reclined against the pillows surveying her steadily. 'There's something I must say.'

'My lord?'

'I'm so sorry, Lara.'

'For what?'

'For dragging you along on this trip against your

wishes. For failing to protect you as I should have. For failing to anticipate the enemy and for exposing you to mortal danger. Take your pick of the reasons.'

She regarded him in genuine astonishment. 'Your reasons for bringing me along were well intentioned. What happened after wasn't your fault.'

'You are generous.'

'But it's true. You couldn't read Steingrim's mind.'

'I couldn't read his mind but I should have considered the possibility that he might double back. Five men died for that short-sightedness, and you were almost—' He broke off, and took a deep breath. 'I know why you had that sword in your hand, Lara.'

'You know?'

'Folkvar hasn't been slow to spread the word.'

'Oh.' She eyed him uncertainly. 'I know it must seem foolish to you but it was all I could think of at the time.'

His gaze met hers. 'Aye, it was foolish all right, and clever and quite astonishingly brave.'

She stared at him uncertain she'd just heard aright. However, there was nothing in his expression to suggest he was teasing. The possibility that he might have meant it resurrected a familiar glow inside her.

'I had to persuade Steingrim to give me a weapon.'

'*In extremis*, you would have used it on yourself, wouldn't you?'

'Yes, but it didn't come to that because you saved me.'

'Thor's blood, does that make me a hero now?'

'It does in my mind,' she replied.

For a moment he was silent, his face hard to read. She would have given a great deal to know what he was thinking.

'I don't deserve the honour,' he replied, 'but I promise that I'll try to do better in future.'

'I think I could not wish for better.'

Some unidentified emotion flickered in the grey eyes and his gaze became intent.

'Then…you do not entirely regret ever having set eyes on me?'

'No, I don't regret that.' She smiled faintly. 'I thought marriage would be dull but it has turned out to be quite the opposite.'

In spite of himself he laughed. 'I'm sorry, my sweet, but I regret to tell you that I mean to put a stop to that kind of excitement.'

Her smile faded a little as she considered the implications. Did he mean that she would be left behind while he went adventuring? Would she become an inconvenience that he could do without and would forget as soon as she was out of sight?

'But not to all excitement I hope,' she replied.

'No, not all.'

'That's a relief.'

'I should have thought it would be more of a relief to know you were safe.'

'Safety is one thing—tedium quite another.'

'I will do my best never to be tedious,' he replied.

Her eyes met his. 'I'll hold you to that.'

'I hope you will.'

She nodded and rose from her stool. 'I should go and prepare some more willow-bark tea. Why don't you get some rest in the meantime?'

When she had gone Finn turned over that conversation in his mind. He hadn't missed her altered expression just now or the doubt behind it. What was it that she feared? Not her new role of wife, surely? She had been preparing for that all her life. Was it the thought of being an abandoned wife perhaps? He frowned. He'd made that mistake once before and if Lara imagined he would leave her for months on end she was mistaken. With her he intended to have a very different relationship. Loneliness wasn't going to feature. On the contrary he intended them to have something much more intimate.

That turned his thoughts in a different direction. Although he hadn't said so, he hadn't missed her altered appearance just now. The mauve gown was soft and feminine and it enhanced her elfin beauty. He'd have liked to think it had been for his benefit but he wasn't so conceited. Lara had done it to please herself and he could not blame her for it. Any woman would prefer to look her best rather than be dragged across the country and forced to live rough among a group of warriors. When he'd insisted upon her accompanying them he had been thoughtless and selfish. He sighed. It seemed he had a lot to atone for one way or another.

As Lara returned to the hall she met Alrik. He enquired after Finn and looked relieved when she said he was lucid and free of the fever that heralded the onset of wound rot.

'He's lucky, then.'

She nodded. 'The wound was clean. What he requires now is rest and food to build up his strength again.' She paused. 'Speaking of which, is there any chance of you taking some men out hunting in the near future? We could do with the meat.'

'Leave it with me.'

'Gladly.'

Alrik smiled wryly. 'You've certainly been thrown into deep water, haven't you? First a war, then a new home, an injured husband and numerous mouths to feed.'

'I like a challenge.'

'That's fortunate, isn't it?'

'Ravndal seems to be well organised and the stores still reasonably plentiful.'

'You're welcome to use some of the ship's supplies if you need them,' he said.

'I appreciate it. I haven't really been able to make a proper estimate of the situation yet. I need to have a look in the barn and the granary and the other storage sheds. Then I'll have the whole picture.'

'Why don't we do it now?'

'Would you mind?'

'Not at all, if you don't object to the company.'

'I'd be glad of it.'

She really was. Alrik was an agreeable companion and he would bring another perspective to the task.

For the next hour they made a tour of the farm. It bore out her previous assessment that it was well run. Although it wasn't especially large, the whole place looked quietly prosperous. Lara viewed it with satisfaction. That at least augured well for the future.

Chapter Fourteen

As the wound began to knit and Finn regained some strength he began to take note of his appearance.

'Will you bring me a bowl of water and some soap so that I can wash?' He wrinkled his nose. 'Even I am beginning to find my own smell offensive.'

Lara grinned. 'As you wish.'

'I notice you didn't contradict me just then so I fear that means I'm right.'

'Well…'

'I knew it. Could you fetch a comb as well?'

When she had provided him with the required items Finn gingerly swung his legs over the side of the bed, biting back a curse as his wound twinged. He shifted to a more comfortable position and dragged off his shirt. Then he looked at Lara.

'Would you mind holding the bowl for me?'

She cleared her throat. 'Not at all.'

She tried not to stare but the sight of Finn without clothes was difficult to ignore, especially when he was only a foot away from her. Her gaze kept returning to the hard-muscled torso and the line of gold-brown hair leading the eye from his chest to a narrow waist and lean flanks and groin. He was beautiful, like a hero out of a saga. Moreover, he seemed at ease with his body in its naked state, even in the presence of a woman. She wished she could feel the same, but proximity was causing her overheated imagination to conjure all manner of sensual images that did nothing for her peace of mind.

Apparently unaware of the mental turmoil he was causing, Finn bathed his hands and face and then, taking up the cloth provided, moved on to his neck and torso. Glancing up he intercepted her gaze and smiled.

'I look forward to an hour in the bathhouse eventually.'

She gathered her wits. 'The wound needs to remain dry for a bit longer.'

'I'll make do.'

He took the linen towel from her arm and dried himself. When it was done he rubbed a hand over his chin. 'I need to get rid of these bristles too.'

'You could grow a beard.'

'I tried once but the itching nearly drove me mad.' He glanced towards the pile of war gear across the room. 'Would you bring me my seax?'

Lara set the bowl on the stool nearby and went to oblige. Like his sword, the knife was beautifully crafted. The hilt was made of walrus ivory and intricately carved; the blade six inches of polished steel with a wicked edge. She eyed it with misgivings.

'Is your hand steady enough for the task at present or would you prefer to let me do it?'

'Are you afraid I might cut my throat?'

'It's a possibility, and if that were to happen a cut throat would be much harder to sew up than a leg.'

His eyes gleamed. 'To be honest I wouldn't care to put the matter to the test so I'll bow to your judgement.'

In fact he was not averse to the idea. Apart from any considerations of safety, the idea of having her close to him was a temptation he didn't want to resist. So he sat very still, every nerve and sinew attuned to her. She smelled of fresh air and herbs, perhaps from the box where she stored her gowns. Underneath was the scent of the woman, sweet and warm and exciting. As she worked the fabric of her gown brushed his arm sending a charge along his skin. He might almost imagine that the light touch of her hand on his face was a caress. His imagination removed her clothing and drew her down on to the bed beside him, pressing her nakedness to his. The image created a wave of warmth from his gut to his loins. He took a deep breath and forced his mind away. Any more thoughts like those and he would be hard in seconds. In contrast Lara looked perfectly cool and collected, clearly untroubled by any such erotic visions, and the blade continued to glide smoothly over his cheek and jaw. That was just as well under the circumstances. Much as he would have liked to ruffle her serenity now was definitely not the time.

When at length she had done he dried his face and ran a hand over his chin once more. The skin felt smooth and clean again and he smiled.

'Thank you. That feels much better.'

'It looks much better,' she replied.

'Does that mean you prefer a man without a beard?'

'It depends on the man. Some faces look better with a beard to hide them.'

'I hope mine isn't among them.'

'No. It is tolerable without.'

'Only tolerable?'

'Stop fishing for compliments and comb your hair. It looks as though you've been out in a gale for a week.'

He laughed. 'I can always rely on you to keep me firmly grounded.'

In fact her assessment wasn't too exaggerated and it took him some time to tease out the tangles and restore order. However, he felt better for having done it. He handed back the comb.

'Would you fetch me a clean shirt from the chest?'

Lara raised an eyebrow. 'You're thinking of getting up then?'

'That's right.' He paused. 'Were you thinking of arguing about it?'

'No. I wouldn't waste time on a lost cause. Besides, gentle exercise probably won't do you any harm.'

'You never fail to surprise me.'

She fetched the shirt and a pair of breeks. 'You'll need these too. The ones you were wearing before were fit only for the fire.'

Finn donned the shirt and then carefully began to pull on the breeks. 'I'll need to stand. Would you lend me a shoulder just in case?'

Lara nodded and moved closer, watching him carefully. Cautiously he stood up, grimacing as the wound sent a fresh twinge of pain along his leg. It didn't go unnoticed.

'Is it still bad?' she asked.

'Not bad but making its presence felt.'

'Do you need any help?'

It was tempting. It was very tempting. He wrestled with his baser instinct and reluctantly overcame it. 'No, I think I can manage.' He tucked in the shirt and pulled his breeks up the rest of the way before fastening them. 'Socks and shoes may be a different story.'

He was right about that. Bending and stretching were more than just uncomfortable and he didn't want to tear the wound. He sat down again and Lara knelt in front of him, her small deft hands sliding hose on to his feet and then fastening his shoes afterwards. Finally she fetched a clean tunic from the chest and watched while he pulled it on before handing him the belt. Then she stepped back, regarding him critically.

'Well?' he asked.

'You'll do.' She paused. 'You might want to use a stick until the leg gets stronger.'

He tried a couple of steps and then nodded. 'I think you're right.'

'I'll have one of the servants find one for you. In the meantime you'll have to make do with me.'

'I'm too heavy to impose on you in that way.'

'I'm tougher than I look.' She put an arm around his waist and then glanced up. 'Ready?'

Finn leaned lightly on her shoulders. 'Ready if you are.'

They set off slowly. Her slenderness and fragility had never seemed more apparent than now and he made a determined effort to take most of the weight because he was fearful of crushing her otherwise. At the same time her nearness and her warmth acted as an antidote to the discomfort in his leg. It felt good to hold her; good and right.

It was also good to get out of the building and into the fresh air again and, being in no hurry to relinquish her company, he steered her to a bench behind the hall and called a halt for a while. Lara eyed him in concern.

'Are you all right?'

'I'm just out of practice, that's all.'

'It's hardly surprising.'

'It could have been a lot worse. But for you I'm sure it would have been.' He paused, holding her gaze. 'I'd like to thank you in my own way.'

The kiss was light, almost tentative, taking account of her cut lip. It looked to be healing well but he didn't want to risk hurting her so he let his mouth brush hers in an act of gentle homage.

'I must apologise for yet another tame offering,' he said, 'but if I were to kiss you properly it would likely tear your lip again.'

'Will you kiss me properly when the cut is healed?'

He was very still, his gaze intent. 'If you want me to.'

'I do want you to, Finn.'

His heart made a sudden irregular leap. With an effort he controlled his voice. 'Do you mean that?'

'Yes, I mean it.'

'Then you have my word on the matter.'

Lara had no idea where she'd found the boldness to say such things but now the words were spoken she couldn't be sorry either, not when her blood was racing from that so-called *tame offering*. She wanted him to do it again, wanted him to kiss her as he had on the day of their wedding, only next time she didn't want him to stop. The knowledge of what she did want made her blush.

By and by they resumed their walk to the hall to be greeted warmly by those present. In short order Finn was provided with a walking stick so that he could stand independently. She might have slipped away then and left the men to talk but he kept an arm lightly around her waist preventing it. The gesture was by no means unwelcome since she had no real wish to go. Besides, it not only established her significance in the scheme of things but also suggested that he wanted her with him, that her company was congenial to him. She wanted to believe that, to think that she might mean more to him now, that one day his affections would be engaged as well.

That evening they dined in the hall with everyone else. It pleased her to see Finn in good spirits and keeping up his part in the conversation. There was no doubt that he was glad to be up and about again. Nor could she blame him. Being forced to lie abed was desperately dull but he'd remained surprisingly even tempered throughout.

Although he was enjoying the change of scene and ate with a good appetite, Lara noticed he wasn't drinking as much as the others, limiting his consumption to two cups of ale. Perhaps in that too he needed to take things slowly. Nor was he inclined to stay late that evening. When she rose to take her leave he came with her, excusing himself from the company with a plea of fatigue. Most of them seemed to accept it, though she noted one or two sceptical smiles. It wasn't hard to work out which way their imaginations tended either. She smiled ruefully. If they knew the truth, how shocked and disapproving they would be. After all, who would credit that a married man would not insist on his rights from the outset?

Finn could have done that but he hadn't. He's not like the others. Suddenly she would very much have liked to know what his motivation was.

When they returned to his sleeping quarters she helped him undress, gathering his clothing as he removed it and laying it neatly aside. If she'd thought his nakedness disquieting before it became downright disturbing when he was on his feet, not least because the sensations it created were centred on something quite different from fear. Finn slid into bed and, having settled himself comfortably, laced his hands behind his head and looked on as Lara began to make her own preparations for the night.

It wasn't the first time she had undressed in front of him but now anger and resentment were entirely absent. She wanted his interest; wanted to increase his curiosity and to stimulate his desire. For perhaps the hundredth time she found herself wishing for experience in these matters but all she had to go on was instinct. So, unhurriedly, she began to undress, unfastening her girdle and removing the overdress and gown. *Is he watching?* She couldn't look up to check; couldn't make it so obvious. When she was down to her shift she turned away a little and then bent to remove her stockings taking good care to offer him several seconds' view of her lower leg in the process. *Is he looking?* Laying the stockings aside with her other garments she took up her comb and strolled back to the pallet, keeping the lamp behind her. The stuff of her shift was thin and with any luck the light would make it semi-transparent. *If he notices, of course.* With every assumption of casual ease she sat down to comb her hair.

Finn's gaze never left the quiet figure across the room, his entire being aroused by the sight of that casual disrobing. It was sensual and provocative and if he hadn't known better he might have thought it deliberate. That was nonsense of course. Nonsense or not, by the time she'd got as far as her stockings he could feel the familiar coil of hot tension form in his groin. The glimpse of her figure backlit by the lamp only intensified the sensation. She had barely begun on her hair before he felt himself growing hard. Mentally he finished undressing her and laid her down on the pallet with the fiery mass of hair spread around her shoulders… He bit his lip to stifle a groan.

As she worked she took care not to look at Finn directly, pretending to be totally absorbed in her task. However, she could feel the weight of his attention now. The very atmosphere was charged with it. Her flesh tingled in response. The sensation travelled all the way from her breasts to the place between her thighs.

She risked a glance his way. Her breath caught in her throat as the grey eyes locked with hers. She needed no experience to read the expression there now. It thrilled through her, hot, avid and dangerously exciting. *When you decide you want to become a real woman let me know.* She laid aside the comb. Then, without taking her eyes off him, she slowly removed the shift. The re-

sult was a sharp indrawn breath from the direction of
the bed. Pulse racing, she got to her feet and crossed
the room.

Finn threw back the edge of the coverlet and then
eased himself across the mattress to give her room to
join him. She slid in beside him. The linen was warm
where he had lain; warm too the strong hands reaching
for her waist. His mouth brushed hers but in deference
to her damaged lip didn't linger there, moving lower
instead, his breath feathering her skin as he nuzzled
her neck and throat. Her breathing quickened. Gods,
how could she have guessed how good this would feel?
Don't stop. Please don't stop. As if in answer to the
thought she felt him tug gently at the lobe of her ear and
then the tip of his tongue probed a little deeper sending
a delicious shiver the length of her body.

The pad of his thumb brushed the peak of one breast.
The sensation was exquisite. As the caress continued,
the nipple hardened swiftly in response. Lowering his
head he took the peak of her breast in his mouth, circling it with his tongue, teasing, sucking, creating a
ripple of pleasure in its wake. *How did he do that?
How do I arouse him?*

'Tell me what to do, Finn. Show me how to please
you.'

'Just relax and follow my lead, sweetheart. If you
enjoy what I'm doing the chances are I'll enjoy it if you
do the same to me.'

And so she imitated him, caressing him in return,
exploring him, enjoying the play of his muscles beneath her hands, revelling in the leashed strength of
him, wanting to discover every part of him. His skin
smelled faintly of soap and musk and beneath it the

man, a heady, sexual scent as intoxicating as mead. Her fingers stroked the warm nape of his neck then did what they had wanted to do from the first and slid gently through his hair. The touch was sensual and arousing and provoked a series of more seductive fantasies.

She could feel his erection hard against her thigh and her mind moved ahead, imagining what it would feel like inside her. How would it feel to be taken by him, to be possessed by him, to yield completely to him? The possibilities swept her with a rising tide of excitement as curiosity mingled with desire. More than anything she wanted to find out. But then, belatedly, a different thought intruded.

'Your injured leg. This might not be…'

His lips grazed her neck. 'What injured leg?'

She felt his hand sweep her waist and thigh and then move to the secret place between, intimate, unexpected and shocking. Delightfully, wickedly shocking. Whatever he was doing she wanted more of it. He drew his fingers slowly through the moist fold of her flesh. As the gentle stroking continued it elicited a rush of slick warmth and the tingling sensation in her loins intensified and tightened into a coil of heat. Relaxing her thighs a little to facilitate him she willed him to continue, her hips arching towards his hand. His fingers found the hard nub they had been seeking and then resumed what they had begun. Lara gasped. And then recalling what he'd said she slid a hand down his belly to his groin and closed her fingers around him, stroking gently in return. She heard a sharp intake of breath and saw him smile.

'You learn quickly, sweetheart.'

She wanted to learn, to find out what would please

him, what would excite him, what would… The train of thought ended on a gasp as the coil of tension tightened further and the heat at its core flared out in a deep ripple of pleasure. It was swiftly followed by another and another, deeper and stronger, until her body shuddered, bucking against his hand.

'Dear gods! Finn, please…'

She was vaguely aware that he moved and parted her thighs; felt the first gentle thrust of penetration. There was a brief sensation of discomfort and he slid deeper until she had all of him. For a second or two he was still, holding her at his pleasure and the grey eyes locked with hers, ardent, hungry, fierce. What she read there made her breath catch in her throat, every nerve vibrating to him. She felt him move inside her, slowly at first, until his own need began to overcome restraint. The tempo changed and became stronger and more assertive. Involuntarily she closed her legs around him, pulling him closer, moving with him, acknowledging the leashed power holding her in thrall. Her body quivered, submitting to his will and thrilling to the possession until eventually she heard him cry out and felt the juddering spasm of his climax and his hot seed inside her.

He rolled aside and collapsed, breathing hard, but she saw him smile. 'You have no idea how much I've wanted to do that.'

'Have you? I thought…'

'Thought what, sweetheart?'

'That it didn't matter to you whether I lay with you or not.'

He laughed softly. 'I had to keep a few shreds of pride intact.'

'You mean you would have…you wanted…'

'Yes, I certainly would have. I've wanted you from the day I first clapped eyes on you.'

'You hid it well.'

'Self-preservation, my sweet, in the face of uncompromising resistance to my advances.'

'I was angry at the time, and confused.'

He kissed her softly. 'I know.'

'I'm sorry.'

'Shh. You have no need to apologise. It's I who should be doing that.'

She shook her head. 'You have been patient.'

'It was worth it.'

'Was it? For you, I mean?'

'Most definitely.'

'I'm glad it was. I didn't want you to be disappointed.'

'*Disappointed* is the last word I'd use.' He drew her closer. 'In fact you never cease to astonish me.'

He had spoken the exact truth. Although he had anticipated her eventual capitulation he had never imagined the circumstances under which it might happen. Nor had he expected to be the one so completely and skilfully seduced. Until she stripped off her shift he'd had no idea that he'd been watching a calculated performance. His hand idly stroked her fiery hair and he smiled. A performance calculated to inflame his senses and drive him wild with desire. The little witch cast a powerful spell and no mistake. He couldn't remember wanting a woman as much or waiting for one either. And it *had* been worth the wait. That too was true. This time reality had exceeded expectation but instead of sating desire it left him eager for more. Somehow he'd managed to use restraint but it had taken every particle of self-control he possessed. Now his mind moved ahead, exploring other possibilities with her, thoughts that only served to fuel passion. He controlled the urge to indulge them. It was too soon. What they'd just shared had been good beyond belief but to repeat it now would be a mistake. He had no wish to hurt her or make her reluctant by being careless or selfish. Next time he made love to her he wanted her as eager and willing as she was tonight.

Chapter Fifteen

Lara awoke just after dawn to a sense of comfortable warmth and well-being. She stretched lazily and turned her head to look at the man beside her. Her gaze met his and he smiled.

'Good morning.'

'Good morning yourself.' She eyed him curiously. 'Have you been watching me?'

'Aye, I have.'

'Why?'

He grinned. 'Because it pleased me.'

'Do you always do what pleases you?'

'Whenever I can.' He stroked her waist. 'But I should also like to do what pleases you as well.'

'Really?' She smiled in return. 'Well, I have some ideas about that.'

'Oh? What ideas?'

'I'm not sure I should tell you.' In fact she was certain that she should not in view of the effect those same ideas were having on her pulse rate. Since when had she become such a wanton? *Since last night. Definitely since last night.*

His hand moved to her breast and stroked lightly. 'Why not?'

Resolution began to waver. 'I'm afraid that if I do it might cause harm.'

'What harm?'

'Such energetic activity might tear your wound.'

'What wound?'

Her body quivered and it became harder to think. 'It…it could cause a relapse.'

He rolled and pinned her to the bed. 'I'll take full responsibility.'

The sun was much higher before they eventually emerged from the sleeping quarters. Contrary to expectation he showed no signs of wanting to be rid of her company and offered to show her around instead. She agreed readily and forbore to mention her previous excursion with Alrik. The thought of spending time with Finn was most agreeable and, as he had to walk slowly, the tour was likely to take a while. All the same she didn't want him to be in pain on her account. When she mentioned the point though, he brushed it off.

'To be honest the leg feels better when I'm moving around. Sitting too long causes the muscles to stiffen up.'

'It's healing well.'

'That's because of the expert care I've received.'

His smile warmed her, like his closeness now. They strolled on a little way in amicable silence but then curiosity overcame her. There was so much she wanted to know.

'Has Ravndal been in your possession long?'

'Since my father died. That's about nine years now.'

'It's a fine steading.'

'I'm glad you think so. Not everyone has been of the same mind.' He sighed. 'My first wife hated it.'

'What was there to hate?'

'In truth it wasn't the place that Bótey hated. It was the fact that I was absent for long periods of time.'

Lara bit her lip. The same thought had been on her mind and he'd just given her an opening.

'I can understand why she would have disliked being alone. I think I should not care for it either.'

'You are stronger than she was. She lacked the inner resources to cope.'

She eyed him obliquely. Was this conversation intended to prepare her for his forthcoming departure? Would she too have to bear months or even years without him? The possibility filled her with dismay.

'You once said that in your experience absence does not make the heart grow fonder.'

'That's right. Others may find it otherwise, but for Bótey and me it was a disaster. Mostly my fault, I admit. If I'd listened things might have turned out differently.'

'You would still be married to her.' She hesitated. 'Do you miss her very much?'

'I used to, but not now. She's a memory I have, some of it good and some of it not.'

'You told me she found someone else.'

'Yes.'

'What did you do when you found out?'

'I went after them and when I caught them I challenged her lover to a fight. Then I killed him.'

Lara shivered inwardly. This was a side of him that

she hadn't seen before—ruthless, vengeful and implacable. And yet it wasn't so surprising that he or any man should seek to hold what was his.

'You acted within your rights.'

'Aye, I did. I didn't question it, at the time.'

'So you never considered letting them go?'

'No, I wanted her back, and I wanted the blood of the man who tried to take her from me.'

'But she refused to go with you.'

'Correct.'

'So…you divorced her for infidelity.'

'No, we were never divorced.'

Lara blinked. Suddenly there were all manner of disturbing undercurrents that she didn't much care for and which might be best avoided. Except that if she shied away now she would never learn the truth.

'I don't understand.'

'Bótey also died that day.'

Her mind reeled with the implications. Surely he wasn't suggesting… That couldn't be. He wouldn't… Yet how much did she really know about him? Who was he really? Part of her dreaded to ask the next question but there was no way to avoid it now. In any case, it was better to know than to live with uncertainty no matter how ugly the truth might be.

She moistened her lips. 'You…you slew her as well?'

The grey eyes locked with hers, their expression as wintry as a fathom of fjord ice. 'No, I did not. She took her own life.'

The relief was almost too much and yet the reply threw up more questions, all equally difficult. He spared her the necessity of asking them.

'That too was my fault,' he went on. 'I just wanted

to talk to her, to take her home again. I had some crazy idea that if we returned we could somehow make everything right between us. Goodness knows what I was thinking at that moment.'

'It wouldn't be easy to think at all at such a moment.'

'At all events, I should have known better than to advance on an already distraught woman with a blood-stained sword in my hand.' He drew a deep breath. 'She assumed, wrongly, that I meant to use it to despatch her as well, imagining a painful and lingering death, no doubt.'

'Great heavens.'

'She used her lover's seax to kill herself. I never guessed at her intent until it was too late. She died in my arms a few moments later.'

Lara swallowed hard. 'I'm so sorry. So very sorry. I didn't mean to resurrect such hurtful memories and yet I'm glad you told me.'

'Well, at least you know I'm not a wife-slayer.'

'I was reluctant to think it of you.'

Some of the tension left him. 'Under the circumstances I suppose it was a natural suspicion.' He smiled mirthlessly. 'Bótey certainly believed it.'

'I imagine she wasn't thinking clearly either.'

'It never occurred to me that she would *ever* think such a thing. That she could ever have imagined I'd harm her.'

'She panicked, Finn. You said she was distraught.'

'It only emphasises the gulf that had opened between us. She didn't know me at all.' He sighed. 'But then I wasn't around long enough for her to find out, was I?'

'She knew you followed the whale road before she married you.'

'But she always hoped I'd give it up.'

'That seems unrealistic to me.'

'It was. I was young and headstrong and selfish—certainly not prepared to listen or to recognise what was happening until it was too late.'

'It's easy to be wise with hindsight.'

'As you say.' He paused. 'If I'd been wiser I wouldn't have lost her.'

'You loved her very much, didn't you?'

'I loved her with a young man's passion—hot and heady and wild. Fortunately, I'm past such foolishness.'

Her heart sank. 'Is it foolish to love, then?'

'Love doesn't last. Affection and respect are a safer bet.'

I don't love you any more than you love me. Once upon a time that statement had been entirely accurate. She didn't know exactly when her feelings for him had begun to change, only that they had. While she had never been indifferent to him, what she had come to feel was not mere physical attraction but something much stronger. It had only been enhanced by the incredible night they had just shared. He had awoken more than her sensuality. She was in great danger of losing her heart. Unfortunately he didn't want it. His love was *dead* in every sense of the word.

'Many marriages are built on far less,' she replied.

'Quite so.' He surveyed her steadily. 'But I think we do have those things now. Am I right?'

It was partly true. She did respect him. It was just that *affection* didn't describe her feelings for him. To confess to more would be foolish and make her vulnerable. Finn wouldn't let her get any closer. He'd just made it clear that his days of indulging the grand passion were over. At least there was some comfort in knowing he did hold her in affection.

'Yes, you're right.'

'Then it's enough,' he said. 'I am content.'

They walked on again in reflective silence. Lara debated inwardly for a little while and then decided that she might as well take advantage of this present mood to find out what she really wanted to know. Living with uncertainty would be worse.

'Is it your intention to return to the whale road?'

'No, or not in the way you mean. I shall not go a-viking again. Any voyages I undertake will be for the purpose of trading and they will not be of long duration.'

'And in between times?'

'In between times I shall be here. I mean to work the farm and raise a family.'

Relief mingled with other emotions as she recalled an earlier conversation. *I shall want half-a-dozen fine sons to continue my line and that you must produce them...* The present arrangement hadn't only been about men and swords; it was also about the need to get heirs. Finn had played a long game because he could afford to. Time was on his side and he knew that inevitably she would become his wife in fact as well as in name. After that the rest would follow. She guessed that now she had begun to share his bed that he would be most assiduous in his attentions there. He knew how to please a woman but he also had an objective beyond pleasure. His involvement was physical and mental; the emotional connection didn't go so deep.

'The fine sons you spoke of?' she replied.

'Just so.'

At least he was honest about it. The thought of bearing his children did not displease her. On the contrary, it would be a great thing to bring new life into the world, to watch a new generation grow and thrive, to make a real home. If he had only loved her as well it would have been perfect. However, life wasn't perfect and affection and respect were better than nothing.

'Some of them might be daughters instead.'

He smiled faintly. 'I have no objection to that— lively red-haired daughters with their mother's beauty and spirit.'

'But perhaps not her temper.'

'I thought it was part of the package and that it came with red hair.'

'That is a generalisation. I'm sure there must be mild-tempered redheads out there too.'

'It may be so, but I don't find the notion appealing. A mild-tempered redhead sounds insipid to me.'

'She would be meek and obedient.'

He laughed. 'And deadly dull. Give me the fiery version every time.'

'So you are satisfied with your bargain, then.'

'Very much so.' His eyes met hers. 'But I am one half of the bargain, Lara. I know that now and I promise to do my part.'

It chimed uncannily with what her father had said before. *Half of what happens hereafter will be of your making.* Even if it wasn't perfect, she *did* want to make something of this marriage. She *did* want to build a future with him.

'And I will do mine.'

He raised her hand to his lips. 'Then it is well.'

As well as it would ever be. She summoned a smile. 'Yes, it is well.'

Chapter Sixteen

When they returned from their walk sometime later they met Guthrum. He greeted them with his usual cheery grin.

'It's good to see you on the mend, Jarl Finn.'

Finn smiled back. 'It's good to be on the mend.'

'I'm glad I found you. I need to speak with you.'

Lara looked from one to the other. 'I'll leave you two alone then.'

'No need, Cousin. What I have to say is not private. It's merely that my men and I are planning to return home.'

'Oh. I see.'

'Now that Steingrim's power is smashed there is no reason for us to remain,' said Guthrum. 'And to be honest we're keen to see our families again.'

'Of course you are. That's understandable.'

Finn nodded. 'Lara's right and I'll not be the man to delay you any longer. Nor will I forget the service you have done me. Without you and your men the outcome would have been very different.'

'It was a pleasure, believe me,' replied Guthrum.

'My only regret is that we haven't got Steingrim's head on a spear.'

'Well, we can't have everything.'

'True. Besides, I may run into him again one day.'

'When are you planning to leave?'

'First thing tomorrow.'

Finn clapped him on the shoulder. 'Then we shall feast you well tonight.'

It was a convivial gathering with much laughter and banter among the men. Lara took little part in the conversation being much occupied with replenishing cups and ensuring the smooth service of food. Fortunately the servants were competent and willing. Nor did any question her right to make decisions and see them implemented. She was mistress of Finn's household and they deferred to her. Perhaps being thrown straight in at the start had been a blessing after all.

'It's going to be a lot quieter without Guthrum around,' said Alrik as she filled his cup. 'I'll miss him.'

'So will I,' she replied.

'Well, he always was larger than life.'

'He wants to get back to Greta. She's expecting their third child soon.'

'Their third? Didn't they just have their first?'

She laughed. 'That was a while ago, Brother.'

'I suppose it must have been.'

'What about you? Is there no lady you've set your heart upon?'

'Ladies there are, but none of them has my heart.'

'There's plenty of time yet.'

He grinned. 'One day I may fall head over heels for a pretty face but that day is not yet.'

'I look forward to the event.'

'I'll be sure to let you know.'

Lara returned the grin and moved on, making her way among the groups of men, pausing occasionally to exchange a few words here and there. Among those she spoke to was Folkvar, now on his feet again albeit with the aid of a crutch.

'I'll be able to dispense with this thing soon,' he informed her.

'But not too soon,' she replied. 'Give nature a chance.'

'I shall, my lady.'

'It's only that he can't stand the teasing,' said Ketill. 'The lads have taken to calling him Folkvar the Halt.'

Folkvar gave him a haughty look. 'Sticks and stones...'

'Well, you have the stick part right.'

'Aye, and I know where I'm going to shove it in a moment,' growled his cousin.

The men guffawed.

Lara shook her head. 'Let them say what they will. I shall always think of you as Folkvar Stoutheart.'

He reddened but his pleasure was evident. His companions eyed him with mock resentment.

'He'll be unbearable now,' said Ketill.

Vigdis feigned dismay. 'What, worse than before?'

'Impossible,' said Sturla.

Lara laughed and they laughed with her, including Folkvar this time. He looked around at the others.

'You're just jealous.'

'Of course we're jealous, you ugly oaf,' replied Sturla. 'For some reason that none of us can fathom, you have managed to win this lady's good opinion.'

Ketill shook his head. 'It's too much. Sickening in fact.'

'So it is,' said Vigdis. 'Give us another drink, my lady, that we may drown our sorrows.'

From across the room Finn watched the little scene closely. He couldn't hear the words but the laughter carried. His men were obviously enjoying his wife's company and she theirs. He didn't imagine that the conversation was anything other than light-hearted banter and it was ridiculous to feel excluded. *No*, he amended, *not excluded: jealous*. Although his relationship with Lara had undergone considerable change for the better she never laughed in quite that way with him, never seemed quite so relaxed around him. Almost at once he felt annoyed with himself. It was still early days. They'd already come a long way and in difficult circumstances. It was ridiculous to compare a casual conversation among friends with that of a husband and wife. Lara was just being a good hostess. Another burst of laughter erupted across the room. Finn took another swig of mead and forced himself to smile. *Let it go. What on earth is the matter with you?*

A short time later he saw Alrik wander over and join the group. He saw Lara smile and put her arm around him. Alrik smiled and kissed her cheek. Finn drew a deep breath. *Alrik is her brother, you idiot. She loves him. It's right that she should*. It occurred to him that Lara had a great capacity for loving, and not just Alrik either. She had loved Asa too, very deeply. Finn sighed. What she felt for him was quite different. On the other hand affection and respect were more than he could once have hoped for. A few hours ago he had declared himself content with that. He realised now it wasn't true.

When at length they retired he undressed her and took her to bed. What followed was passionate but restrained; a slow-burning and intense coupling in which he used all his skill to arouse and excite. Physical surrender wasn't enough; he wanted every part of her. She was his. It must be he who dominated her thoughts, his touch that set her alight, his lovemaking that she craved. Possession must be absolute. Only once before had he felt so strongly about a woman and he had lost her through his own carelessness. That wasn't going to happen again, and so he used every means at his disposal to reawaken desire and to bring her with him; caressing, teasing, exploring possibilities, alive to every response and then making her wait, holding her at his pleasure and hearing her plead before he granted the wish. And when he took her she cried out, the blue-green eyes dark with passion, her expression tense and ecstatic, her body arching against his, her nails raking his back. And his whole being was suffused with the sheer blood-leaping joy of it.

Afterwards they lay together, weightless, drowsy with contentment and temporary satiety. For some time he watched her, his gaze taking in every detail of her nakedness and the pale skin flushed with his lovemaking, and he breathed the hot sweet scent of her. Then desire rekindled and he made love to her again and the night was far advanced before they slept.

Lara woke with the light and her body still throbbing. Every last detail of that skilled and protracted possession was imprinted on her flesh. Tender and ardent and demanding by turns, he had roused her to a pitch of desire so intense that everything else ceased to exist save the hunger for him, the fierce longing that only he could satisfy. And he had, twice over, until every part of her was resonating with it, thrilling to his possession of her. Submission to his will was exhilarating; it made her feel triumphant and supremely alive. The joy of it bound her more strongly than chains. He had awakened something in her whose existence she had not guessed at until now and which would not die until she did. The knowledge was bittersweet. His lovemaking was motivated by a desire to get her with child and, at this rate, it wouldn't take long. Perhaps even now his seed had taken root inside her. Her only regret was that his actions were not motivated by love.

Later they went together to bid farewell to Guthrum and his men. Lara was sorry to see them go, although she understood their need. The ties of home and kin were strong and they had more than fulfilled their part of the bargain with Finn. Her bargain with him was just beginning.

'I shall return before too long,' said Guthrum.

'With news of a fine new child,' she replied.

'I trust so.' He grinned. 'Perhaps by the time I get back you'll have the like news for me, eh?'

Her cheeks reddened a little. 'Who knows? In the meantime be sure to give my love to Greta and the children.'

'I will.' He wrapped her in a hearty embrace and

then turned to Finn. 'I hope we shall meet again very soon.'

'It is my hope also,' he replied.

When all the words had been said the crew went on board and soon afterwards the *Sea Snake* was moving away from the jetty. Lara watched her go with mixed emotions. It wouldn't be long before Alrik departed too, she realised, and with him the last link to her family and her home. The past couple of weeks had been an interlude only. After this she and Finn would truly begin married life in earnest. They would establish the routines of daily living. They would discover more about each other, argue sometimes and learn where the boundaries of tolerance were. The quarrels would be fierce but the making up would be passionate too. She threw him a sideways glance. No doubt Finn would try to have his way by one means or another.

He intercepted the look and raised an eyebrow. 'That was a very speculative expression. I'd like to ask its origin only I'm afraid you wouldn't tell me.'

'In truth I was thinking about the future.'

He put an arm about her waist. 'What were you thinking?'

'That this is really the start of normal married life.'

'Yes, I suppose it is, since what went before can scarce be described as normal.'

'No, but it was exciting, wasn't it?'

'Have you not had your fill of adventure?'

'I could do without the deadlier kinds, but not all.'

'Well, there are other options left to us. All manner of exciting possibilities.' He bent to nuzzle her neck. 'Like the ones we experienced last night.'

She had no trouble interpreting the real meaning

of this. Now he had dealt with his enemies he would turn his attention to getting her pregnant. He would make the process enjoyable but what he wanted were the sons he'd spoken of before. Would he love her if he got them? Could real love ever be conditional? She wished that she could take a more dispassionate view because then she would care less and it wouldn't hurt as much. As it was, the only possible response was to put a brave face on things.

She summoned a smile. 'You are insatiable.'

'You have no idea.'

'I think I do.' *I think I know all too well.*

'Well, perhaps the general idea is now clear to you,' he conceded. 'It's the details I shall have to explain.'

'Only to explain?'

'Explain and demonstrate—at some considerable length.'

In spite of her present mood the words created a little shiver of anticipation. He held the key to pleasure, to sensations she wanted to repeat. It annoyed her that she did. It annoyed her that, deep down, a part of her still clung to the hope that physical intimacy might one day let her reach him and touch his heart. Mixed up with that was the fear that she might not succeed and an underlying resentment that she now had no choice but to try. He had ascendancy over her in every possible way and he'd accomplished it with very little effort. It was a potent combination of conflicting emotions and its effect was to increase mental confusion.

As Lara had anticipated, the departure of the *Sea Snake* was the signal for Alrik and his men to think about taking their leave also. Now that the adventure

was over they would look for another. She felt a sudden
strong twinge of envy that they had the freedom to do
as they wished and go where they wanted whereas a
woman never had that kind of choice. Her destiny was
marriage and even that was decided by others. It created an unwonted feeling of entrapment. She guessed
it must be akin to what a wild animal felt when caught
and caged.

'We must find something lucrative this time,' said
Alrik.

'Be careful, Brother. Don't let greed for silver over-
ride common sense.'

He grinned. 'I shall heed the advice.'

'I'll miss you. Be sure to return soon.'

'I shall. After all, it's not so very far to come.'

'You and your men will always be welcome here.'

He surveyed her steadily. 'And you take care as well
while I'm gone. No more adventuring. You must settle
down and become a good wife.'

At the back of her mind the cage door slammed shut
with cold finality. However there was no way to share
that sensation and nothing to be done about it if she
did. With an effort, she summoned a smile. 'Must I?'

'Certainly. After all, you have a good husband, do
you not?'

She could think of worse ones. 'In truth I think so.'

'Well, then, you have no grounds for complaint.'

A woman must accept her lot, you mean. 'I have
none to make.'

'Good. He too seems content with the bargain. I see
the way he looks at you.'

'Oh? What way is that?'

'Like a man much smitten,' he replied.

No, a man who wishes to get a child. 'I believe he has some affection for me.'

'I'd say he has all of that and more. I saw his face when he saw you in the clutches of Steingrim's thugs. It's the first time I ever saw a warrior's face turn pale.'

The conversation stayed with her long after Alrik and his companions had departed. In the melancholy aftermath of that event she hugged her brother's words close, wanting to believe they might be true. Finn had been enraged that another man should lay hands upon her, but had there been more to it than that? Had he cared at a deeper level than a trespass on his rights? If so, might there not be a real chance for affection to grow and become stronger; to become love?

It was impossible to deny what she felt for him; impossible to deny that she had lost her heart. She had denied it until that awful day when his ship returned and she couldn't see him and feared him dead. The horror of that moment was greater than any she had ever experienced. A world without him in it would be a cold and unattractive place indeed. If anything had happened to him a part of her would have died too. Yet if she could not win his love there would be another kind of dying, one slower and crueller by far. In her early association with Finn, she'd been in a position of strength. Emotional involvement undermined it leaving her weak and vulnerable. Sometimes she hardly recognised the woman she was becoming.

When the skalds recited poems about love it was always a mutual passion they described. A man and a woman so deeply committed to each other that nothing could part them save death, and not always then.

Great love sometimes transcended death. Did not the warrior Helgi return from the dead to spend one last night with his beloved Sigrún? Did she not weep tears of blood at their parting? There surely was a great and tragic passion. The poems did not mention unrequited love. They certainly did not speak of affection and respect although those emotions were implicit in the relationships they described. Lara sighed. How did a woman inspire love in a man? How did she conquer his heart? Having inspired such a love, how did she then contrive to keep it? Just then she would have given a great deal to know.

Chapter Seventeen

The steading seemed very quiet after the departure of the two ships. Those men who remained and were fit enough to work began to occupy themselves with tasks about the farm or else they went fishing or practised with weapons. Finn was very often out of doors with them and in his absence Lara inevitably became far more involved in the day-to-day business of running a household. He encouraged her in this.

'It's your home now so feel free to order domestic affairs as you see fit.'

It pleased her that he took such a view of things because it gave her autonomy in one sphere at least.

'Thank you.'

He held out his hand. 'You'll need these.'

She glanced down and realised he was giving her the keys to the stores. It was an important symbolic gesture on several different levels: it did her honour because it demonstrated his trust in her abilities and underlined her status as a wife. It also spoke clearly of the division of labour within the household and it revealed what she was expected to be from now on. For all sorts of reasons it was a momentous occasion and it called for a suitable response.

'I hope my ordering of affairs will meet with your approval, my lord.'

He bent and kissed her cheek. 'I'm sure it will.'

Lara attached the keys to her belt. They felt heavy, as though responsibility had suddenly achieved mass and weight. *No more adventures for you, my girl. That's over.* She took a deep breath. From now on she must try to be a good wife as Alrik had advised.

'By the way,' he went on, 'I'm going on a hunting trip in the mountains tomorrow with some of my men. We'll be gone a couple of days.'

The casual tone could not disguise the true import of this. *I* and *we*, but not *you*. *I and we may make choices about where we go. You may not.* It was ridiculous to feel hurt and annoyed but she did all the same.

'I see.'

'It's been a while since we last got up a proper hunting party. I think we've all missed it.'

She kept her voice level. 'I expect you have.'

'I'm sure Ravndal will be in capable hands while we're gone.'

A good wife would surely feel pleased that he thought so. She *was* pleased that he thought so. It wasn't her only emotion though and it conflicted with the rest. A good wife would not feel at all disappointed or resentful that she must remain behind and tend to mundane chores while her husband went off to enjoy himself with his friends. That was the way of things. *You're not required to like it. You have to be mature about this.* Lara dredged up a brittle smile.

'I'm happy to know you have such confidence in me.'

He returned the smile. 'Of course I do. It's already clear that you've been well trained to fill your new role. I can think of no one who'd do it better.'

Lara feigned to smooth a wrinkle from her skirt and thus occupy her hands. A good wife would never wish to hit her husband. 'It's kind of you to say so.'

'We're going after deer and boar. Obviously you'll wish to roast some when we return but, with any luck, there will be enough meat left over for you to salt as well.'

'I'll look forward to that.'

A good wife didn't use sarcasm either but she hadn't been able to help herself. However, Finn seemed blithely unaware of it.

'We'll need some provisions to take with us.'

'I'll have the servants organise it.'

'Well, then, I think that's everything.'

She was careful to maintain an impassive expression. 'If you find you've forgotten anything be sure to let me know.'

Finn departed at dawn. Lara was still asleep and he was reluctant to wake her. She'd been busy since Guthrum and Alrik left, which was probably why she'd been looking a little tired recently. It occurred to him that she'd been quieter than usual too. No doubt she was still finding her feet. He realised it couldn't be easy adjusting to a new life in a new home. It would take a while but she was brave and resilient so she'd get there in the end. He bent and dropped a kiss on her forehead. She stirred but didn't wake. He'd miss her while he was away but it was only for two days and they could make

up for lost time when he got back. He collected his gear
and went out to meet his companions.

'A good day for it, my lord,' said Vigdis.

'That it is,' he replied.

'I'm looking forward to some hunting. It'll make
a change.'

'A change is as good as a rest,' said Unnr. 'That's
what my father used to say anyway. After a winter at
home he was always ready to put to sea again.'

'You're right,' said Vigdis. 'And we all need a
change, don't we?'

'I'm not ready to stay in one place all the time,' replied Unnr. 'I reckon I'm good for a few more adventures before I decide to settle down. No offence, my
lord.'

'None taken,' replied Finn. 'Marriage is a different
kind of adventure, that's all.'

'My brother, Sveinn, would likely agree with you.'

'But you don't?'

'I'm willing to be convinced—just not yet.' Unnr
grinned. 'In the meantime, let's go and have some fun.'

When Lara woke Finn was gone and when she
reached out a hand to touch the place where he had
lain, the linen was cool. She hadn't heard him leave.
By now he and his companions would be far away. She
sighed and climbed out of bed. There was work to be
done, instructions given to the servants. Mentally she
ran through the list.

By now she was familiar with Ravndal and the people who lived there. Most she knew by name, others by
sight. Soon she would know all the names. It was her
duty to do so. In the meantime, between the hearth and

dairy and weaving shed, there was plenty to keep her occupied. Like all girls she had been trained to competence in everything pertaining to household duties. However, it wasn't stimulating or challenging work and it left her mind free to roam.

In her mind's eye she could see Finn striding through the forest with his companions, perhaps pausing to admire a fine view or to examine the trail for spoor; could imagine the conversation and laughter when they stopped to make camp. His thoughts would be on the here and now. The steading would be relegated to the back of his mind and she along with it. In truth she was little more than a convenient steward in his absence.

She wondered where her brother was now and what he was doing. Not churning butter or making cheese or spinning wool that was for sure. The repetitious nature of the tasks involved meant that each day at Ravndal had begun to blend and blur with all the rest until they became indistinguishable. Having briefly tasted adventure the contrast was all the more pointed. She tried to put such thoughts to the back of her mind. They wouldn't help. Nothing was going to change the situation. This was all there would ever be. *No, not all. Soon you'll be pregnant and then you'll have children to take care of as well.* That would have been a pleasing prospect if Finn had loved her but he didn't. In that respect she was the equivalent of a brood mare.

For one brief moment she wondered if it wouldn't have been better if Kal had run her through. Almost immediately she upbraided herself. *Self-pity is no good. You need to snap out of it and accept the fate that the Norns have woven for you. It is the same fate they weave for all women. No one cares whether you like it or not.*

Her present state of mind gave her a fresh insight into how Bótey must have felt. If a brief hunting trip could bring on such gloomy thoughts what must it have been like to be left for months on end? Lara swallowed hard, reminding herself that she wasn't being left for months or even weeks. It was a couple of days. Men went hunting sometimes. That was all. Finn would be back soon enough. She just hadn't expected to miss him so much. It was downright foolish because he certainly wouldn't be thinking about her. He'd be enjoying male companionship and the camaraderie that went with it. He'd only think about her again when he returned.

The rest of the day passed uneventfully and came to a weary conclusion. Lara retired to the sleeping quarters and drew the curtain screen across the entrance. Then she went to her personal chest and opened it and took out the sword. It felt good to hold it again. She hadn't practised at all since coming to Ravndal. A good wife had no business with a sword and her abstinence had been out of deference to notions of appropriate behaviour. A flicker of rebellion kindled to life and she smiled to herself. Finn wasn't here and what others didn't know wouldn't hurt them.

The following morning she rose early and slipped out unseen. Finding a quiet and sheltered spot well away from the steading she unsheathed the blade and, closing her mind to everything else, put in an hour's practice. It felt liberating, as though, for a little while at least, she was herself again. She didn't know how Finn would react if he knew about this: the topic of sword practice had not arisen since their coming here and she hadn't mentioned it. Would he consider it incompatible with her position as his wife? Surely he couldn't be so hypocritical as to stop her now, not after what had gone before? *I'll look after his hall and do what's required, but I need something for myself too and this is it.* If that meant standing her ground she was prepared to do it. Otherwise the old Lara would be lost completely and she would become a mere cipher. Her jaw tightened and she slashed at a clump of thistles, slicing off the heads. *Over my dead body.*

Finn looked at the two dead boars with satisfaction. The hunt had gone well and not only for his group. Vigdis and Folkvar had brought down a fine deer. There would be meat to spare in the days to come. No one would go hungry. His thoughts turned to Ravndal and to Lara and he smiled. No doubt she had everything under control while he was gone. It was a relief to be able to leave the place in trusted hands. Much as he'd enjoyed the thrill of the chase and the company of his sword brothers he'd missed her over the past couple of days. He'd missed her fiery beauty and quick wit and her mischievous smile. He'd missed her in his bed at night. His smile widened. It would be good to get home.

Lara was in the weaving shed when a servant announced the return of the hunting party. At once, gloom was forgotten. *He's back.* Pausing only to tidy her hair and gown she hurried off. The huntsmen were standing in a group around the trough. Most of them had stripped off their tunics and shirts to sluice away the sweat and dirt from their recent expedition. Her gaze searched the assembled group and found Finn at once. For a moment or two she studied him unnoticed. With his lightly tanned skin and gold-brown hair and easy smile he was heart-stoppingly handsome and his athletic frame exuded rude health and energy. Water droplets glistened on his breast, enhancing the powerful musculature of his torso and the thick corded biceps beneath his arm rings. Just to look at him created a fluttering sensation in the pit of her stomach.

As though sensing himself watched he looked round and saw her and then she was the one under scrutiny. His smile widened. Detaching himself from his companions he crossed the intervening space to join her. The fluttering sensation increased. With an effort she controlled it.

'Welcome home, my lord.'

He drew her close for a resounding kiss on the cheek. 'It's good to be back. Did you miss me, wife?'

She had missed him terribly and there was no point denying it when every fibre of her body tingled with awareness of him. 'Of course.'

'I'm glad to hear it. I missed you too.'

'Did you?'

'Can you doubt it?'

She *had* doubted it. Part of her still did. 'I thought you'd be too busy.'

'Not that busy,' he replied.

'Did you have good hunting?'

'Very good hunting—two boars and a deer. Some of the servants are flensing the carcases now.'

'Oh.' Then mindful of what he'd said in an earlier conversation, 'Perhaps I should go and supervise.'

'It can wait a while. Let's go indoors. My men and I would like some ale.'

'Yes, of course.'

They walked together to the hall and then Lara went off to organise the required refreshments. The men smiled at her as she filled their cups and then resumed their conversation. Once or twice she caught Finn's eye and he smiled at her as well but he made no attempt to keep her by his side. Disappointment swelled like a tide. He hadn't missed her at all. It had been words only, the outward form of courtesy. Suddenly she felt an absurd desire to cry. Furious with herself she fought it. A glance around revealed that everyone had a drink, and two of the servants were refilling cups. The room was filled with the sound of conversation and laughter. It would be a good moment to slip away. No one would notice.

She was barely fifty yards beyond the door before she heard Finn's voice behind her.

'Lara? Where are you going?'

She turned around to face him. 'I thought I'd check on that meat.'

'That's very diligent but there's no hurry.'

'Now or later makes no difference. It'll still have to be done.'

'Well, then, why not stay awhile longer?'

There were several reasons she might have given but, equally, knew that she wasn't going to. After all, she had her pride.

'I think I'll deal with it now. It'll be one less thing to think about.'

Finn closed the distance between them. For a moment or two he surveyed her in silence and his eyes narrowed.

'You look a little pale, sweetheart. Are you all right?'

'I…yes, quite all right.'

He traced a finger lightly across her lips. 'That cut looks to have healed at long last.'

'Cut?' She forced her brain to catch up. 'Oh, that cut. Yes, it has.'

'I'm very glad to hear it.'

'Thank you.'

'Don't thank me. My reasons are entirely selfish.' Seeing her puzzled expression he smiled. 'It means I can kiss you properly now, you see.'

Her heart gave a sudden erratic lurch. He was too close and this conversation was becoming dangerous. Dangerous because of his nearness and because of the sensations it awoke.

'You didn't kiss me properly before?'

'I couldn't. I didn't want to hurt you.'

It's not kisses that hurt. 'That was very considerate.'

He put an arm around her waist and drew her closer. 'It has cost me dear. You have very kissable lips.'

She wished she could believe him. She wished she hadn't missed him and that his touch didn't matter. 'Do I?'

'Yes, you do, among other things of course. The subject has been much on my mind of late.'

'I think wild boars were much on your mind.'

'And yet I felt no desire to kiss one.'

'Just as well, I'd say.'

His eyes gleamed. 'You fear for my safety?'

'Well, of course, but it would also be mortifying

to discover that I must compete with a pig for your affections.'

He laughed softly. 'Thor's blood, I have missed you.'

Without further warning his mouth descended on hers. There was nothing tentative or gentle about it this time. On the contrary it was assured and persuasive, the kiss of a man experienced with women. It spoke of contained passion that sought her response. And passion woke in its turn and of its own volition her mouth opened to him, her tongue tilting with his. He tasted of ale, strong and heady. She swayed against him, sliding her arms around his neck, caressing the warm skin at the nape, breathing the erotic musky scent of him. Her touch sent a tremor through his flesh and then his arms closed around her, his tongue thrusting deeper. Lara felt her blood leap in reply. A few moments more and she knew it would become much more than a kiss. The barn was just yards away, cosy, private, just right for a lovers' tryst. *Except that he doesn't love you. What he wants is to get a son.* He would consider it as nothing more than an agreeable interlude in the pursuit of an aim. He'd pleasure her thoroughly and then go back to the hall with barely a break in his stride. Desire began to fade and somewhere, deep inside, the spark of rebellion flickered into life again.

Finn felt her tense and draw back. 'What is it, Lara? Am I hurting you?'

She summoned a brittle smile. 'No, of course not.' *Not in the way you think anyway.* 'It's just that I…I really must go and speak to the servants about that meat. There's the evening meal as well.'

'I told them to roast a haunch of venison. They've probably started.'

'Possibly, but I'd rather make sure.' She stepped back. 'I must leave you to your ale and your men for the time being.'

Reluctantly he let her go. 'Very well, but I promise you it *is* only for the time being. Next time I get you alone you won't get away.'

The implications did nothing for her equilibrium and giving him an ambiguous and fleeting smile she hurried away. Finn watched her go, his brow creased in bemusement. Mingled with it was disappointment. Her kiss was sweet and arousing and it turned his mind away from everything else. He would have liked to take things further than a kiss. It had been in his mind to carry her into the barn and take her until she swooned. Two days of sexual abstinence were more than enough. Or they were when the woman in question was Lara. Not only had he not tired of her, whenever he took her he found himself looking forward to the next time. He'd thought just now she might be amenable to the idea. He certainly hadn't imagined the warmth in her response. What had happened to change it?

Lara paced around behind the barn for a while until she felt calmer. By that time she was annoyed with herself. She shouldn't have reacted like that. If she hadn't been feeling out of sorts it wouldn't have happened. She'd let herself get sidetracked by daydreams. It was stupid and pointless. Men had adventures, women became wives. That was the way of things. Finn was not a bad husband: he didn't beat or abuse her but he did expect her to give him a son. Half-a-dozen sons, in fact. If he fancied a roll in the hay so what? What did it matter where the children were conceived? She sighed. *It isn't the where, it's the why. He just wants heirs to continue his line and all you can think about is love. That's not the real world, Lara. He doesn't love you.* He had told her where she stood. She had affection and respect. Only a fool longed for the unattainable.

Later that evening everything was back on an even keel, outwardly anyway. Finn made no reference to what had passed between them and neither did she. Possibly he hadn't even noticed the brief awkwardness. When they retired that night he made love to her as she knew he would. Nor could she pretend to herself that she didn't want him too when his very touch set her afire. He was ardent and eager and if she hadn't known better she might have thought his passion was rooted in something deeper than mere affection. *But she did know better.* The truth was that he wanted a wife who could run his hall efficiently and who would bear his children. That was the lot of every woman and she was no different. She didn't want to let him down but at the same time she had to be true to herself.

'Finn?'

'Mmmm?'

'I need to talk to you about something.'

He yawned. 'Can it wait until morning, sweetheart? It's been a long day.'

She conquered disappointment. A few more hours wouldn't make any difference. 'All right.'

He kissed her shoulder and then rolled on to his side. Within a few minutes he was asleep.

Lara stared at the rafters. *It doesn't matter. Don't take it personally.* In spite of that it was hard not to. *Survival means not letting yourself feel hurt. Finn has learned to cope with pain even though he lost Bótey.* It was a salutary reminder to keep a sense of perspective. Sword craft was part of her self-preservation strategy, something that she could have for herself outside of the mundane round of domestic existence. That was worth fighting for.

Chapter Eighteen

When Finn woke the next morning the space beside him was empty. He knew from the light that it wasn't long after dawn yet Lara's clothes were gone. It suggested that she wouldn't be coming back to bed. He experienced a powerful surge of disappointment. Although they'd made love last night he'd been too tired to give her the degree of attention he would have liked. The degree of attention he'd like to devote to the matter right now.

He was faintly surprised. Even for Lara this was an early start. He already knew that she was industrious and conscientious. She'd stepped into her wifely role with ease. Food was well prepared, clothes washed, wool spun, cows milked, butter churned, cheese pressed and cloth woven. She had a natural authority with the servants too. He never heard her raise her voice but they obeyed her at once. It was most pleasing and he had no fault to find, except her present absence from his bed. Without her the thought of remaining there lost much of its appeal, a point he was going to take up with her very soon.

He got up and began to dress. As he did so his memory returned to the incident outside the barn when she'd made an excuse to leave. He admitted that the meat had needed attention and that Lara was diligent about such things. Perhaps there was a similarly good reason why she had left his bed this morning. If she hadn't seemed so tense yesterday he might have let it go. Furthermore, she'd wanted to speak to him about something last night. In which case why had she left so early?

She was finishing up the practice session behind the barn when he appeared. He made no attempt to interrupt, waiting until she had sheathed the sword before strolling across to join her.

'So this is why I was forsaken.'

She eyed him cautiously. 'Are you angry with me?'

'*Angry* is not the right word,' he replied. 'Say rather, *disappointed*.'

Her heart sank. 'Do you dislike it so very much?'

'Of course I dislike it. What man would not?'

It was going to be harder than she'd thought. 'I wanted to talk to you about it last night but you were tired.'

'If you'd told me last night it wouldn't have happened because I'd have forbidden it.'

She paled. 'Are you serious?'

'Of course I'm serious. How could you think otherwise?'

'You didn't mind before so I thought…I hoped you'd understand. Obviously I was naive.'

He stared at her. 'I didn't mind what before?'

'My learning sword craft. It didn't bother you then

because I wasn't your wife and perhaps it had a novelty value or maybe it helped you stave off boredom.'

'What?'

'Now we're married you forbid what you accepted then, because what you really want is a wife who will conform and content herself with domesticity. I can't blame you for that because I know it's what I should be but—'

'Wait—stop there. You think I came out here to forbid you to practise sword craft?'

'Didn't you?'

'I woke and found you gone so I came to find out why you'd abandoned my bed.'

'Oh. I thought…you said—' She broke off in confusion and looked away.

Finn's gaze never left her. 'I think there are a few things we need to get straight.' He paused. 'Look at me, Lara.' When she had obeyed he went on, 'Do you really think me such a hypocrite as your words suggest?'

'I…we were speaking at cross-purposes.'

'But the doubt was in your mind, wasn't it?'

'At that moment I didn't know what to think.'

'And now?'

'I see I was wrong.'

'I hope you do,' he replied.

She drew a long shuddering breath. 'I'm sorry. It's just that I couldn't bear to lose this.'

'I'm not going to take it from you.'

'It means a lot to hear you say that.'

'I'm glad to have set your mind at rest. Now come here.' He put his arms around her and drew her closer.

She rested her cheek against his breast and let herself relax a little. Although she felt somewhat foolish for having misread him, the feeling was outweighed by relief. He had been kind. She would still be able to retain something for herself.

Finn glanced down, his mind very much on the recent conversation. Ostensibly it had been a misunderstanding but there were deeper undercurrents that he didn't like. Lara never complained but he was more attuned to her than he'd ever been to any woman, and he sensed that something was wrong. Having foolishly ignored warning signs in the past and lost a woman as a result, he couldn't afford to let this slide.

'I would never want you to be unhappy and yet I think that you are. It's not just about sword craft either, is it?'

She glanced up at him, uneasily, wondering where this was leading.

'Won't you tell me what's wrong?' he went on. 'Is it something I've done?'

A lump formed in her throat. She swallowed it quickly. 'You've done nothing wrong, my lord. I am treated well. I have no complaint to make.'

It was an evasion but an honest answer was impossible. What could she say? *I want you to love me and you don't. I want your heart and you can't give it.* Gods, how pathetic it would sound. She'd cut out her tongue rather than tell him that. His pity was the last thing she needed. All the same Finn was persistent and he was perceptive. He'd know at once if she tried to fob him off with a lie. The best option was to tell him something he'd find convincing. Therefore, whatever she said next would have to be as honest as she could make it.

'I… It's not that. It's just…'

'Just what?'

'I've been feeling a bit homesick, especially since Alrik and Guthrum left.' That much was true at least.

'It's only natural that you would miss your home and your family when you've been uprooted and taken to live in a strange place.'

She drew a deep breath. 'And then, well, I...I've missed adventure too. I've done my best to keep busy but it's not the same somehow.' That too was true. The repetitious daily round of household chores wasn't the same at all. 'I know it's foolish. I know very well that there aren't going to be any more adventures. You told me that.' And he had, so she hadn't lied there either. There were three partial truths that sidestepped the central one. 'I'm sure I'll get used to it in time.' She eyed him anxiously. 'Are you angry?'

'No, sweetheart, I'm not angry.' He stroked her hair. 'And I didn't say there would be no more adventures— only that there would be no more of the kind that could get you killed.'

'Oh.' The words created a flicker of hope. 'Really?'

'Yes, really.' He smiled. 'I have to go down the coast to pick up a cargo of iron and salt next month. Why don't you come with me?'

Her spirits began to lift a little. 'I'd like that very much.'

'Then it's settled.'

'It will be good to have a change of scene again.' Then realising how that might have sounded she hurried on, 'I didn't mean to imply that there's anything wrong with Ravndal. What I meant was—'

He stopped the words with a finger to her lips. 'It's all right. I know what you meant, sweetheart.'

Finn had spoken the truth. He had a very good idea of what she had meant and he blamed his short-sightedness for letting this happen. It should have occurred to him that she might be homesick. It should have occurred to him that domestic chores would not be enough to stave off boredom and unhappiness. Lara wasn't like any woman he'd ever met and he realised, belatedly, that if he failed to take account of the difference he was heading for disaster. She was not only beautiful, but intelligent and spirited and passionate. They might not be the qualities that made for a meek little housewife but they were the qualities that had first attracted him, the qualities he didn't want to change. That she should try to suppress her true nature to conform to some abstract ideal of womanhood was not only painful, it was dangerous. A spirit like hers would break free eventually and when it did he would lose her. He had lost a wife once before because he hadn't taken her needs into account and he wasn't about to let it happen again. He was glad now he'd confronted the problem and got everything out in the open.

'I know how accomplished a housewife you are,' he said. 'No one could do better. But you mustn't think that's all there will ever be. Ravndal is your home. It's not a prison.'

She lowered her gaze and made no reply and he realised with chilling clarity that prison was how she did perceive it. The implications sent a sharp jolt to his solar plexus. Along with that was a dawning understanding that if the daily round of chores on a steading wasn't a perpetual source of fun and stimulation for him, that if he felt the need to escape from time to time, then perhaps the same might be true for a woman.

One couldn't just assume that the accepted norm was right for every woman just because she was a woman. Some might well be satisfied with the *status quo* but not all. Experience had shown him that.

'I'm sorry that you should have thought so,' he said. 'It was never my intention.'

'I thought I'd be able to adjust more quickly. I want to be a proper wife to you, Finn.'

'You are a proper wife to me. You always have been.'

She smiled ruefully. 'Well, not always. Not at first, but I'm trying to improve.'

'There is nothing to improve, Lara, and nothing I would change. I like you exactly as you are. I always have.'

The blue-green eyes met his. 'Do you mean that?'

Her expression cut him to the heart. How could she have doubted it? Had he somehow given a false impression? If so, it was time to correct it.

'Yes, I do mean that.' He took hold of her hand. 'Come with me.'

'Where are we going?'

'Back to the sleeping quarters.'

He set off drawing her along with him. Nor did he make any attempt to shorten his stride so that she was almost running to keep up. She had no doubt about how he meant to demonstrate the sincerity of his words. Had he not complained about her rising so early? She smiled wryly. At least she wouldn't have to do that any longer because there was no need for her to sneak out to practise now.

When they reached their quarters she fully expected that he would demand her immediate return to bed. However, Finn released his hold on her hand and turned instead to his sea chest. Under her quizzical gaze he opened the lid and took something out. Then he came to join her.

'There's something I want to give you,' he said. 'Something I hope will please you and also demonstrate the truth of what I told you.'

She looked up at him in surprise. 'A present?'

'Yes. I never did give you a morning gift so it's long overdue. Besides, I wanted it to be something personal, something unique to you.'

He offered her the item in his hand. The cloth-wrapped package was long and narrow and surprisingly heavy in relation to its size. She sat down on the edge of the bed and laid the package carefully across her lap while she undid the fabric. Then she gasped in astonishment. Inside was a sword in a fine leather scabbard with a silver chape and mounts.

'Oh, Finn.'

For a moment she was stunned, staring at the gift in total disbelief. The five-lobed pommel was made of silver, each indentation delineated with silver wire. Below it was a carved boxwood grip overlaid and bound with fine leather. The curved guard was also silver and cunningly decorated with a pattern of interlacing stems. She closed her fingers around the grip. It was smaller than usual but a perfect fit for her hand. Slowly, she rose from her seat and drew the sword. It was lighter than a man's weapon but perfectly balanced in an ideal ratio of weight to size. Her gaze drank in the soft lustre of blue-grey metal and the wondrous patterns flowing through the fuller and down the blade.

He watched her closely. 'Do you like it?'

'It's beautiful,' she breathed. 'I never saw anything so fine before.'

'I gave the smith very precise instructions so the blade took a while to make. I only collected it yesterday—a detour on the way back from hunting.'

'It's the most wonderful surprise ever. Thank you so much.' Sheathing the blade again she laid it carefully on the bed then put her arms around his neck and gave him a lingering kiss. 'No one ever gave me so fine a gift before.'

He linked his hands around her waist. 'I'd noticed you were neglecting to practise so I thought this might provide some fresh motivation.'

Her face lit in a smile. 'It will, believe me. Thank you a thousand times for this. I can't begin to tell you how much it means.'

'I know what it means, sweetheart. Have I not felt the same?'

'I shall try to do justice to the gift.'

'Then perhaps you'd care to resume lessons.'

'You would still teach me?'

'Who else?' he asked.

'That would be wonderful.'

'We're agreed, then.'

Her expression grew serious. 'I stopped practising because I thought you would not like it.'

'Why should you think that?'

'It's not how men expect their wives to behave.'

'Different things please different men. You are *my* wife and I'm proud of it, too much so to want to change you. I would never have you pretend to be someone you're not just because you have some idea that it's what I expect or that it's what I want. It isn't, on either count.'

'Then...what do you want?'

'I want you to be yourself and most of all I want you to be happy.' He kissed her gently. 'Don't ever doubt that.'

She hugged him tightly. 'I do love you, Finn.'

The hand that had been stroking her back was suddenly still and there was silence. For a moment or two the only discernible movement was the light rise and fall of his breast beneath her cheek and the rhythmic thudding of his heart. Lara shut her eyes and cringed inwardly. *You idiot! What on earth possessed you to say that just when everything was going so well?* In fact, the words had been quite involuntary, before she was even aware of the thought or could guard her tongue. That didn't detract from their truth but now she had put him in an awkward position because he couldn't reciprocate. He had been kind and generous in ways she could never have expected or dreamed of, and he would be a good husband, but he couldn't give her his love. What he offered was affection and respect. She'd known that all along. Now, with one thoughtless comment she'd made a fool of herself and possibly spoilt a very special moment. *Say something. Cover your tracks. Pretend nothing happened.*

She summoned a bright smile and adopted a tone to match. 'Can we practise tomorrow?'

Finn cleared his throat. 'Yes, of course.'

She maintained the smile. *Keep it light. You've already been stupid enough for one morning. Don't make it worse.* 'I'm afraid I'm going to be a bit rusty, unlike the sword.'

With an effort he rallied. 'Light rust, perhaps, and soon removed.'

'With expert tuition I'm sure you're right.'

'I warn you, I'm a hard taskmaster.'

She didn't care about that, only about being with him, of having his undivided attention for a while. 'I'll do my best.'

'I know.'

Later, as he was forking hay for the horses, Finn tried to order his thoughts. It gladdened him that his gift should be so well received. He'd made the right choice and it had been worth every penny of the cost. There could be no doubting her surprise and delight. He'd hoped that would be the case. What had taken him completely aback was the remark she'd made afterwards. Was it part of a spontaneous expression of general pleasure or had she meant more by it? He'd been caught so off guard that he was temporarily speechless. By the time he'd recovered his wits enough to speak the conversation had moved on and the light tone suggested that he ought not to read too much into what had probably been a throwaway comment. The word *love* could be used in so many ways. If he'd asked for clarification it might have created awkwardness or embarrassment. He didn't want her to feel pressured into expressing more than she felt just to please him. He didn't want her ever to pretend with him. What he did want was to hear her say those words and mean them.

He sighed. When he'd agreed to this marriage he'd had no idea that Lara would get so deeply under his skin. He'd had no idea that she would revive passions he'd believed to be long dead, or that he would be knocked so completely off balance. That he'd fall so hard a second time. It had happened though. Disquieting as that was he could no longer pretend otherwise, at least not to himself. She had found a place in his heart that no one else could fill. One day he would tell her these things but not yet, not until he was more certain of her real feelings for him. To do anything else was too dangerous and left him too vulnerable, too exposed. Lara had the power to hurt him and he wasn't sure his heart could survive another disaster.

Chapter Nineteen

With regard to sword craft, Finn was as good as his word. Lara was woken abruptly the next morning when a ruthless hand dragged back the bedcovers and delivered a lusty smack across her rump. Uttering a startled yelp she opened her eyes to see him looking down at her. He was already fully dressed.

'Your lesson starts in ten minutes. Woe betide you if you're late.'

With that he sauntered out. Shaking off the remnants of sleep she jumped out of bed and hastened to her clothes chest. Rummaging around in the bottom she found the items she was looking for. Within a couple of minutes she was dressed in tunic and hose. Then she tied her hair back, grabbed the new sword and hurried after Finn.

He was sitting on the old tree stump outside the barn, casually watching her approach. Feeling the power of that penetrating gaze she felt suddenly self-conscious. She'd taken a risk wearing these clothes but they were comfortable and practical, affording greater freedom of movement than a gown. Would he object? Her father would have had a fit. She'd only ever dared wear these things when he was well out of the way. Only Alrik knew about it but then he wasn't remotely bothered. Finn was a different matter, an unknown quantity in this respect. Taking a deep breath she waited for his reaction.

However, he made no comment on her change of attire. Instead he drew his sword. 'We'll warm up first. You know the drills.'

She nodded, relieved by the businesslike tone, and drew her own blade. For the next ten minutes they moved through the exercises in silence. Lara lost her self-consciousness and settled into the familiar rhythm realising how much she had missed this. It didn't take her long to get used to the new sword: it was strong but it was also light and felt as though it belonged in her hand.

After the warm-up the lesson began in earnest. She had truly expected her skills to be rusty after weeks of neglect, but after a couple of run-throughs the moves came back easily and then it all flowed again. When he saw that she was back into her stride Finn came to join her. He taught her a couple of new manoeuvres and then made her repeat them, watching critically, stopping her, correcting when necessary, then making her do it all over again. When he was satisfied he intervened and made her practise with him.

At that point the whole nature of the session changed and went up several notches to become much more exciting and infinitely more challenging. Lara did her best but no matter how hard she tried she was unable to break through his defence. He, on the other hand, could have killed her several times if he'd wanted to.

Moreover, she suspected he wasn't even trying. By the end of the practice she was perspiring freely whereas he hadn't even broken into a sweat. It was galling but at the same time exhilarating and she knew she wouldn't have missed it for anything.

Finn sheathed his sword. 'We'll leave it there for today.'

'It was fun.'

He smiled. 'You did well.'

His praise created an inner glow. 'It came back more quickly than I thought it would.'

'Once learned, the skill is never lost. It's just that practice makes you quicker and better.'

'I like the sound of that.' She sighed ruefully. 'As it is, if we'd been fighting for real I know I'd have been dead a dozen times.'

'Once would be enough.'

It drew a reluctant laugh. 'Yes, quite enough.' Retrieving the scabbard she sheathed her blade. 'I haven't found a name for my sword yet.'

'No need,' he replied. 'When the time is right the sword will tell you its name.'

She eyed him askance. 'Can a blade speak, then?'

'Aye, it can. All you have to do is to listen.'

For a second she wondered if he were teasing but the look in his eyes suggested quite the opposite. It sent a little shiver down her spine. Everyone knew that the relationship between a warrior and his sword was special, mystical. From the day he received it when he reached manhood he carried it with him always. He slept with it at his side. He looked after the sword and the sword looked after him. When he died it went with him to the grave or, if he had a son, it was given to him and so on through the generations. The names of the greatest swords passed into legend. For as long as skalds recited verse, the names of Hrunting and Naegling, Gram and Tyrfing would be remembered and thus achieve immortality like the warriors who once wielded them.

Her throat tightened and in that moment she truly understood the nature of the gift that Finn had given her. She would never possess his strength and probably only a small fraction of his skill but, symbolically, when he gave her the sword he did her honour by raising her to the status of an equal. It was a statement of the utmost respect and no little affection since it had undoubtedly cost a fortune. The knowledge was humbling. Most women never won the kind of regard from their husbands that he had shown her. He had given as much as he could; had shown as much as he could. Why then should she bemoan the fact that she couldn't have his heart as well?

'I'll listen,' she replied.

He nodded. 'I know.'

His words filled her with pride. She would have liked to get closer, to show her thanks in a more personal way but she held back for fear that it would spoil the present mood. Besides, she was fascinated by what he was telling her because it offered an insight into a world that women didn't usually enter.

'Was that how you and your brother learned the names of Foe Slayer and Foe Bane?'

'That's right.'

'It must be a magical moment when it happens.'

'It is. It begins the bond between the warrior and the weapon.'

'I can see that.'

By tacit consent they began to stroll back towards the house. She glanced up at him. 'Have you received any news of your brother or cousin since you left them?'

'No, not yet, but I will as soon as they're able to send word.'

'You do not fear for them in the meantime?'

'I have a keen interest in their welfare but they are both strong men and mentally tough. Survivors, in other words. They will come through this too.'

'I should like to meet them one day.'

'You will.'

'I know so little about your family. Is your brother married?'

'He was, but it ended badly.'

'What happened?' She checked abruptly, realising that she might have gone too far. 'Forgive me. That was an intrusive question. You don't have to answer it if you'd prefer not to.'

'Don't be uneasy. It's history now in any case.'

'But painful perhaps.'

'Painful is right. His wife fell into a black melancholy after the birth of their child and the balance of her mind became disturbed.' He paused. 'She tried to kill Leif and the baby.'

'What!'

'Leif survived, the child didn't.'

'Oh, Finn. What a terrible thing.'

'Yes, it was. Leif was a changed man after that.'

'It could not have been otherwise.' She hesitated. 'Did he…did he avenge himself for what she had done?'

'The thought was in his mind but he couldn't do it. Leif has never used his sword or his strength against a woman. It has always been a taboo among the men in our family. He divorced her instead and her kin took her into their keeping.'

'He was merciful. Truly a good man I believe.'

'I think he is. Besides, he had once loved her very much and he couldn't forget that.'

Lara smiled sadly. *As you loved Bótey and cannot forget her.* 'I take it he never remarried.'

'No, although I did think there was a woman who might have healed him, in time.' He shook his head. 'It was she who warned us of the planned attack by Prince Hakke's men.'

'It sounds as though she cared.'

'So I think. However, the situation was complicated and we had to leave in a hurry shortly afterwards so I don't know how it worked out between them.'

'If he cared for her as much as she did for him then he will not give her up.'

He smiled. 'Love will find a way?'

'Yes, of course.'

'You have a strong romantic streak, don't you?'

'Is that wrong?'

'No, not wrong,' he replied, 'but real life usually isn't romantic.'

Lara looked away but she hadn't missed the message. Love and romance didn't figure in Finn's world view. Perhaps he was right. Perhaps such things were only found in songs and stories. If only she could persuade herself of that how much easier life would become.

'Let's just say that, in this case, I'm optimistic and hope for a positive outcome.'

'I hope you're right.'

'But you doubt it.'

'As I said, the circumstances were difficult.' He grinned. 'On the other hand my brother could never resist a challenge and he's tenacious. If there's something he wants he goes after it and he doesn't give up until he wins.'

'Like a hero from legend.'

'He'd be delighted to hear you say so.'

'Is he handsome?' she asked.

'I suppose he is. Why?'

'Oh, no reason.'

His eyes narrowed. 'You take a great deal of interest in him. I'm beginning to feel jealous.'

'Do I have the power to make you feel jealous?'

'Aye, you damned well do. Perhaps I shan't let you near my brother after all.'

She glanced up mischievously. 'Is your cousin handsome too?'

'Erik?' He shrugged. 'Some women have found him so, I believe, but it was always a moonless night and they were drunk. Come to think of it, Leif looks better in the dark as well.'

The words drew a gurgle of laughter. 'When we do meet I'll tell them you said that.'

'What, and risk early widowhood?'

'Hmm. Perhaps not, then. What will you give me to keep silent?'

'A kiss?'

'Oh, I think I'd want more than that.'

'Two?'

She shook her head. 'Don't imagine you'll get off so lightly.'

'Three? Four?'

'At least.'

'You drive a hard bargain but, since my life hangs in the balance, I suppose there's nothing for it but to pay up.'

'That's right. At a time and place of my choosing, of course.'

'So be it.' His eyes glinted. 'I warn you though I shan't forget this injury or the shameless way I have been exploited, and I shall seek revenge.'

As imagination supplied the possible forms his revenge might take, her pulse quickened in response. She regarded him speculatively. 'Should I be worried?'

'Oh, yes,' he replied.

They returned to the sleeping quarters to put up their weapons. Lara glanced at her clothing.

'I need to make myself respectable again.'

He sat down, stretching his legs in front of him. 'Please go ahead.'

She raised an eyebrow. 'Are you going to watch?'

'Of course I'm going to watch. It's a husband's privilege after all.'

Lara drew off her tunic and tossed it aside. 'A husband's privilege?'

'Just so.'

'Don't I have any say in the matter?'

'Certainly not.'

She removed the hose in leisurely fashion, leaving only the linen shift, then surveyed him coolly. 'There's just one thing you've overlooked, my lord.'

'And what is that?'

'You owe me certain payment.'

'Payment?'

'Earned from my silence?'

'Ah, that.'

'Yes, that. I require the first instalment now.'

'Now?'

'Indeed.'

'Very well.' He rose from his seat. 'I must accede to your demands, lady.'

'Yes, you must. Moreover, I must be entirely satisfied that the payment is just.'

'I'll try not to disappoint.'

He stepped closer and held her lightly in his arms, then slowly bent his head towards hers. His mouth grazed hers, soft, teasing, his tongue running along her lower lip. The touch created a shiver of anticipation. His teeth gently tugged at her lip and then the pressure on her mouth became a little more assertive, more persuasive. She opened to him, felt his tongue teasing hers and then the familiar flame kindling deep inside her. His thumb brushed across the peak of one breast and she drew in a sharp breath.

Finn drew back a little. 'Does it please you, lady?'

'It wasn't bad,' she replied, 'but I cannot say I am completely satisfied yet. I should like the second instalment now.'

'As you command.'

He resumed, his mouth on hers light and teasing and seductive, one hand caressing her back, the other her breast. The touch sent a flood of heat from there to her pelvis. She leaned closer, sliding her arms around him, breathing his scent, tasting him, her mouth yielding to his. The kiss became a little deeper. Lara groaned softly.

He paused, looking into her face. 'My lady?'

She found her voice. 'Better. The third instalment, now.'

He pulled her against him and his mouth slanted across hers, hard, searing, passionate. Her arms twined around his neck and she swayed against him. His hold tightened. She could feel the start of his erection, suggestive and arousing. More than anything now she wanted to continue this, to inflame him, to cast off all restraint and make him forget everything else.

Deliberately, provocatively, she rubbed herself against him. The response was a stifled animal growl in the base of his throat. He crushed her closer, forcing her head back as the kiss grew fierce and demanding, his hands clasping her bottom, pulling her against him and letting her feel the growing hardness there. Heat flared in response, flooding her pelvis, causing slick warmth between her thighs. She fisted her hands in his hair and returned the embrace, avid, hungry for him. And then restraint was abandoned and he gave rein to desire until her lips were burning and she was breathless and aware of nothing save him and the fire in her blood. The grey eyes glinted as his gaze locked with hers, predatory, dangerous and wickedly intent. Their expression sent a shiver of anticipation down her spine.

'Finn?'

He picked her up and carried her to the bed. 'I did warn you that I meant to have revenge, didn't I?'

Chapter Twenty

Thereafter their sword practice became an established part of the day. Inevitably it also became common knowledge. Lara's unorthodox attire caused a raised eyebrow here and there but no one made any comment. If it pleased the jarl to teach his wife to fight and permit the wearing of such clothes, that was his business. Besides, they already knew that the lady was something out of the ordinary so the mental adjustment to these developments was less than it otherwise might have been. Some of the men even rose earlier to watch the proceedings secretly from a discreet distance.

'It's only natural when you think about it,' said Unnr. 'She's a redhead after all, and we know about the redhead's warlike temperament, don't we?'

Folkvar grinned. 'We certainly do.'

'She learns quickly. He only taught her that footwork a couple of days ago but she's got it already.'

'Better on the downstroke too,' said Vigdis.

Unnr nodded. 'Much better.'

'Needs to lunge a bit faster though,' said Sturla. The others fell silent and, under the combined weight of several frosty stares, he hurried on. 'Still, it's early days yet and she has made good progress. Anyone can see that.'

Mollified, they looked away again and returned their attention to the combatants.

Lara moved in to the attack and the strokes came thick and fast, Finn parrying deftly. She concentrated, forgot everything but the two swords, moving instinctively, seeking the opening that would let her through his defence. And then, almost without her being aware, the point of her blade slid under his guard and came to rest against his shoulder. She checked there, staring at him in disbelief.

'A hit! At last!'

'Aye, you little wretch, it was,' he replied.

She grinned. 'I did it. I really did it!'

'You're not going to let me forget this, are you?'

'Not likely.'

The onlookers burst into spontaneous applause. Unnr capered and let out a whoop of delight.

'Thor's stones, she got him!'

'A blow like that would've really hurt too,' said Vigdis.

'No question. Would've laid him up for a fortnight, I reckon.'

Sturla nodded. 'I told you she was making progress.'

The two combatants turned in surprise and saw their audience some thirty yards away by the root store. Lara caught Finn's eye and laughed. By tacit consent they sheathed the swords.

He sighed. 'You realise this has done incalculable damage to my reputation. I may never live it down.'

'I won't tell.'

'You won't have to.' He jerked his head towards the onlookers. 'They will be only too pleased to do it for you.'

'I didn't know they were there, did you?'

'Unfortunately not, or I'd have spitted them all first to ensure their silence.'

She giggled. 'You sound aggrieved, my lord.'

'I am aggrieved and demand retribution. Come here.'

'No.'

Finn raised an eyebrow. 'Come here.'

He tried to grab her but Lara danced out of reach. 'Shan't.'

'Oh, but you shall.'

'You can't make me.'

He advanced menacingly. 'Would you care to wager on that?'

She grinned and retreated, staying just out of reach. 'I'll wager you can't catch me.'

'You'll lose. I *will* catch you, you little wretch, and when I do…'

'You'll what?'

'You'll find out soon enough.'

Without warning he darted forward to grab her. Lara dodged and fled. She had no intention of letting him catch her, not yet anyway. She raced round the end of the barn but had gone no more than a dozen yards when she stopped so abruptly that Finn almost cannoned into her.

'What the—?' He broke off and his grin faded when

he saw why she'd stopped. Six armed warriors barred the way—all of them strangers, save for one.

Lara's breath caught in her throat. 'Steingrim.'

The warlord surveyed her dispassionately for a moment then looked past her to her companion. 'Well met, Jarl Finn.'

Finn returned the stare. 'You and your men are harder to get rid of than lice. Wasn't our last encounter enough for you?'

The mercenaries glared at him, hands hovering over sword hilts. Lara's stomach churned.

The warlord's eyes glinted. 'Did you think it would be?'

'I didn't think you'd be fool enough to come back for more.'

'You're mistaken. I've been hoping to run into you again for some time, but you've done it for me.'

His companions bared their teeth in feral grins that never altered the cold, hard light in their eyes.

'Glad to oblige,' replied Finn. Seizing hold of Lara he pushed her firmly behind him. As he did so he lowered his voice. 'Run, Lara.'

'I won't leave you.'

'Go. Fetch reinforcements. I'll try to hold them off.'

Her throat dried. She knew full well that she wouldn't have enough time to get to the hall and back. By then it would be too late. Finn was good but odds of six to one were hopeless. With thumping heart she backed away to the corner of the barn and darted a glance towards the root store. Unnr and his companions were no longer anywhere in sight. Her heart sank.

Finn drew his sword. 'Come, then, Steingrim. Let's end it now. Just you and me.'

The warlord smiled. 'I mean to end it all right. All debts between us shall be paid.' With that he drew his sword and, flanked by his companions, advanced on Finn.

Lara's eyes widened. This couldn't be happening. Sucking in a deep breath she cried out at the top of her lungs, 'Unnr! Folkvar! Vigdis! Help us!'

There was no reply. *Where are you?* Lara called out their names again, darting frantic looks between the hall and the intruders. *Answer me, for the love of Odin.*

Steingrim laughed. 'There's no one coming to save you this time.'

Finn shot a sideways glance at Lara. 'Run!'

She shook her head. 'No. I stay with you.'

'Touching loyalty,' said Steingrim. 'Too bad it's misplaced.'

Finn's voice grew harsh. 'Lara, in the name of all the gods, I command you to go.'

'It's no use, Finn. It's my choice and I will make my stand with you.'

For a moment there was silence. Steingrim surveyed her with grudging admiration. Then he nodded. 'So be it. We'll give you a quick death. You deserve that much.'

'No!' Finn's voice rang out. 'You have no quarrel with the woman. Your quarrel is with me.' He turned to look at Lara. 'Your loyalty *is* misplaced. Don't throw away your life in a foolish romantic gesture.'

She frowned. 'I'm your wife. How is it foolish?'

'Because I'm not worth it. Because the woman I loved is already dead and you'll never take her place. Because I don't want your death on my conscience. Take your life and go.'

He had never used that tone with her before and it
stripped away the last vestiges of hopeful fantasy to
leave her in no doubt of his true mind. It hurt more than
being punched because the pain went right to the core
of her being. Speech was impossible and for a second
it was hard even to breathe.

Steingrim frowned and jerked his head towards her
line of escape. 'It's good advice, wench. You should
heed it. In truth I'd be loath to slay *you*.'

Mentally reeling she began to back away. The pack
watched but no one tried to stop her. She retreated
round the end of the barn and slumped against the wall,
blinking back the water in her eyes.

Steingrim turned to look at his opponent. 'I never
thought I'd live to see the day, but for once I actually
agree with you. You're not worthy of her. It'll make
killing you all the more enjoyable.'

'We'll see about that, won't we?' replied Finn.

The clash of steel rang out on the quiet air as he
launched himself on Steingrim. The warlord stepped
forward to parry the blow. There followed a swift and
fierce exchange in which each man sought an early advantage, but they were well matched and too experienced to offer a weakness that might be exploited. At
every turn Finn's attack was blocked. Steingrim was
strong and his reflexes fast. The warlord alternately
defended and attacked, keeping up the pressure, looking for the opening that would allow him under his
opponent's guard.

For a little while his companions looked on without
interfering, no doubt expecting that their chief would
dispatch his enemy quickly as usual. However, it didn't

happen. Moreover, the sound of the conflict carried and with each passing minute discovery became more likely. If reinforcements arrived from the hall then the intruders were done for. When it became clear that the swift victory they'd anticipated was going to be denied, the rest began to close in.

Finn smiled grimly. He meant to sell his life dear but even so he knew he would die today. What mattered was that Lara would live. It had been worth the lie to bring that about. The look on her face hurt more than anything Steingrim and his wolves could do to him. The only consolation was that it wouldn't haunt him for long.

Lara shut her eyes and took a deep breath. Finn had never lied to her about the way he felt. Even at the end he refused to do that. However, he was wrong about being unworthy. No man was more so in her eyes. He was a man worth living with, a man worth dying with. It wouldn't take long. Anyway, the alternative was a lifetime without him.

She retraced her steps and drew her sword. Steel whispered against wood and leather: *Death Kiss*. Lara felt the hairs rise on her arms.

'I hear you,' she murmured. Then, tightening her hand round the grip, she leaped into the fray.

The man closing on Finn's left side didn't even see her coming. The first and last he knew of her presence was the cold steel plunging deep into his ribs. He froze in mid-stride with a stifled cry. Lara gritted her teeth and tugged the blade free, whirling round just in time to parry a blow aimed at her head. The force of it jarred the length of her arm. Her assailant sneered.

'Well, well, the miniature Valkyrie returns.'

Heart pounding, Lara sneered back, 'I couldn't resist the chance to kill some giant nithings.'

His smile faded. 'You should have run while you had the chance, bitch. Now I'm going to carve you into little pieces.'

'I'm trembling.' That was no lie—only it was from anger now, not fear. Only a nithing would consent to a fight with such cowardly odds. The scum didn't deserve a shred of respect.

'You will be,' he said.

'In your dreams, craven.'

He threw himself at her. Lara stood her ground and faced him, fighting for her life and for Finn now, using every skill she'd ever learned. Half-a-dozen times she turned aside a death blow. Even so, her enemy's strength was greater and slowly, relentlessly, he began to drive her backwards, step by step. Out of the corner of her eye she could see a second man approaching on her right in a pincer movement. *Where in Hel's name were Unnr and the others?* Her assailant pressed harder. Defending desperately, she took another pace back and then another. Then she hit the barn wall and there was nowhere to go. Her opponent grinned and raised his arm for the killing blow. She threw up her sword, parrying instinctively. The force of the descending blade sent a jarring shock through her arm and shoulder and slammed her against the timber planking. A gust of fetid breath hit her in the face.

'Little pieces, bitch.'

Lara spat at him. 'Nithing.'

He drew back his arm. A second later his eyes bulged and he grunted, doubling over in agony as she brought her knee up hard between his legs. Without hesitation she swung the sword and felt it bite deep. Hot blood sprayed from the cut in his neck, splattering across her tunic. Somewhere in the distance she heard the sound of running feet and shouting and moments later several armed men flashed across her line of vision. Her heart leaped. *Unnr. Vigdis.* All was not yet lost. Breathing hard, she whirled round to look for Finn but her vision was blocked. She had a swift impression of a helmet, a bearded face and a studded leather tunic before the pommel of a sword clubbed her savagely across the side of the head. Then the ground rose up to meet her and everything went black.

Finn stepped away from Steingrim's body and whipped round, grimacing at the sudden pain in his leg as the old injury protested. Instead of the opponent he'd been expecting to see, the entire area was a sea of fighting men as his sword brothers hurtled to the fray. Within two minutes it was over and the mercenaries lay dead. He barely spared them a glance, his gaze searching frantically for Lara. *She'd come back. Even after everything he'd said, she'd come back.* He'd seen her account for one of his enemies and go on to tackle a second but then there was no more time to look. Now he couldn't see her at all. Cold dread settled like a stone in the pit of his stomach. *Sacred All-Father, let her be all right.*

'You're hurt, my lord,' said Unnr.

Finn glanced down, belatedly becoming aware of the

gashes across his chest and arm. 'It's nothing. A couple of scratches.' He looked around again. 'Where's Lara?'

'Over here, my lord,' said Folkvar.

Finn hurried across the intervening space and then the cold stone in his stomach became a large rock as his gaze fell on the still form sprawled at their feet. Her bloodied sword lay by her outstretched hand. His jaw clenched. *Not dead. She couldn't be dead.* He fell on one knee and very carefully turned her over, terrified of what he might see. Grim-faced he took in the waxen pallor of her cheek and the great splatter of gore soaking into her tunic. *Where was the hurt? How bad was it?* A swift check failed to find a wound. *Not her blood, then.* His gaze moved on to the cut on her head and the blood matting her hair and his heart sank. He felt her neck for a pulse. For one awful moment he couldn't find one. Then his fingers detected it, weak but there at least.

'I need to get her back to the hall for tending. The rest of you get Steingrim and the other carrion underground.'

'Consider it done,' said Unnr.

'Bring Lara's sword with you when you come.'

Finn bent and lifted his wife carefully, with no more effort than if she had been a child. His throat tightened. She weighed nothing. Nor had she ever seemed as fragile or as vulnerable as now.

He carried her back to the sleeping quarters and fired off a series of instructions to the startled servants. While they bustled about fetching water and cloths he laid Lara on the bed. Then he undressed her. He used his seax to cut away the tunic and shirt. The skin beneath was cold and alabaster pale but it was unblemished. He was right. The blood on the fabric wasn't hers. That was something at least. Gently he turned her head and examined the cut there. Like all head wounds it had bled copiously but what bothered him more was the spreading black-and-red swelling around the cut. It must have been a heavy blow. Had it cracked her skull? Depressed the bone? Was there internal bleeding as well? He cleansed the injury as best he could and covered her with blankets and furs to keep her warm. Then he sat down to wait.

A little later Unnr appeared on the threshold bearing Lara's sword. 'I brought this, my lord, like you said.'

Finn nodded. 'I thank you. Put it over there in the corner.'

Unnr duly obliged and then looked at the still figure in the bed. 'How is she?'

'As you see.'

'She'll be all right, won't she? The lads will want to know.'

Finn dredged up a wan smile. 'She's a fighter. She'll come through it. She has to.'

'Aye, right. Of course she does.'

'I'll let you know when she comes round.'

'Good.' Unnr hesitated. 'Best get those cuts tended to, my lord. You won't be much use to her if they get infected and you're off your head with fever.'

'You're right. I'll attend to it presently.'

In truth Finn had forgotten about his injuries. Without the protection of the chain mail byrnie he couldn't hope to escape unscathed but it might have been much worse. But for Lara the odds would have been even greater. She'd taken out two of his opponents. His fear for her had lent strength to his arm. Either that or Steingrim was so confident of winning that he became careless. Finn broke through his guard and sped him with a single thrust through the gut, one of the most satisfying strokes he'd ever delivered. He didn't have long to celebrate though because two others attacked him and he was hard-pressed for a while, losing sight of Lara. The few short minutes between then and the arrival of his sword brothers had been enough for the harm to be done.

He looked at her and his throat tightened. *Why did you come back? Why didn't you save yourself?* He'd done his best to make her go, to turn her away from him. To achieve it he'd been prepared to say anything, no matter how cruel or how untrue. He really thought it had worked at first but then she came back. Incredibly, improbably, against all reason she came back. Lara wasn't conceited about her fighting skills. She must have known there was a better than even chance of getting killed, of them both getting killed. Yet she'd chosen to stay with him, to die with him. *I do love you, Finn.* He shut his eyes, remembering that conversation. It hadn't been a throwaway comment at all. She'd meant every word. Her actions today proved that beyond doubt. There was no greater love.

The knowledge smote him, more painful by far than the cuts he had received in the fighting. He should have told her the truth. The chance had been there and he'd let it pass. Now there might never be another. She might die believing every lying word he'd uttered today.

He remained where he was for some time but without seeing any change in her condition. Eventually he permitted one of the servants to bathe and bind his injuries, and then donned fresh clothing. Having done that, he arranged for a straw palliasse to be fetched and set down near the bed. He wouldn't risk disturbing Lara so he was going to have to sleep on the floor for a while. It would also mean he would be on hand if she needed anything.

For the remainder of that day and all of the night he watched over her but Lara did not stir or wake. In the meantime the bruising had darkened and spread, a hideous red-black mass discolouring her brow and temple and cheek. The lump at the site of the blow was the size of his palm. With great care he laid a cold compress over it, changing it regularly. Still she didn't move. Sometimes he checked for a pulse just to reassure himself that she was still alive.

'Don't die, my darling girl. Please don't die.'

The thought of a future without her filled him with dread. If he lost her he would lose a part of himself and nothing would ever be the same again. He loved her. If she lived he would tell her that; he would demonstrate it to her every day. First though he was going to have to beg her forgiveness.

Chapter Twenty-One

There days went by and Lara still didn't regain consciousness. In all that time Finn hardly left her side, praying to every god he'd ever heard of that she might wake and be herself again. Occasionally Unnr looked in and reported back to the others in the evenings while everyone was gathered at table, but his sombre expression told them all they needed to know.

'I am sorry to hear that the lady is no better,' said Folkvar, 'but what of Jarl Finn? We haven't seen or spoken to him in days.'

'I tell you frankly I don't like it,' replied Unnr. 'I've never seen him like this before. He hardly eats or sleeps. He looks terrible. If she dies I fear for him.'

The others exchanged troubled glances.

'We have to do something,' said Vigdis.

Unnr raised an eyebrow. 'Such as?'

'I've been thinking. Maybe we should make a sacrifice to Odin All-Father and ask for his intercession.'

His companions looked thoughtful, weighing his words carefully. Several people nodded.

'Vigdis is right,' said Sturla. 'Lady Lara was injured

in battle so if anyone can save her it's surely the god of war. We must seek Odin's help in this.'

A rumble of agreement spread through the gathering.

'I have seen it done before,' said Vigdis. 'The people sacrificed a fine bull and drained its blood into a large tub. Then they cut the body of the animal into pieces and added those as well.'

His companions listened intently. Pleased by their evident interest he went on.

'When it was done they placed the injured warrior in the tub and he bathed in the contents while the spae-wife spoke the ritual words. In that way the strength of the animal passed into the patient and he was cured.'

The men exchanged thoughtful glances.

'Impressive,' said Sturla.

'That's powerful medicine all right,' said Folkvar, 'but will it work for a woman as well as for a man?'

'She *is* a warrior. But whether a bull is the appropriate sacrifice in this case is more than I can say. Somehow it doesn't seem quite right for the transference of female energy.'

'Good point. Come to that, is Odin the correct deity to ask? Might not one of the Valkyries be better? Eir for instance.'

'Eir is known to be a great healer,' said Sturla.

'And, being one of Odin's attendants, could still intercede with him if necessary. Inside influence as it were.'

The others nodded solemnly.

'We would need to consult a spae-wife before we could be absolutely sure,' said Sturla.

'The woman Gyrda is known for her skill as a seidrworker and her dwelling is no more than an hour's sail from here. She could easily be fetched to perform the relevant rite.' Folkvar looked at his companions. 'What say you?'

'I say we give it a try,' said Unnr. 'All those in favour raise a hand.' His gaze scanned the room. 'That's unanimous, then.' He paused. 'Obviously Jarl Finn will have the last word on this matter. I'll speak to him right away.'

Finn heard Unnr in silence. He hadn't been expecting anything like the suggestion put before him now, but it was a serious and sacred thing they were proposing and it behoved him to consider it carefully.

'I will think on this,' he said, 'and let you know my decision in the morning.'

'As you will, my lord.'

Finn knew about healing rituals and had seen some performed. The fact that his shield brothers had conceived of the scheme spoke louder than words of the esteem in which they held his wife, and he was grateful for their care of her. That they should even have considered the bull sacrifice made him feel particularly proud. It was an honour usually reserved for warriors of high rank. He had already asked for Odin's help but as yet the All-Father had not answered his prayers. Of course, if his shield brothers were right and male energy was not appropriate that would explain it. Perhaps an approach to Eir might be more successful.

He glanced at the still figure in the bed. He'd never felt so helpless in his life. Never before had he sat around waiting for something to happen: it was entirely opposed to the world of action he usually inhabited. In that world if what you wanted wasn't happening then you made it happen. This sitting and waiting was excruciating. The opportunity to do something, anything, that might help gave him a slender straw of hope to clutch at. If there was the least chance that a healing ritual might save Lara he was willing to try. It would take a little time to organise and time was running out. He knew what answer he would give his men in the morning. Feeling marginally better for having made a decision he returned to his chair beside the bed.

The spae-wife, Gyrda, arrived the following day, escorted at a respectful distance by half-a-dozen warriors. Although not young she was far from being the ancient crone of Finn's imagination. She was tall for a woman and of upright bearing which lent her natural authority. With its strong bone structure her face was distinctive, even handsome, the brow and cheek bones tattooed with mystic patterns. The dark eyes missed nothing. She was clad in the blue gown of her calling over which she wore a leather cloak decorated with feathers and beads and the skulls of mice and small birds. More feathers adorned the brown hair which she wore loose over her shoulders. A leather scrip hung from the belt at her waist.

Gyrda examined the patient carefully her eyes narrowing at the sight of the head wound. 'A blow from a sword pommel you say.'

Finn nodded. 'Can you help her?'

'If the gods will it,' she replied.

When she had completed her examination they returned to the hall to speak to the waiting men. Conversation died away and was replaced by expectant silence as all eyes turned towards the spae-wife. She surveyed them steadily, her expression sombre.

'Ordinarily when treating a wound like this I should have sought Odin's help directly,' she said, 'but the case is unusual and complex. You are right in thinking that we need the help of Eir.'

The men exchanged looks of satisfaction that their view should have been endorsed by such a respected medical practitioner.

'In addition,' she continued, 'we must invoke the aid of Gmot and Ran.'

'A powerful trinity,' said Finn.

Gyrda nodded. 'You speak true, lord. Gmot not only controls the tides of the sea but also the female cycle and its related energies.'

Understanding began to dawn in the faces of those around.

'We must ask the moon god to rebalance the patient's disordered energies,' she went on, 'and request the goddess Ran to send cleansing waves and wash away the evil seidr that currently prevents Eir from healing the injury.'

The men listened with close attention.

'Tell us what we must do,' said Finn.

'At the rising of the moon you must carry the patient down to the sea upon your shields. The number of the shields must be nine—one at her head and the rest overlapping beneath her body, for nine is a powerful number and great magic attaches to it.'

'It will be done.'

'The bearers must wear iron and steel to counteract the strength of the evil weapon that caused the injury,' said Gyrda. 'Then you, my lord, must bear the patient

into the waves and immerse her thrice while I speak
the words of the healing ritual. The black seidr shall
be washed away and the strength of the husband shall
be imparted unto the wife.'

'This also I will do.'

'Finally,' said Gyrda, 'the patient must drink a
healing potion which I shall prepare. It is a powerful
brew made from special herbs picked at the full of the
moon. She must continue to drink it for three days afterwards.'

For the first time in days Finn was hopeful. He'd
be willing to tackle a pack of starving wolves armed
only with his belt knife if it meant that he could have
Lara back.

'All shall be done as you command.'

Lara floated up slowly through a sea of darkness
towards the pale orb of light dimly discernible above
her. She wanted to reach the light but her limbs felt
heavy and sluggish and her head ached abominably.
The sound of the waves seemed very loud. In spite
of the dark sea all around, her throat was dry and she
felt thirsty. She groaned, striving for the light again.
The water was cold against her flesh and she shivered.
There was a voice as well, female, but it spoke words
she didn't understand in a strange sing-song chant.
Then the water closed over her and she thought she
was lost. She fought the darkness, willing herself to
rise above it and somehow, blessedly, she was borne
up. Twice more it happened but each time she sur-
faced. Her eyelids fluttered open but all she could see
was a silvery blur. Suddenly there were other voices,
male this time, but, again, she couldn't make out in-

dividual words only a ripple of sound. It swelled and
faded again. The chanting intensified and reached a
crescendo and many voices roared the names of Gmot
and Ran and Eir. Thrice they roared. The din seared her
brain. Then it ceased abruptly. She thought that someone called her name: the woman, but the voice sounded
distant. It spoke again, clearer this time.

'Lara, you must return. It is time.'

Her eyelids flickered again. She tried to peer
through the blur but it refused to clear and the effort
made her headache worse and she groaned once more.

'She wakens.'

'The gods have heard our prayers.'

'All praise and thanks to the gods.'

Many voices called out the name of Eir once more,
this time in exultation. Strong arms lifted her effortlessly from the cold sea. Someone placed a cup to her
lips and bade her drink. The liquid was warm and it had
a slightly bitter taste. After that she was borne away
and then the darkness was replaced by a pool of mel-
low light. She had a sense of a sodden garment falling
away to be replaced by something soft and warm. It felt
good, safe. She knew now that she would not drown.

'Lara?'

It was a voice she had heard before. She thought
she ought to know it. Gradually as the blur cleared she
could make out a man's face bending over her.

'Lara, my love.'

She tried to speak but all that came out was a dry
croak. Very gently a hand lifted her head a little and another placed a cup to her lips. She drank a little water.
It tasted sweet and good so she drank some more, eagerly this time, but he removed the cup.

'Not too much all at once.'

She lay back against the pillow gratefully. 'My head hurts.'

'That's not surprising. It took a heavy blow.'

'Oh.'

'Don't you remember?'

'No.'

He smiled at her. 'Never mind. It doesn't matter. It's just good to have you back again.'

She regarded him curiously. 'You…you look familiar somehow but I can't recall your name.'

For a fleeting moment the smile faded and she saw a different emotion flicker across his face but before she could identify it, it had gone.

'It's Finn, sweetheart.'

'Finn?'

'Don't worry about it now. It'll come back to you later. All you have to do is rest.'

Rest sounded very attractive so she shut her eyes and let the comfortable warmth take her.

Finn looked down at the sleeping figure, his heart full. He had her back. After five days of fear and dread he had her back. The gods had been merciful and answered their supplications. They had restored Lara from the dark limbo where she had drifted between the world of the living and the land of the dead. Now the healing process could truly begin. At first it dismayed him that she should not know his name but then he reflected that it was not uncommon for a blow on the head to cause confusion. It would clear soon enough. He must be patient.

In the meantime he would bathe and shave and

change his garments. Then he would have a servant bring him some food. He couldn't recall the last time he'd eaten or what it was. After that he must speak with his shield brothers. He had neglected them of late although their care for him was undiminished. The spae-wife, Gyrda, had been sent off with a purse full of silver in recognition of her services. It was the least he could do.

Summoning a servant to sit with Lara in his absence, Finn took himself off to the bathhouse feeling better than he had for a week.

It was light when Lara woke again. Her head still ached but not as badly as before. As her vision cleared she could make out details of the room: wooden rafters and walls, a red curtain across the entrance. The room seemed vaguely familiar. Nearby a man lay sleeping on a straw palliasse. He was the man she had seen before: Finn. In the corner behind him was a pile of war gear. She stared at it and frowned. It was significant some-how but she didn't know why. Closing her eyes again she tried to remember and couldn't.

Lifting a hand to check her head she was surprised to feel the lump beneath her fingers and then a hard crust of dried blood. Exploring a little further she found more of it in her hair. *A result of the blow he had mentioned? Possibly.* She glanced at her hand and arm and her frown deepened. *That's odd.* They didn't look different but the skin felt drier than usual. It smelled slightly salty. Her hair felt sticky and it too smelled faintly of brine. When she ran her fingers through it they found tangles. She grimaced, wondering how that had happened.

Before any answer presented itself the sleeping figure stirred. Then he opened his eyes. Seeing that she
was awake he smiled.

'How are you feeling today?'

'A little better, I think.'

'Good. Would you like some water?'

When she nodded he got up and crossed the room.
Lara blinked. For a start he was physically impressive and second he was stark naked save for a bandage
around one arm and another around his chest. All this
was significant too, and required analysis. *Better start
with the bandages.*

'You're hurt.'

'Not really. Scratches only.'

'How did you get them?'

'In a fight.'

'Oh.'

She watched him pour water into a horn cup. Having done it, he perched himself on the edge of the bed
and carefully lifted her head a little so that she could
drink. Now that he was closer she was aware of his
warmth and the pleasant musky scent of his skin. It
stirred something at the back of her mind but the memory refused to surface.

'I can't remember. I can't remember anything.'

'You will,' he replied. 'It will just take time.'

She fought down momentary panic. 'What if I never
remember?'

'You will, sweetheart.' He set the cup down and
lowered her gently back on to the pillow. 'Don't try
to force it.'

She lifted her hand to her head again. 'Is this connected to the fight you spoke of?'

'Yes. Someone hit you over the head with a sword pommel.'

'That was unkind.'

He smiled at her, a lovely warm smile that went all the way to his eyes. 'Your attacker paid a heavy price for his unkindness.'

'I'm pleased to hear it.'

'Do you know you're beginning to sound like yourself again?'

'Am I? Right now I don't know who she is.'

'She's not far away, I'm sure of that.'

She regarded him speculatively. 'Are you and I… are we…husband and wife?'

'That we are. Have you remembered?'

'No, but it seems a fair assumption, given that you're naked and sitting on my bed.'

He laughed. 'Good point.'

Laughter lit his face. He really was very attractive. If he was her husband then she must have shared his bed. The notion was disturbing. No, disconcerting, she amended. Disconcerting because he could remember every detail and she could not. Perhaps he was remembering now. The possibility did nothing for her equilibrium. It was time to change the subject.

'I should like to bathe. I feel so unkempt.'

'All right. I'll organise it. In the meantime, could you manage to eat something?'

'I think so.'

He dressed and departed for a while. Lara shut her eyes. *I will remember. I must remember.*

Chapter Twenty-Two

Finn returned a little later with a bowl of broth. He set it down on the stool and rearranged the pillows so that Lara could sit up. The broth was hot and savoury and she managed to swallow half of it. Finn looked on with approval.

'It's good to see you eat again.'

'How long was I unconscious?'

'Five days.'

Her brow creased. 'That's a long time.'

'In truth it seemed like an eternity.' He let out a long breath. 'For a while I was afraid I'd lost you, Lara, but the gods were kind and restored you to me.'

'Kind indeed. I'm glad to be back.'

'You are most precious to me. I think I did not know how precious until then. I love you and I want you to know that right away.'

She was silent, uncertain what to say. This man was her husband and it was therefore right and good that he should love her. Nor could she doubt his care and kindness. She must have been fortunate in this marriage. How had it come about? Had they married for love? She thought it a strong possibility. It wouldn't be hard to love such a man.

He saw her confusion and squeezed her hand gently. 'There will be a time to speak of such things later, when you're stronger.'

She summoned a smile. 'As you say.'

'Do you still want that bath?'

'Very much.'

'I'll come back when everything is prepared.'

He hauled the water himself and heated it in the bathhouse cauldron while a servant went to fetch soap and towels. The usual steam bath wouldn't serve this time. Besides, a hot tub might enable Lara to relax and so feel better in which case it might help her memory to return. He tried not to think about the alternative. Eir had given back the physical form of the woman but their prayers had not specified anything else. Had the goddess taken them literally? *Let her mind recover as well. Let me have all of her back again.* Mixed up with that hope was guilt that his actions had helped to bring this situation about. He had given her the sword. He had taught her how to use it. Had he not done so, she would never have been hurt. Better that he had died than see her irreparably harmed.

He took a deep breath and mentally upbraided himself for negative thinking. *She is going to recover. Look at the progress already made. Three days ago you could never have dreamed this much. Eir has been merciful and you should be grateful. All we need is time.*

He finished preparing the bath and then returned to the sleeping quarters. On the way he bade the servants strip the linen sheets from the bed while his wife was bathing, and change them for clean ones. If she felt more comfortable it might aid her recovery. Then he went to collect Lara.

As Finn entered she looked up and smiled. How tall he was and how strong he looked. His presence seemed to fill the room.

'Your bath is ready.'

'Would you help me up?'

He drew back the fur covers. She saw then that she was wrapped in a blanket although it smelled slightly fusty. Beneath the blanket she was naked. Before she could decide what to do about that he bent and lifted her, blanket and all.

'Allow me.'

Although she was taken aback, argument was impossible at that point. Part of her felt inclined to argue all the same. That part warred with the rest which knew she needed his help. It was just that he was so unsettling a presence; so overwhelmingly male. He was also used to being in charge. *And to being obeyed.* Probably she ought not to have been surprised, as he had an air of natural authority about him. It might not have been so disconcerting if he hadn't made her feel gossamer light. Annoyingly it was hard to dislike the sensation.

Unaware of this inner conflict, he carried her to the bathhouse and heeled the door shut before setting her down by the tub. A glance around revealed towels, soap and comb set out nearby.

'You seem to have thought of everything,' she said.

'I hope so. If not I'll just have to fetch whatever is missing.'

'I wouldn't want to put you to further trouble.'

'It's no trouble.'

Under her puzzled gaze he stripped off his tunic and shirt and tossed them on to one of the wooden benches by the wall.

'What are you doing?'

'I don't want to get my clothes wet.'

'No, of course not.' She paused. 'I thought the bath was for me.'

'It is for you.'

'Then you mean to…'

'Help you wash. Yes.'

'No!' Although he was her husband he was also a stranger, a physically imposing stranger whose semi-clad state was doing nothing for her composure whatever.

'I beg your pardon.'

'I'll bathe myself.'

'You'll never manage.'

'I can try.'

'But you won't.'

The tone was quiet but uncompromising, like his expression now. Both bore out her earlier impression that he was used to taking charge. The implications made the bathhouse feel a lot warmer.

'It isn't decent.'

He raised an eyebrow. 'You are my wife and I have seen you without your clothes on many occasions before.'

'That may be so but I don't remember.'

'Perhaps it may come back to you.'

'No.' The notion of stripping off in front of this man was too much.

He sighed. 'I tell you what. I'll turn my back while you get into the tub. You can drape the blanket over it afterwards if you wish.'

She hesitated. The water looked tempting and the urge to be clean was strong. 'Very well.'

He turned around. She threw him a swift glance to make sure he wasn't watching and then stepped into the tub. Lowering herself into the water she draped the blanket across the edge so that the majority of her was concealed from view.

'Can I turn around now?'

'All right.'

His eyes gleamed. 'There, that wasn't so bad, was it?'

She pretended the question was rhetorical. 'The water feels good.'

'Soon you'll feel even better,' he replied. 'Shall I help you wash your hair?'

It was tempting to refuse but common sense dictated that it would be easier with help. 'Very well.'

He smiled faintly, and knelt beside the tub. 'Lean forward a little.'

She complied and felt him draw her hair back over her shoulders. The light touch set her skin tingling. It was suddenly as though all her senses were sharpened, every last nerve ending aware of him.

He reached for a jug and poured warm water over her head until she was soaked. Then he lifted a small pot from beside the tub. From that he poured a little soapwort into his hand and applied it to her hair, rubbing gently, taking care to avoid direct contact with the site of the injury. His hands were strong and gentle, lightly massaging her scalp.

'Am I hurting you at all?'

'No.' She paused and then, because silence was just too intimate, 'How did I get so sticky and salty?'

'It's a long story.'

'I'm not going anywhere.'

'True.' He rinsed her hair and then began to wash it again. As he worked he told her the details of the ritual they had performed. 'The gods heard us and you awakened.'

Astonishment began to displace awkwardness. 'You did that for me?'

'The idea originated with my sword brothers. It was they who fetched the spae-wife. To be honest I could hardly think at all by then because I was so afraid that I was going to lose you. I would have done anything to get you back.'

The sincerity in his tone was unmistakable. It was also humbling to think that he and his men should have undertaken to consult the spae-wife on her behalf.

'I thank you, though it seems little enough to say in the circumstances. Such a rite must have been costly.'

'Not nearly as costly as losing you would have been.'

Her heartbeat quickened a little. It seemed he really did care. Did not his actions show it? Surely theirs must have been a love match. It could not be otherwise. Why then should she feel so discomposed by him? *He's the kind of man who would make most women feel the same.*

He rinsed her hair again and set the jug aside in favour of a cloth. He soaped it thoroughly and handed it to her.

'Here. I'd offer to wash the rest of you but...'

Lara's pulse quickened. 'I can manage, I thank you.'

'How did I know you'd say that?' He grinned and turned his back again.

Seizing her chance she set to work. Once or twice she glanced over her shoulder but Finn didn't move. His behaviour was honourable even if his presence was disturbing. Would she have felt the same way about this situation if she hadn't lost her memory or would she have accepted his offer? Had their relationship really been as intimate as his offer suggested? The possibility of being bathed by him created a flush of heat that was quite unrelated to the temperature of the water.

'Are you all right?'

His voice jerked her out of thought. 'Yes, perfectly.'

'Relax for a while, then. It'll do you good.'

He drew up a stool and sat down near the tub. Her gaze followed him. Even sitting down he was still an imposing figure. Too imposing by half. Did he know it? Did he have any idea of the effect he was having? How could he look so completely at ease?

She took a deep breath. 'I need to ask you something.'

'Ask.'

'Was our marriage arranged or was it a love match?'

'It was arranged. The rest followed.'

She nodded thoughtfully. 'How long have we been married?'

'Not long. A few weeks only.'

'Ah. Were we…I mean are we…compatible you and I?'

'Highly compatible,' he replied.

'Oh. That's good, then.' *But it would be better if I could recall the details.*

'It's very good.' He smiled. 'You'll start to remember things soon enough. In the meantime why don't you lean back and relax while I comb your hair?'

She knew now that he was to be trusted and so she obeyed and surrendered to the touch of his hands. He was careful, painstakingly teasing out the tangles, avoiding the injury, taking care not to pull or do anything that might cause pain or discomfort.

'You're very good at this,' she observed. 'Have you had a lot of practice?'

'Not as much as I hope to.'

'Hmm. Why do I have the feeling that I shall rediscover a very wicked streak in you?'

'Because, unfortunately, it's true. There is a wicked streak in me but it is capable of amendment. The process has already begun.'

'What began it?'

'I date it back to marriage with you.'

'Oh? Am I a strict wife, then?'

'No, you are a perfect wife and I would not change you.'

The words were like an echo but just a little too far away to hear properly. The more she reached for it the more it eluded her grasp. Nevertheless it pleased her to know that he valued her so highly. How had that come about? How had she managed to win this man?

He finished combing her hair and then rubbed it lightly with a linen towel. 'Are you ready to get out now?'

She nodded. He reached for another linen sheet, opened it wide and held it up to provide a screen. She rose and wrapped it around her, conscious of the man just inches away. He extended a hand to steady her as she stepped out of the tub, a firm warm clasp that set her tingling.

'Here. I don't want you catching cold.'

He swathed her in the remaining towels and, having donned his shirt and tunic again, scooped her up and carried her back to the sleeping quarters. His nearness was still disturbing but at the same time protective. It just took a bit of getting used to, that was all.

On their return he found her a clean shift and turned his back while she put it on. Then he helped her back into bed. The servants had changed the old linen and the clean sheets smelled sweet and fresh. Lara was tired now but the overall feeling of well-being was wonderful. That was directly due to his efforts on her behalf.

'Thank you, Finn.'

'You're welcome.' He smiled. 'I think you should try to sleep for a while.'

'I believe I shall.'

'Good. I'll bring you some more food later.'

He bent and kissed her cheek, a caress whose effect was out of all proportion to the lightness of his touch. With that he took his leave. Lara smiled and closed her eyes, her mind filled with him and a hundred unanswered questions.

Chapter Twenty-Three

Finn sat down on the old stump outside the barn. The hour in the bathhouse had been a test of self-control but he'd come through it. Lara was making real progress now and that part of the matter was an enormous relief. Her wariness around him was something different. It felt like they'd gone back to the early days of their relationship. Perhaps not all the way back, he decided, but far enough that he seemed a stranger to her. That hurt. He wanted to help, but not to force things to the point where she became upset and possibly alienated. For that reason he'd tried to adopt a casual and relaxed approach to the situation, giving what help she would accept and backing off when she wouldn't, but the pretence had not been easy to maintain.

He reminded himself that it was only temporary. Very soon she would be well again, and very soon her memory would return. He wanted that, but dreaded it too. Her recovery would create a host of different problems because then he would have some serious explaining to do. He sighed. It wasn't going to be an easy conversation. He just had to hope she would understand and forgive him.

* * *

Lara slept a lot over the next few days but each time she woke she felt a little stronger. Before she departed, Gyrda had left some more of the herbal potion with Finn, along with instructions for its administration. He had been diligent in following them and ensuring that Lara took the medicine at the prescribed intervals. For all that it tasted bitter she had to admit it made a difference. The headache was gone. What remained was some tenderness at the site of the injury but that was growing less and would disappear eventually.

During her convalescence Finn had continued to sleep on the palliasse. He made no demands on her at all. At first it had been her concern that he might; he was her husband after all, and it was his right. However, the concern was unfounded. He made no move to touch her, much less force himself on her. Of course marital relations would recommence at some point and then it would be like starting again. She would have to re-learn him, discover what pleased him. Without memory there were no points of reference. Again he had the advantage. All she had to go on was instinct. Would it be enough? In other respects instinct had served her well in this situation. It told her that he could be trusted; that he wouldn't hurt her, and that she could believe what he told her. After all, his behaviour thus far had been honourable. He had been kind and patient, putting her needs above his own. She was fortunate to have married such a man.

Propping herself on one elbow she looked at the sleeping figure on the palliasse, studying him closely, tracing the contours of his face. A strikingly handsome face, especially in repose. Her gaze lingered on his mouth. He had kissed her cheek; memory had no trouble recalling that or how it made her feel. How would it feel if he kissed her properly, on the lips? How would it feel if he...?

Before the thought finished itself Finn opened his eyes and as their gazes met she saw his expression warm. It was almost as if he knew what she'd been thinking. *That's ridiculous. He couldn't know. Could he?* Then she saw him smile and it was hard to think at all.

He glanced at the space beside him. 'Would you like to join me?'

Finn saw her hesitate but resisted the urge to say anything else. Nor did he move. Lara must come to him not the other way around. It must be her choice and freely made. Hardly daring to hope, he waited. Another dozen heartbeats passed and still she didn't stir. *She won't come. It's too soon.* Even knowing that, disappointment was acute; more so than he could have anticipated. He closed his eyes and took a deep breath, fighting it. *There's plenty of time yet. Be patient. It'll be worth the wait.*

He was drawn from thought by a small sound from across the room. Instinctively he looked that way and then all thought deserted him as he saw Lara slide out of bed and cross the space between them. When his brain caught up he shifted across the palliasse to give her room and then drew back the edge of the blanket in invitation. Heart thumping he watched as she lowered herself on to the mattress and slid under the covers next to him.

As he gathered her close she turned to look at him, her expression enigmatic. Then, slowly, her lips brushed his. The contact sent heat flooding through him and he felt his body stir in response. It felt like a lifetime since she'd shared his bed and he'd missed her terribly, missed her warmth and the touch and taste of her. It was tempting to give passion free rein but he was too experienced to do it, knowing he must let her set the pace.

What followed both astonished and delighted him as it became evident that flesh had its own memory. Nor had her touch lost any of its power to arouse and excite. She took her time to relearn him, an unhurried sensual exploration that was a heady and thrilling combination of curiosity and eroticism.

He reciprocated, unhurried too, caressing, stroking, teasing, bringing her with him to the heart-stopping pleasure of mutual climax. Afterwards he held her, unwilling to relinquish her, knowing beyond doubt what she meant to him and how terrifyingly close he had come to losing her.

'I love you, Lara. Never forget that.'

'I won't forget.'

'Good. Not that I should allow it anyway.'

'Ah, you would remind me often.'

'Very often. And demonstrate it too.'

'As you did just now?' she asked.

'In that and every other way I can. I would leave no room for doubt.'

'How could I doubt it when you make such a convincing case?'

Finn kissed her gently by way of reply. He could only hope that she would continue to feel convinced.

When Lara woke she was alone and the quality of the light suggested that the hour was advanced. From the hall she could hear the sounds of the servants' voices as they went about their tasks. It hadn't been her intention to lie abed so long but there was something delightfully decadent about it all the same. She stretched lazily, filled with a sense of well-being. She had no problem recalling what had taken place earlier; her whole body resonated with it. She smiled to herself, warmed by the words of love he had spoken. There could be no doubting the strength of his feeling.

She glanced around the room and, as so often before, her gaze fell on the pile of war gear in the corner: shield, spear, axe, sword, helmet and byrnie. Suddenly, as though a dam had burst, memories flooded back: the voyage and the fight with Kal and how Alrik and Guthrum's forces had joined with Finn to defeat Steingrim.

The recollections were accompanied by excitement and relief. Bit by bit everything was falling into place. After they had dealt with the foe, Finn brought her here to Ravndal and he'd given her a gift, an astonishing gift. She looked around trying to locate it and her eye came to rest again on the pile of war gear. Her heart beat a little faster. Getting to her feet she crossed the room.

Among the war gear were two swords. One was Finn's: Foe Slayer. She reached for the other and drew it part way from the scabbard. The blue-grey metal gleamed softly, the patterns flowing through it like water. Steel whispered against wood and leather. *Death Kiss...*

In an instant all the rest came back and with it, loud and clear, the words that Finn had spoken. *The woman I loved is already dead and you'll never take her place. I don't want your death on my conscience.* Reeling as from an impact, she put a hand against the wall to stop herself from falling. If she'd once thought the pain in her head was bad it was as nothing compared to the hurt in her heart now. Finn didn't love her and he never had. This latest display of concern was about guilt, nothing more. All the loving words were lies; intended to make her feel better perhaps, but lies nonetheless. Nothing had changed. In that moment she wished he hadn't interceded with the gods at all.

'Lara?'

His voice reached her from the far side of the room. She remained quite still, apparently contemplating the pile of war gear. 'You were right when you said that the sword would tell me its name. It's called Death Kiss.'

'Most apt.' He paused. 'Did it tell you just now?'

'No. It was the day that Steingrim returned.' Slowly she laid the weapon down again and turned to face him but his image blurred through the water in her eyes. 'I remember now. All of it.'

A muscle jumped in his cheek. 'It was only a matter of time, my love.'

'Don't, Finn. There's no point in pretending any more. Besides, I'm strong enough to bear the truth.'

'I'm glad. This conversation is long overdue.'

'Yes, I suppose it is.'

'What I said that day was a lie, Lara.'

'No, what you told me this morning was a lie.' As the extent of the deception became clear the fragile hold on her emotions began to unravel. 'How could you do it? Were you secretly hoping my memory would never return?'

'Of course not.'

'And yet it would have been most convenient for you, wouldn't it?'

'I never wished any such thing. I swear it.'

'You have learned how to be convincing, as you hoped you would be.' She shook her head in self-disgust. 'And I fell for it. I really believed you.'

'You were right to believe.'

'No, I was a gullible fool, eager to be told what I most wanted to hear. Your experience of women must have shown you that.'

'Do you truly think me so devious?'

'I'm no longer certain of anything, Finn.'

He paled. 'I did not lie to you.'

'Odds of six to one tell a different tale.'

'I think you'd better explain because I'm clearly missing the point.'

'You believed that you were going to die when Steingrim returned that day. That's why you told me the truth. You knew you had nothing to lose.'

His gaze locked with hers. 'You're right about the first part. I did expect to die, although I thought I might account for two or three of them before the others cut me down.' He paused. 'But you couldn't be more wrong about the rest of it.'

'What possible reason could you have for lying at such a time?'

'The best of reasons.'

'Ah, yes, you didn't want my death on your conscience.'

'I wanted you out of there and I had to say something to make you leave so I deliberately chose the most hurtful thing I could think of.'

A lump formed in her throat. 'You chose well.' *Better than you'll ever know.*

'I wanted you to live. It was all that mattered.'

'I'm grateful for the thought.'

'Damn it, Lara. I didn't say it in the expectation of earning your gratitude. I said it because I love you.' He drew a deep breath. 'If I'd had any sense I would have told you long before. I'd have told you the day you declared yourself only…'

'Only what?'

'I was afraid it had been just a casual comment.'

The blue-green eyes grew stormy. 'A casual comment? Do you really imagine I would ever say such a thing without meaning it?'

'Now? No. At the time… Those words were the ones I'd most hoped to hear you say and when you eventually did…well, it seemed too good to be true.'

'You didn't trust me.'

'I didn't trust myself.' He sighed. 'After what happened before, with Bótey, my relationships with women have been of a certain kind. I never expected to love again. I told myself that marriage with you was just a business arrangement. I tried to pretend I wasn't attracted to you and eventually I tried to deny my deeper feelings.'

'Why should you deny them?' she demanded.

'Such feelings make us vulnerable. I learned that the hard way. A man who loves nothing fears nothing. But that day when Steingrim returned and I thought he might kill you I *was* afraid and I knew then that I loved you more than my life.' He paused. 'Instead of saving yourself like any sensible woman ought to have done, you came back. That was when I knew beyond all doubt that you'd meant what you said before.'

Lara was silent. Such an interpretation had never occurred to her. Was it possible to have got things so wrong? She tried to think. In all the time she had known him Finn rarely revealed his deeper feelings, never mind discussed them, concealing them behind the barrier of his wit and apparently imperturbable manner. By laying his heart bare he made himself dangerously vulnerable, the one situation he had always sought to avoid. He'd given his heart once before and been betrayed. By offering it again he was taking a terrible risk. He couldn't give his heart without also giving her the means to hurt him badly. It was a measure of his trust that he had done it. Not only that, he'd been prepared to lay down his own life to save hers.

Anger evaporated and suddenly she was blinking back tears. 'Even if you didn't love me it seemed better to die with you than live a lifetime without you.'

He folded her in his arms. 'Oh, my sweet love. Steingrim was right when he said that I wasn't worthy of you. In future I'll try to do better.'

'Steingrim was wrong. So wrong.' The tears spilled over then in spite of all her efforts to check them. 'I'm s-sorry. I d-didn't mean to cry. I d-don't usually.'

'I know and I am ashamed to be the one responsible for it. I have hurt you in so many ways.' He grimaced. 'I even gave you the means to get yourself killed.'

'No, you gave me a gift I value above any other. No one else would have thought of it.'

'A halfway decent husband would have kept you safe not put you further into harm's way.'

'You didn't. You taught me how to defend myself.'

'I never met any woman one-half so courageous or as generous as you. Can you ever forgive me?'

'There's nothing to forgive. I love you, Finn. If I have your love in return it's all that matters.'

'You do have it. You'll always have it.'

'Then what you said about Bótey wasn't true.'

'No. She belongs to the past.' He sighed. 'I was much to blame for what happened but not entirely. I've come to realise that absence and distance don't alter love, not if it's the real thing.'

'I won't try to keep you here if it's your will to be gone.'

'Any absences of mine will be of short duration. I meant what I said about that.'

'I'm glad,' she replied. 'I'd rather have you here with me.'

'That's fortunate since you'd find me hard to get rid of.'

'I don't want to be rid of you. I want to build a future with you. That's something I never thought I'd say to any man.'

'It's an honour I have done little to deserve.'

She looked up at him. 'You see me for who I am, Finn. You don't find fault and you don't try to change me.'

'Why would I want to change you when you're perfect as you are? My brave, beautiful, indomitable Lara.'

He bent and kissed her, a lingering and tender embrace that conveyed more eloquently than words what was in his heart.

* * * * *

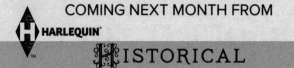

REQUEST YOUR FREE BOOKS!

 HARLEQUIN® HISTORICAL:
Where love is timeless

2 FREE NOVELS PLUS 2 **FREE GIFTS!**

YES! Please send me 2 FREE Harlequin® Historical novels and my 2 FREE gifts (gifts are worth about $10). After receiving them, if I don't wish to receive any more books, I can return the shipping statement marked "cancel." If I don't cancel, I will receive 6 brand-new novels every month and be billed just $5.44 per book in the U.S. or $5.74 per book in Canada. That's a savings of at least 16% off the cover price! It's quite a bargain! Shipping and handling is just 50¢ per book in the U.S. and 75¢ per book in Canada.* I understand that accepting the 2 free books and gifts places me under no obligation to buy anything. I can always return a shipment and cancel at any time. Even if I never buy another book, the two free books and gifts are mine to keep forever.

246/349 HDN F4ZY

Name _____ (PLEASE PRINT) _____

Address _____ Apt. #

City _____ State/Prov. _____ Zip/Postal Code

Signature (if under 18, a parent or guardian must sign)

Mail to the **Harlequin® Reader Service:**
IN U.S.A.: P.O. Box 1867, Buffalo, NY 14240-1867
IN CANADA: P.O. Box 609, Fort Erie, Ontario L2A 5X3
Want to try two free books from another line?
Call 1-800-873-8635 or visit www.ReaderService.com.

* Terms and prices subject to change without notice. Prices do not include applicable taxes. Sales tax applicable in N.Y. Canadian residents will be charged applicable taxes. Offer not valid in Quebec. This offer is limited to one order per household. Not valid for current subscribers to Harlequin Historical books. All orders subject to credit approval. Credit or debit balances in a customer's account(s) may be offset by any other outstanding balance owed by or to the customer. Please allow 4 to 6 weeks for delivery. Offer available while quantities last.

Your Privacy—The Harlequin® Reader Service is committed to protecting your privacy. Our Privacy Policy is available online at www.ReaderService.com or upon request from the Harlequin Reader Service.

We make a portion of our mailing list available to reputable third parties that offer products we believe may interest you. If you prefer that we not exchange your name with third parties, or if you wish to clarify or modify your communication preferences, please visit us at www.ReaderService.com/consumerschoice or write to us at Harlequin Reader Service Preference Service, P.O. Box 9062, Buffalo, NY 14269. Include your complete name and address.

HH13R

The warmth of her body against his, the scent of roses that always clung to her, her low, brandy-soaked voice all intoxicated him as much as the brandy had intoxicated her. At this moment he did not wish friendship from her, but something more. Something between lovers.

He resisted the impulse, but he did not release her. "I will bid you a friendly good-night, then."

He placed his cane against the wall and searched for her face. Touching her cheek and cupping it in the palm of his hand, he leaned down until he felt her breath on his face. He lowered his face and touched his lips to hers, slightly off-kilter. He quickly made the correction and kissed her, as a man kisses a woman when desire surges within him.

"Mmm." She twined her hands around his neck and gave herself totally to the kiss.

He was acutely aware of her every curve touching his body. His hand could not resist sliding up her side and cupping her breast, her full, high breast. He rubbed his fingers against this treasure and she pressed herself against him, her fingers caressing the back of his neck.

He wanted to take her there in the hallway, plunge himself into her against the door to her bedchamber. She would be willing. Never had a woman seemed more willing.

"Daphne," he whispered.

Some rational part of him heard footsteps on the stairs.

"Someone is coming." He eased her away from him. "We had better say good-night before we do something two friends might regret."

"I wouldn't regret it, Hugh!" She tried to renew the embrace.

"Not now." He pushed her away gently.

The footsteps were coming closer, nearly at the top of the stairs, he guessed. He opened her door and picked up his cane.

"Oh, madame!" an accented voice said. "I—I have come to assist you. If—if I do not disturb you."

"You must be Monette," Hugh said. "I have walked Mrs. Asher to her room. She is a bit unsteady."

He heard Monette rush over to her. "Madame! Are you ill?"

"Not ill," Daphne said. "Feel wonderful. Am dizzy, though."

"She drank some brandy," Hugh explained. "Without realizing the effects."

"*Je comprends,* sir," Monette said. "I will take care of her."

He felt the two women move past him and walk through the doorway. The door closed behind them and Hugh was left to find his own way back to his bedchamber to await Carter's assistance to ready himself for bed.

Sleeping would be difficult this night, he feared.

Don't miss
A LADY OF NOTORIETY,
available from Harlequin® Historical
July 2014.

HARLEQUIN®

HISTORICAL

Where love is timeless

COMING IN JULY 2014

The Scarlet Gown
by Sarah Mallory

What is he hiding from her?

When impoverished Lucy Halbrook arrives at Lord Adversane's estate she knows her assignment is unusual—not only will she act as hostess at his Midsummer's Eve play, she must also pretend to be his fiancée!

What Lucy doesn't know is that Ralph is hiding something dark and dangerous. He must uncover the truth behind his wife's death—and Lucy is the key. She challenges him at every turn and, as each day passes, unlocks a little more of Ralph's guarded heart....

Available wherever books and ebooks are sold.